PENGUIN BOOKS

As the River Rises

Drawing from her earlier life as a rural midwife, Fiona McArthur shares her love of working with women, families and health professionals in her books. In her compassionate, pacey fiction, her love of the Australian landscape meshes beautifully with warm, funny, multigenerational characters as she highlights challenges for rural and remote families, and the strength shared between women. Happy endings are a must.

Fiona is the author of the non-fiction book *Aussie Midwives*, and lives on a farm with her husband in northern New South Wales. She was awarded the NSW Excellence in Midwifery Award in 2015 and the Australian Ruby Award for Contemporary Romantic Fiction in 2020.

Find her at FionaMcArthurAuthor.com

Also by the author

Red Sand Sunrise
The Homestead Girls
Heart of the Sky
The Baby Doctor
Mother's Day
The Desert Midwife
Aussie Midwives
The Bush Telegraph
The Farmer's Friend
The Opal Miner's Daughter
Back to Birdsville

FIONA McARTHUR

As the River Rises

PENGUIN BOOKS

This book is dedicated to the great Australian resilience.

PENGUIN BOOKS

UK | USA | Canada | Ireland | Australia
India | New Zealand | South Africa | China

Michael Joseph is part of the Penguin Random House group of companies
whose addresses can be found at global.penguinrandomhouse.com.

Penguin
Random House
Australia

First published by Michael Joseph, 2023
This edition published by Penguin Books, 2024

Copyright © Fiona McArthur, 2023

The moral right of the author has been asserted.

Cover photography: woman by PeopleImages.com – Yuri A/Shutterstock;
landscape by Rene de Haan/Stocksy
Cover design by Louisa Maggio Design © Penguin Random House Australia Pty Ltd
Typeset in Sabon LT Pro 11/18 pt by Midland Typesetters, Australia

Printed and bound in Australia by Griffin Press, an accredited
ISO AS/NZS 14001 Environmental Management Systems printer

A catalogue record for this
book is available from the
NATIONAL LIBRARY   National Library of Australia
OF AUSTRALIA

ISBN 978 1 76134 967 6

penguin.com.au

MIX
Paper | Supporting
responsible forestry
FSC® C018684

We at Penguin Random House Australia acknowledge that Aboriginal and Torres Strait Islander
peoples are the Traditional Custodians and the first storytellers of the lands on which we live
and work.. We honour Aboriginal and Torres Strait Islander peoples' continuous connection
to Country, waters, skies and communities. We celebrate Aboriginal and Torres Strait Islander
stories, traditions and living cultures; and we pay our respects to Elders past and present.

Prologue

Hannah

A thin crack of light appeared around Hannah's mental door of entrapment, offering a possibility of escape.

An invitation? Dr Hannah Rogan traced the bouncy blue bear holding a birthday cake with a big number one front and centre, and felt the warmth of the sender as if Gracie was right there talking to her. Warmth. Not the Central Queensland heat beating down on her head in the middle of Roma in summer, but freely given, real, friendship warmth. She'd almost forgotten how that felt. It was funny how some people seemed to think if you were a doctor, you didn't need reassurance or support.

Glancing around to ensure she was alone, she grabbed her phone and pressed the 'call' button. Even as she did so, she couldn't help wincing that the situation had come to this.

Holding the phone to her ear – not on loudspeaker in case he'd paid someone to watch her – Hannah rubbed her other arm as if to calm herself. When had she become so paranoid that somebody might hear her plans?

Stop it, she silently commanded, sliding her hand away when she recognised the protective gesture. What had she turned into?

The call connected. 'Hannah?' Gracie's familiar voice came through light and teasing, but Hannah caught the faint shimmer of her friend's underlying concern at the last few months of radio silence. 'Are you okay? You got the invite? I thought you'd forgotten me.'

Hannah's shoulders drooped just a fraction, her eyes stinging in remorse at the words. Her kind-hearted, wonderful friend had a right to be upset with her.

They'd forged their friendship on mutual trust and professional respect when they worked together, Gracie as the midwife and Hannah as the consultant obstetric GP caring for inland birthing mums in the town of Roma. They'd stuck together in support, the glue set rock solid after a pair of unpreventable emergencies, where they'd combined their skills to manage successfully and save the day against all odds. They'd got tipsy afterwards with relief. And Gracie had become her discreet and reliable friend, one who shared history and stood steadfast. Most precious of all was that Gracie made her laugh.

Yes, Hannah had felt sorely the loss of that friendship when Gracie and her husband had moved away to New South Wales last year.

'I've missed talking to you, too.' She drew a breath, swallowing the tightness in her throat. 'I'd love to come to my godson's birthday.' Then she made herself add, 'So much in fact, I'm angling for an invitation to extend my visit to a few extra days.' Her throat tightened again, and her voice dropped lower. 'Um, I need to get away.'

'Yayyyy. And we need you here.' The response made Hannah smile. 'Awesome. Absolutely. We'll have you for as long as you want. Though, you know I'll be nagging you to relocate.'

Gracie had mentioned before about creating a midwifery group practice in her new local area down in New South Wales and she needed a GP. Hannah wasn't stepping into that role – she just needed space to recover and be inconspicuous. Notoriety didn't sit well, and nor did being ostracised in her own town by fairweather friends, even if she'd only become notable by association.

'Come as soon as you can.' Gracie burbled with delight. Relief seeped through Hannah as her friend enthused, 'Come now. Help me get organised for the party.'

Hannah wished, but she had work to finish and loyal patients to ensure care for. 'You're the most organised person I know.'

'Not.' Gracie laughed. 'It's harder with a one-year-old. So? When? Your bed's ready.'

'Next Thursday. That gives us two days before the party. And can I stay for a week?'

'Done. Booked,' Gracie crowed. 'You can't change your mind now.'

Chapter One

Hannah

Hannah glanced at the map on her dashboard – fifteen kilometres to go. She was stranded behind a slow-moving tractor, half her brain on driving and half on admiring the green and rocky countryside. She'd left the southbound New England Highway an hour ago.

Now, she edged past a heavy, black metal sliding gate, one that opened with a code box and screamed *keep out*. The gate seemed at odds with the celestial, and quite beautiful, name of the station – Luna Downs.

Beyond the gate, she could see rolling green hills and clumps of rising monoliths of granite dotting the landscape like little altars. If they were altars, then the supplicants would be the black-and-white spotted cattle. The cows grazed or lounged under shade trees and milled around two newly dug, clay-sided dams, half-full of water. She'd been watching the rainfall down this way with interest, and she'd bet the dam builders were happy the rain had come.

Last year it had been fires. This year they'd been inundated with wet weather. *Better watch that*, she thought. The last thing she needed was to be flooded in New South Wales and miss work.

4

Her patients would add 'unreliable' to the grumbling suspicions they had about her, personally.

Casting one final sideways glance at the boulder-strewn paddocks, she admitted there was something compelling and mystical about the picturesque land behind those long fences. And yet, there was the unfriendly gate. In light of her recent experiences, it wasn't surprising for her to consider the person inside might have something to hide.

The tractor turned off to the left, and she pushed the thought away and increased speed. Now she was driving uphill, through winding tunnels of green overhangs and then swooping down around bends with tumbling creeks to the side. Every now and then a gateway flashed past, side roads leading to other properties with cattle and stock yards and clearings, and rarely, visible houses.

As she approached the last rise, the overhead tree tunnel opened out into clumps of olive against the gold hills, and a cloud of pink cockatoos cawed in the sky in front of her as she swept the bend. One kilometre to go.

A valley spread before her. A village. It lay inland from the sea, but there was a coolness here she hadn't expected to find in summer, especially compared to Roma. Because of the recent rain no doubt, the paddocks glowed emerald. They stretched away as she drove slowly down the hill, taking it in. She saw a number of houses and a church spire. The swollen creek snaking on the left and the wide green paddock beside it, the spotted cattle grazing, some sitting as if so full they couldn't eat another blade of grass.

When she reached the spread of houses that lay on each side of the one main road, after almost eight hours of driving, she'd arrived. Thank goodness.

She crossed the bridge and the 'WELCOME TO FEATHER-WOOD' sign appeared like a whoop of delight. Population one hundred and seventy. *With me, one seventy-one for a while*, she thought.

'Thanks for the welcome,' she murmured as she gazed around, following the road into the scatter of small houses, some timber, some brick, some a mix of both.

Chimneys perched like ochre gnomes over most of the roofs, as if winter meant wood fires and warm clothes. But with the hot air that rushed into the car as she lowered her window, it was hard to imagine them ever being used.

Hannah breathed the scent of eucalyptus and mowed grass, mixed with the aroma of cows and diesel from maybe a tractor she could hear rumbling in the distance. There was the school on a flat pancake of land past the bridge, with the two small brick buildings edged in white timber. 'Featherwood Public School,' she said out loud. She could almost see future Gracie in the tuckshop making lunches, and the thought made her smile.

There was a big hall on stilts beside a small white church kneeling delicately on a slight knoll, with a tall, square, solid-looking bell tower and narrow arched windows. Its lawn was surrounded by a painted picket fence and a matching gate that led through to the graveyard on the right. It contained a scattering of old graves, but they were well kept. Above the church perched a house, probably the manse supervising the town, with a 'FOR SALE' sign that was slightly crooked and tattered looking.

Where was Gracie's house? Yes. There it was. Opposite the church sat the Farmer's Friend, Gracie's husband's rural store.

Eager now, Hannah's gaze slid past to the farm gate. 'Ah, just like you said,' she breathed.

She purred into the store's driveway, past the shop front to the far gate. Behind that, raised on stumps above the paddock surrounding it, and well back from the road, stood Gracie's dream home, silver and serene, exactly as she'd described it to Hannah.

The aged-grey wood-sided residence appeared bigger than Hannah had expected. While narrow, it was quite long, stretching back towards the creek, with brightly flowering pots on the front verandah and a freshly painted sky-blue tin roof. The bull-nosed verandah circled the house, and though the walls stood naked in the spotted khaki-silver of old wood, the sturdy wooden rails and the posts holding up the roof were sparkling white.

Three big, brick-coloured chimney pots poked out of the roof, one on each side at the front and one at the back, and she remembered Gracie saying there were fireplaces and that she'd learned to cook on the old fuel stove.

A wiry, petite figure with red hair in a ponytail threw open the front screen door and danced out onto the verandah with a small blond-haired child in her wake. As Hannah drove up to the door, Gracie's smile beamed out like a lighthouse in the storm of Hannah's life.

Gracie had one of those faces that radiated sunshine; a glad-to-see-you face. Relief and a strange sense of homecoming soaked into Hannah as she climbed from the car to meet her friend.

Gracie skipped down the stairs. 'Welcome to Featherwood,' Gracie cried and flung her arms around her.

*

It took Hannah only minutes to unpack her bags and settle her things into the old-fashioned bedroom with the polished rosewood bedstead and so many colourful heaped pillows at the head of the floral bedspread.

Then it was to the kitchen, where the windows drew the eye over the paddock and back to the road and the store. But Hannah was watching Gracie because she couldn't believe she was there.

Gracie stood at a scrubbed central table swiping jam on scones and dolloping cream as they both listened to one-year-old Oliver babble unintelligible words at them. He wasn't shy with her at all.

'Seems young Oliver has your social aptitude,' she teased the doting mother.

Gracie filled the jug with milk and put it on the table. 'If not the language skills, just yet.'

'Not true. We just don't understand his language. I need to brush up on my babble.'

Gracie smiled and poured the tea. Then came to sit quietly opposite Hannah at the table, folding her hands in her lap, as if trying not to startle her. 'Jed will be home after five when the shop shuts. We've an hour to talk, though probably more. How are you? Why haven't you answered my calls?'

Where to start? Hannah didn't even want to. She blew out a breath. 'I told you about Beau Porter.' Even saying his name made her skin grow cold. She'd been such a fool.

Gracie nodded. 'The hunky bad boy who chatted you up in the car park?'

Beau Porter – *Call me Porter*. Buff. Handsome. Charismatic. He'd certainly been hunky. And the first time she'd seen him, she'd been poleaxed by his machismo. Except now she'd seen him do things with that impressive strength that chilled her to the bone. 'Yep, that one.'

Hannah didn't want to talk about the seismic shift that had happened in her world while she had watched the real Beau Porter disintegrate into drug dependence and wildness, because she was still coming to terms with it. Even though he was safely locked away in jail for the moment. She'd feel angst for the man he had lost if she didn't feel so sorry for herself.

'Yes. Well. After the flowers and the chocolate, came the drugs, mostly ice, and he morphed into more of a bad boy than I expected.' She hadn't had an inkling that he had criminal fingers in secret pies, or that those white-powdered digits reached as far and as viciously as they did. Or that his paranoia would drive him to have others watch her when he hadn't been able to himself. In Roma, though. Not here. Hopefully, they didn't know she was here.

'He didn't hurt you, did he?'

Hannah thought about the subtle pressure on her behaviour, the accountability he demanded, the increased isolation from her closest acquaintances. 'No. Not physically.' Not me. 'But I was pretty stupid not to run screaming after the first signs appeared. And things got worse quickly.'

'Ice dependence is a horrible thing.' Gracie's compassionate gaze soothed. Her friend's engagement in her plight contained no judging, just concern for Hannah. 'It's okay if you don't want to talk just yet. I think you need to, but take your time.'

Yes, she needed time. Years, probably. But she did need to debrief with someone she could trust. 'Let's just say he worked into distributing as well as using, and my reputation went downhill when his exploits became public and he was arrested for trafficking.'

'Ouch.' Gracie pushed a plate with one heaped scone towards her. 'Where is he now?'

'In custody. Waiting for his court case to come up. Drugs, extortion and assault.'

Gracie stiffened and Hannah shook her head. 'The assault wasn't against me.' But she'd seen another occasion, which had been even worse than the one he'd been charged with. Porter off his head with drugs; a young man, one she'd befriended because he'd looked so scared, one of Porter's hirelings, being kicked on the ground. The one she'd walked out on because she hadn't been able to stop him, and instead she had run to the law and told the police about the incident. Unfortunately, she couldn't prove it happened because there'd been no sign of the man when the police arrived. She hadn't seen that young man since.

'Sounds like you made a lucky escape.'

She had. Cold trickled down her neck. 'I hope I have. At least while he's in jail, he can't follow me.'

Gracie's brow furrowed. 'You're safe here.' She leaned forward. 'And his mud can't stick to you. Everybody knows you're an honest and amazing GP. A wonderful human being. What about your dad? What did he say?'

And . . . that was another story. 'I haven't mentioned it to him.'

Gracie's frown deepened as she opened her mouth and shut it again. Yes, Hannah thought, families were complicated. Gracie had nagged her before to give her dad another chance.

'Who in Roma is giving you a hard time?'

Hannah had to smile at the militant glint in her friend's eyes. Gracie's championing made Hannah's chest tighten with gratitude. And relief. She knew without a doubt that her friend believed she was innocent of becoming involved in criminal activity, if very foolish not to get out sooner.

'Just whispers. Small-town stuff. Insinuations that I'd known more than I had.' She spread her hands. 'That I'd consorted with a drug pusher.' She met Gracie's eyes. 'He changed so much, and suddenly he craved money and power above all things. Craved the drugs. I couldn't help his addictions because he wouldn't let me. I saw the sudden uncontrolled violence and finally I left. I grew terrified that he'd spike my drinks and I'd wake up one day not knowing what I'd done.'

'I believe you. That was never you. You're not the first person to find herself in that position, and you won't be the last. I'm mostly angry that anyone would think badly of you.'

It all came out then. The ugliness, the fear and horror. And the guilt. The shame that she hadn't been able to help or heal him. Hannah dragged her fingers across her damp cheeks. When had she started crying? She shook her head. It didn't matter. The relief was overwhelming. 'Thank you, dear Gracie, for listening. I'm sorry to dump it on you, but I am glad I came.'

'So am I.' Gracie reached out and touched her hand. 'This is what friends are for. You would do the same for me. Take time out. Relax – because I think maybe you haven't done that for a while.' She smiled. 'And tomorrow and Saturday, you'll meet the rest of the women here. You're going to love Featherwood.'

Chapter Two

Hannah

On Saturday, as they prepared Oliver's first birthday party with community effort, Hannah stood included and welcomed into Gracie's warm circle of women. It felt like being a part of one of those handmade pottery clusters of faceless feminine forms with arms around each other.

It seemed ages since she'd been free to be with other women without sour looks from Porter. How had she allowed herself to become such a victim? Beau Porter should have been pushed to the kerb at the first sign of trouble.

She shook off the thought. She was a long way from Roma, and once the sun passed directly overhead, the back of Gracie's house and the trees down by the swollen stream she could hear from where she stood would morph into the shady place to be. With the creek fenced off, it was the perfect venue for a children's birthday party.

Hannah felt surprisingly at ease with this multigenerational, vocal gathering of women, despite the brevity of her visit so far. Soaking it all in, she turned and studied her friend.

Gracie's eyes were wearing her sparkling, excited look, but they were also full of mischief. No doubt because the diminutive midwife was determined to take advantage of Hannah's professional state of uncertainty. She'd said it more than once. *'They don't appreciate you up there. Move here. Featherwood needs a GP like you.'* Closely followed by, *'I know just the place that would be a perfect doctor's surgery and house.'*

It was all well and good to dream about permanently escaping, but did Hannah need to risk all her savings on being the solo doctor in this tiny town? The truth of an outlying practice meant there would be emergencies twenty-four seven, plus delayed access to the hospitals that were hours away if needed. She'd be responsible for keeping people alive until they could be retrieved. More paramedic than general practice doctor.

But then again, hadn't she wanted that since she'd been a heart-broken little girl who had lost her mother? Wasn't that why she'd studied medicine in the first place, instead of training to become someone's trophy wife? To save lives? Make a difference? *Yes, it was!*

But more daunting than any of those issues would be the scrutiny in this tiny village. She'd already been under the piercing analysis of a small town watching her every move after the truth came out about Porter.

Those, right there, risking her savings, being the only doctor and the scrutiny of a very small town, were three good reasons to go slow.

But there were also pluses . . . She mustn't forget the pluses.

She would not be isolated. Sadly, now, at home in Roma, she felt so alone. And embarrassingly ridiculous for being blind to

Porter's dark side, because she should have read the signs, tried to save him and left when she couldn't – a long, long time ago.

'Hey. You have a task, here.' Nell, another midwife like Gracie who lived in Featherwood, tied the end of the blue balloon she'd huffed and puffed into shape and took up a yellow one. Hannah liked Nell, so maybe she'd already found another possible friend.

She waved at the chaos. 'Did you have parties like this when you were a kid?'

'Nope.' Nell had mentioned being adopted by very wealthy medical parents and brought up by nannies. Her words and sentiment had created a small bond of two who had known privilege but missed out on the parental love Gracie showered on her toddler.

'I spent a lot of time at boarding school. No personal cooking or decorating for parties. It was all done by experts. My mother would spend a whole day with me shopping to make sure my dress, shoes, hair ribbons and party favours were exactly right. But I'd still manage to do something wrong at the event that embarrassed her.'

'Ouch.' Hannah winced. She'd been there, not with her dad, but the women he'd courted. 'I had more than a few step-aunties like that.' She shook her head as she reached for a cherry-red inflatable challenge. 'This is my first homemade kid's birthday and I am not an experienced balloon-blower.'

Nell grinned. 'I've learned since I came here.'

Hannah could learn too – it was a nice thought. 'We had staged affairs with restaurants or party planners, as well. Richard, my widowed dad, tried, but the day usually ended with him going off with one of the single mothers. I'd go home with my latest nanny.'

Hannah shook her head. 'Throwing money at organisers isn't the same as Gracie pouring love into a rocket-ship cake.' Even if the cake sagged a little to one side, because Gracie had spent yesterday afternoon crafting it for her child and love shone from the splotchy spacecraft like the stars it was aiming for.

'So true. If I have kids I'll make the cake, even if it's not perfect.' Nell, the expert balloonist, looked slightly militant, as if she'd thought about this. Hannah suspected Nell's mum hadn't been the loving type.

Her widowed dad had loved her, but he'd been a man who needed a woman fussing over him. And those women, except for her mother, were not the loving type.

She puffed the last breath into the balloon, examined its size and looked to Nell, who smiled and showed her how to tie the end of the mouthpiece. Hannah guessed her new balloon buddy, who had a long plait of brown hair reaching to her designer-jeaned butt, to be about mid-twenties. She was model trim with a loose silk blouse draped elegantly over her frame.

A glorious Pacific Island gene pool mixed with Asian had created an alluring beauty to Nell's face. Her long legs, visible through the stressed holes in her jeans, showed a deep tan that Hannah suspected rarely suffered damage from the sun. Her eyes were chocolate, almond-shaped, and framed by thick lashes and arching brows, and her mouth and chin held a determined tilt. She made Hannah think of a ballet dancer practising arm floats as she dropped and lifted her elegant hand to her mouth with each new balloon.

Godson Oliver squealed in delight at the next balloon Nell handed him. He was a blond-haired bruiser like his dad, and they both watched him chortle with delight at his prize as he squeezed ruthlessly and released it.

This morning, Gracie and Hannah had moved the kitchen table and a portable bench out onto the long, breezy rear verandah, to prepare the food and hang the streamers along the railing. The party would start soon, right after Gracie's husband, Jed Edwards, closed the town's rural store at midday.

Apart from the bushfires, which had swept the town last year and been a whole other story with this little village suffering like a lot of Australia, Featherwood had been a good move for Gracie and Jed. The big question for Hannah, now that she'd slept on the idea, was: could it be a good move for her, too?

The wooden verandah had become more crowded and she squished up closer to Nell. People seemed to arrive every few minutes and the chatter rose in volume. Everyone in town had been invited – not that it was a big village, but it was more bodies than Hannah had expected – and Gracie said they'd all bring a plate.

'Great to see you, Audrey,' Gracie called out and moved towards a newcomer. A pregnant woman with twin boys carrying popcorn eased in with her big, rounded belly out front. *There really is nothing so beautiful*, Hannah thought. She'd missed this connection and collaboration with others that Gracie seemed to draw around her so effortlessly. But as far as a party went, it felt too chaotic for something to begin in half an hour.

Hannah glanced at her watch. 'Will Jed be late?' she murmured into a sudden silence. The big guy had been tardy with both evening meals since she'd arrived, supposedly with dawdling customers holding him up from closing the doors, though Gracie postulated that Jed liked a good natter and was more responsible for the delays.

'He'll shut on time. Liam will make sure of it.' Nell's face suddenly glowed. 'Liam's ex-special forces. He'll have no problem completing the mission of getting Jed here on time.'

Gracie swung back their way and laughed. 'Liam isn't a pushover for customers like Jed is.' She gave a sidelong look at her friend. 'But don't start Nell waxing lyrical about Liam.'

Nell removed her next balloon from her mouth and let it, half-inflated, whoosh erratically in Gracie's direction. It popped her on the shoulder.

Hannah giggled then slapped her hand over her mouth. She was not a giggler. But these guys were funny. And solid. The kind of solid she needed under her. More tension dissolved and disappeared from the deep well of darkness inside her. Suddenly, the weight on her shoulders felt almost as light as the deflated rubber bag between her fingers. In her mind's eye, she saw again Nell's balloon's erratic flight.

Release, she implored silently. *Stop thinking about Porter. Let his actions go.* They weren't her fault and she'd been an innocent fool. *Bless friends and non-judgemental people*, she added, though she suspected she was the one being the hardest on herself.

'Right. No more sharing rosy-glow anecdotes with Gracie,' Nell said, mock-affronted. She turned pointedly away and blew gustily into her new balloon.

A small black-and-gold bee hovered above Gracie's head. It zipped back and forth like a tiny zebra helicopter. Hannah herself would have stepped away, but Gracie ignored it and continued to sprinkle coloured hundreds and thousands onto the buttered loaf to create fairy bread. Gracie believed in live and let live. Hannah sort of did, or she had, before Porter. But, she narrowed her eyes at the bee, now that she'd been stung, she admitted that she wasn't so sanguine.

Nell paused as she too watched the plump insect. 'Did you know that a third of the state's bees were wiped out by the end of last summer? Between the drought and the fires?'

'Did Liam tell you that?' Gracie teased in an arch voice, and Hannah once again felt how keenly she'd missed the warmth of female companionship. Porter had progressively isolated her. And lied as he had lost himself in the downward spiral. And almost destroyed her career and her life with his machinations and descent into drug-induced evil.

'Beeezzzz,' Gracie whispered, and Hannah realised she'd zoned out. Bees. They were talking about bees. *Stay with the picture.*

'No, Molly did.'

Hannah wondered who Molly was. She was here, somewhere; she'd heard her name earlier. There were so many names. So many women.

Chapter Three

Molly

Molly caught her name and turned from her intended target, dear Audrey and the twins, and tuned into the conversation with Nell.

'Liam only keeps bees because I love them,' she said, smiling at Gracie's Queensland friend's slightly harried expression. 'I'm Molly. Liam's my only sibling.'

'Ah, yes. Hello there, Molly. We did get introduced, but I'm struggling with names. Did I look confused?'

Molly laughed. 'A little.' She'd been watching the newcomer. Dr Hannah had a kind face, as if she wanted to help people but was happy to wait for them to tell her how. A good, patient trait for a doctor. She was blonde and confident, with smart, blue eyes and a not-yet-often-seen – but genuine – smile. 'We'd have a lot less food to eat without bees.'

'True.' Nell, Molly's should-be-sister-in-law-already, held her balloon in front of her mouth to speak like a microphone. 'Since December, there's been a bumper crop of trees and plants, some blossoming for the first time in twenty years. So . . . the bees are back.'

Molly shook her head in admiration. 'I love that you can remember a fact if you hear it once, and repeat it anytime it's needed. I wish I had those skills.'

'You have more useful skills, dear Molly,' Nell said. 'I'm a city girl, settling into the country. I'm the first to say you're the better cook, seamstress and farmer.'

Yes. Yes, I am. And what a waste it is, Molly thought. She'd wanted to be a good mother if she'd had the chance, but she'd been a widow too long now, and at forty-two, it was probably too late for her.

Now she was waiting for Nell and Liam to decide on kids, which didn't look promising when they couldn't even decide when to marry and where they wanted to live. Molly's house, which was the roomier option, or Nell's rebuilt, tiny house. Fingers crossed, it wasn't her that was holding them up.

She concentrated on the new doctor. 'Do you cook, Hannah?'

'I'd like to. I want to make gorgeous sausage rolls like Gracie whipped up this morning. They make my mouth water.'

'I can help you there,' Molly said. In an aside she added, 'Gracie mentioned you're thinking of moving here?'

'Did she now?' Hannah mock-frowned at her friend, who missed it, intentional or otherwise, as she chatted behind them.

Molly smiled. 'Well? Are you thinking of moving here?' She watched the doctor glance around the long porch. The smiling faces. The camaraderie she was accustomed to. Did she detect a slight wistfulness in the younger woman?

'Maybe,' Hannah responded.

After only two days? Now that would be a good thing. 'If you want to know anything about the place you come see me. I've lived here all my life, except for six months after the fires while we waited for our house to be rebuilt.'

The young doctor met Molly's eyes and nodded, then chose a green balloon thoughtfully, as if weighing up what to say. 'Thank you. I'll do that. It's a welcoming valley. Green and happy somehow.'

'That it is. We'd all be even happier with a doctor in town,' she teased, as she sliced Gracie's colourful fairy bread into small triangles and covered it with plastic wrap. She looked up. 'Here's Mavis. Have you met Mavis?'

Molly knew Mavis had turned eighty-one, but darn if the woman didn't still look like a tough and fit seventy. This was no pampered retiree. Mavis was a frumpy, feisty and fabulous woman with opinions. Molly chuckled quietly to herself as she considered Mavis's favourite crimson cardigan teemed with claret-coloured trousers, and as usual she was snorting at someone's comment as she tromped onto the back verandah carrying a big plastic bowl of chopped watermelon.

'Once met never forgotten,' Hannah said. 'I had the pleasure at Jed's store. And I met Archie.'

Molly hadn't seen Archie there, but of course Mavis's great-grandson would be with her. Dear Archie. Molly wished she could mother him herself, but Mavis was doing a fine job. Archie had grown like a bean sprout in the last year.

Nell had said Mavis was the kind of gruff great-aunt she would have loved to have had in her childhood. Then dear Nell had said, 'Or Molly, I'd be happy with either,' and Molly had loved her from then on. She suspected that with Nell's childhood as the not-quite-acceptable adopted child, any real aunts would have made a cosy difference to Nell.

No-nonsense Mavis dumped down her dish of melon and began cutting up the sausage rolls Gracie had put out to cool, placing the bite-sized pieces on an empty plate.

'See,' Hannah murmured. 'I feel like a useless appendage. Why didn't I know I could do that?'

Molly felt for her. Awkward and unsure at how to help. 'You will,' Molly said. 'If you move here, we'll all show you.'

'I'd better get back to work.' Hannah shook her head and waved her limp balloon at Molly, before she began to blow.

When she had inflated then tied it, Hannah looked up. 'How do apiarists make money? Apart from selling honey?'

Molly covered another plate with plastic wrap. 'We sell to agricultural industries that require pollination. Like canola farms. The state lost nearly ten thousand hives last year, but they've nearly all been replaced already.'

'Ha!' Mavis snorted. 'I heard it's the weeds that bees like the best. Apparently.' She paused and gave a happy sigh as she pulled an empty cereal bowl forward and began filling it with tomato sauce to dip the sausage rolls in. 'Patterson's curse is a godsend for beekeepers.'

'A Farmer's Friend,' Molly said.

Gracie reappeared. 'Just like our store.'

'And Jed,' Nell added. The women laughed.

Molly could see Hannah didn't get the joke, but she smiled and looked like she enjoyed the company. She heard her say quietly to herself, 'I thought a farmer's friend was a weed that stuck to your socks.'

She'd learn.

Chapter Four

Hannah

Six weeks later, Hannah was again driving south to Featherwood. This time with the intention of staying.

Her car phone switched from music to an incoming call and she glanced at the screen for the identity of the caller. Something she never used to do. RR – her father. The person she hadn't asked for help when she could have. To answer or not answer?

'Richard, how are you?' He'd asked for that mode of address around the same time he'd exploded out of mourning for her mother into brown Italian loafers and bespoke shirts.

'Excellent as always, thank you, my sweet.'

Hannah winced. It was now either 'my sweet' or 'honey', which would have been fine if the procession of ladyloves hadn't been called the same names.

As a seven-year-old when she lost her, Hannah remembered her darling mother as a quiet and compassionate homebody who loved to cook. And her father's adoration of her had been a warm and wonderful thing without overt displays of wealth or flowery name designations.

23

Everything had changed, got complicated, her father most of all.

Why her father thought he should only date vain and materialistic women he needed to attract with glad rags, she'd given up trying to understand.

Richard's voice intruded on her thoughts. 'How are you, honey? We haven't spoken for a while. Are you driving?'

'I am. I've been meaning to mention it.' She'd been putting it off in case he decided to discover why. 'I'm moving. I'm opening a new practice in Featherwood. With my friend, Gracie.'

'Isn't Gracie down in northern New South Wales?'

How on earth had he remembered that? 'Yes. I'll be coming into Featherwood soon. Everything okay?'

'Just checking on you. You sounded strained the last time I called. Has that got something to do with why you're moving? Let me know if I can help. I could be there as soon as I can get a flight?'

'No.' Then I'd have to tell him, she thought. 'I'll be fine.'

'Is there something I should know about? Did something happen?' he pressed.

'No.' She changed the subject. 'How are you? How's Priscilla?'

'Priscilla and I have gone our separate ways.'

Of course they had. The woman had been beautiful but boring. 'I'm sorry.'

'No, you're not.' She heard the smile in his voice. 'You knew, before I did, that we weren't suited.'

Well, she had, but she hadn't thought she'd shown the fact. Bad Hannah.

He went on to tell her he'd met a new woman and Hannah zoned out as the kilometres passed.

'Did you need something, Richard, or can we talk when I'm settled?'

'Nothing needed, honey, I just wanted to hear your voice. I'll phone next week. You enjoy your new home down there with Gracie. I know you missed her. Bye.'

And how had he known that, as well? She didn't remember ever telling him she had missed Gracie.

The music returned. Hannah reached over and switched it off, ignoring the small tug of guilt. The truth was, she'd stopped sharing her life with Richard a long time ago – in boarding school, really. He'd been so busy searching for the next Mrs Rogan, ostensibly to find her a mother, and there'd been plenty of runners but sadly no warm and fuzzy finalists. Hannah had decided early on not to discuss or ask for anything personal that he'd refer onto the latest woman for advice.

Since she'd become an adult, he was the one to phone her, even though she suspected her father would have liked her to instigate a call. Yes, she admitted, it was her fault that they didn't speak more. But when she was in trouble was the least likely time she'd phone him.

She drove over the Featherwood bridge, sent a friendly nod to the welcome sign, and resisted the childish urge to pull out a black marker pen and change the population numbers to add a one.

Slowing down as she passed Gracie's gate, she turned right off the Featherwood main street into her newly gravelled driveway. Gracie was her friend, not her crutch, and she was more than capable of moving into her new place on her own.

The entrance ran steeply up the hill, past the side of the churchyard, and curved to come out at the site of the recently christened

Featherwood Medical Centre. 'Christened' was an appropri-ate word, she felt, as the older-style house on the hill above the multi-purpose church had once been a many-roomed rectory. The previous owner would surely have christened it.

The large brick dwelling sat on a wide, flat area with a sweeping, circular drive that took visitors to the front parking area. In theory, and hopefully in reality, too, patients would park there and walk down the path into reception at the front.

Past that turn, the drive forked to the triple garage at the back, with carport and an expanse of open area at the rear. For the moment, Hannah parked at the front and climbed out.

Key heavy in her hand, she crossed to the main entrance, turned the lock and pushed open the arched front door. Hannah liked the quirkiness of having an ecclesial and studded doorway and the row of stained-glass panels high on the wall.

The inside shone bright and welcoming, not dark like it had been when she'd first seen the rectory, and her heart leaped a little at the transformation she'd envisaged. It was amazing what a couple of coats of egg-shell paint above the hip-height cedar panel-ling could do to an older building.

The dwelling had five bedrooms and two business offices, plus two sitting rooms – one of which she would turn into the waiting room. Amusingly, she'd discovered the biggest, 1950s-style, tiled bath she'd ever seen in a private home. She wasn't sure where that came from, unless the previous owner had been into full-immersion baptisms in the rectory.

The fact that the house had a wall and door separating the offices from the living areas meant a saving factor for her finances and an absolute delight at the idea of finally having a home of her own. Rentals had always been her preference but, coming to Featherwood, she'd felt the need to commit. And the rectory did feel homelike. Most importantly, it was all paid for and hers.

Hannah blew out a relieved breath as she put her crossbody bag on the kitchen bench. It had been a big week, with an eight-hour drive in the rain. *Go away, rain*, she thought.

The house creaked and echoed, and she stood there, slightly damp, staring at the boxes and the furniture waiting in orderly rows. It was her choice to be unaided. Alone. But she hadn't expected to feel this daunted when she arrived. She was an idiot.

Her father had said he could help. He could have been coming for the company if she'd invited him, but she'd said no, of course, citing that she needed time to settle in. But standing here alone, she was sorry she hadn't told him some of the facts about Porter and why she'd been glad to move.

Just as she was considering calling him, a sudden image of her father's arrival in Featherwood made her pause. In her mind's eye she could see him descending on her, then proceeding to flirt with all the women in town, leaving a trail of broken hearts when he left. Then where would she be as the new doctor in town? *Oh no.* She didn't need that headache.

Decision made, she pushed the thought away. She needed to stop feeling sorry for herself and get some work done.

Half an hour later, Hannah stood in the kitchen surrounded by boxes she'd unloaded from the car, contemplating where to begin. In the lounge, all the furniture was still waiting where it had been left by the removalist.

Suddenly, the idea of pouring a glass of white wine was a much more attractive prospect, even if said wine wasn't chilled. She'd only just turned on the fridge, but no matter. She could just sit and sip . . . except all the chairs had boxes on them.

The *tap*, *tap*, *tap* at the back door lifted her head. When she swung it open, she found Gracie standing with her small son in tow, but that wasn't all. There was Nell, with her towering man, Liam, standing lithe and powerful behind them; and Liam's sister, friendly and always helpful Molly; all smiling expectantly in her direction.

Oh, wow. A welcome committee? Company? A cheer squad? She hadn't realised, but this was exactly what she needed.

'Thank the Lord'—not her usual exclamation of delight, the rectory had to be rubbing off on her already—'for your smiling faces.'

And when her friend walked into the room, it felt as if the sun had come out from behind a cloud of misgivings. A warm hug enveloped her and then she was twirled. 'What fun,' Gracie said as she released Hannah and rubbed her hands together. 'We're here to sort out the furniture and help you unpack.'

Gracie's wondrous words slid some of the tiredness from Hannah's shoulders, as if negative thoughts were sucked through the floor to waiting Mother Earth, leaving them absorbed and Hannah feeling healed. And with her new Featherwood friends here, she didn't feel alone.

Her throat felt tight, but she cleared it and lifted her hands. 'May I say . . . welcome to the new Featherwood Medical Centre.' Her breath whooshed in relief, giving her the sense that everything would be fine. 'All of you. Drinks on me at the pub. I'll fix you a voucher later.' She grinned. 'Isn't the house gorgeous?'

'It came up well,' Liam agreed. He'd been the painter. The man could do anything, Hannah had discovered, and she'd had to force him to take a reasonable pay for his efforts.

Molly gestured for her brother to put a box they'd brought on the bench, and Hannah saw she'd packed a thermos, milk, makings of tea and coffee and cups. 'I thought this might kickstart you after the drive. Just until you get your kitchen set up.'

Molly swung a Tupperware container up beside the box, and Hannah suspected there'd be something incredibly delicious inside. Even from their brief previous acquaintance, she'd learned that Molly could bake like a champion. The scent of fresh quiche filled the air.

'I fancy a cup of coffee,' Molly said. 'Mind if I get it happening?'

Two hours later, her house looked more like a home. Liam and Molly had assembled the beds and Molly made them up in two of the biggest rooms, one for Hannah and one for guests. The sofa bed went in another, and Gracie told her she knew of someone selling more furniture for the empty rooms. She'd sort that out later in the week, she told Gracie, although secretly she was thinking, *As if I'd ever have visitors!* However, she did remember the possibility of her father turning up with whoever his latest love was, and groaned.

Gracie had tackled the kitchen, with Oliver 'sorting' the plastics, and Hannah and Nell were going through the lotions and soaps and shelving towels in the bathroom. It was nearly done. The most important living areas, anyway.

But then she'd have to sort the whole medical practice. From scratch. Panic edged up her throat again.

Nell cleared her throat, and Hannah blinked away the worries for now and paused in the makeup arranging.

'Hannah?' Nell lifted her chin, mouth determined and eyes narrowed, and said slowly, 'I was thinking . . . You'll need a receptionist-slash-practice nurse when you start, but not until you get some patients.'

Correct, Hannah would. Panic.

Nell swirled a long-fingered hand in the air. 'I need a job, so I wondered if you'd be interested in trialling me, for free,' she added hastily. 'I'm still registered as a nurse and midwife. I can type and I know computers. And bookwork.'

Hannah closed her mouth, which had unattractively hinged open, replaying the magic words. *Nurse, midwife, bookkeeper, typist.* Her heart gave a big thump of delight. 'Stop already. You're hired.' This was too good to be true. 'And I'll pay you from day one.'

Nell blew out a breath. 'Phew. I was nervous about asking. Just a trial is fine.'

Hannah shook her head, her brain suddenly clear of the horrid stress fog. 'I've been worrying about how to answer the appointment phone while consulting. Thinking maybe a voicemail and ring them back?' She rubbed her hair. 'It was doing my head in.'

'Even if there aren't enough patients to cover the wages,' Nell said, 'you'd still need help to set up before the first week.'

Hannah nodded, visualising working together with Nell. Like at Gracie's party when she'd visited. Like today. Easy. Efficient. Effortless communication. 'That's what I was thinking. I might not be busy enough for a full-time employee to start, but yes, during the set-up, absolutely. Then, after that, depending on how many hours I need when I open, you'd come in. Would it work to be part-time if that's how it turns out?'

'Part-time is fine. I still have the farm, but I need something else, and I need to get midwifery and nursing hours to keep my registration.'

'You said bookwork? Could you do the practice-manager details? Help me with procedures and protocols for legal requirements? I have it on file. It just has to be reformatted with our letterhead. And can you load the computers with medical software for consultations?'

Nell nodded decisively. 'And if we have software problems, then Liam knows more than I do.' Even Nell looked excited now. 'I could set up the bookwork and ordering the way I like it from the start. Everything would be streamlined, and we'll get a webpage.' She smiled shyly. 'I like to be organised.'

Hannah lifted her eyes to the rectory roof. 'Praise be to Featherwood.' They laughed and Gracie came in to see what she was missing.

Hannah grinned at her. 'I have a new employee.'

Gracie did not look surprised. 'Excellent.' She clapped her hands. 'Everything is coming together.'

So it seems, Hannah thought. Although Roma had been like that. Before. Until she'd blotted her copybook with a bad-choice boyfriend and the sky had fallen in.

Chapter Five

Jude

Jude Waugh stared out of the open kitchen window and across the paddocks of Luna Downs to the cattle. The rain had let up briefly and the herd's sleek coats shone in the morning light. A sense of accomplishment, the first he'd felt for a year, seeped into him with the sight. It had been a battle, emotional and physical, but they were coming out of it, now.

Footsteps sounded and he turned to see his son slip in beside him. The boy sighed as he reached to grab a glass of water from the tap. It was the smell that caught Jude's attention.

'Leo?' Touching his son's shoulder, Jude felt more clavicle than expected. He furrowed his brows. 'Have you been drinking nail-polish remover?'

Even as he said it, Jude heard the crazy in that accusation. Now that he really studied Leo, normally an energetic twelve-year-old, his son resembled a washed-out windsock. Pale, listless, and if he wasn't mistaken, he'd lost weight. Was he sick?

Fear slapped Jude upside the head. *Not cancer. Not again*, he begged. He couldn't do that same road.

How had he missed this? The parental wake-up call nearly knocked him over. Why hadn't he noticed before?

'Mate?' He'd said that too loudly and toned down his voice. 'Leo? Tell me. You okay?'

'I'm tired,' Leo muttered, testiness plain in the way he jerked his shoulder out from under Jude's hand. 'Thirsty. That's all. I'm fine, Dad.'

Thirst wasn't unusual; the kid drank like a camel. But irritable and tired? Like his mother, who'd gone down like a limp kitten when the cancer hit her? Until the pain had made her cry in the night. Which was why Jude had agreed, at first.

His throat closing, he strained to swallow to get his voice going again, being the strong one here and supposedly, the men said, as tough as Thunderbolt's Rock. 'You don't look fine.' Jude pushed panic away and took a steadying breath, forcing out the next words. 'How long since you felt well? Days? Weeks?'

Dammit, Iris wouldn't have missed this change in their only child.

'Since we went back to school.' Leo pushed his flopped fringe of dark hair back off his face. 'I'm not sleeping well, that's all. It makes me tired.'

His son huffed at him and Jude blinked at the sweet stink of his breath. Fear coiled and chewed. He knew in his gut something was very wrong, and all he could think was *cancer*. Where was the nearest doctor's surgery? No way was he going near *that* hospital. The one where Iris died.

He pulled his military-case phone from his pocket. Although he rarely looked at it, everyone here was his responsibility, and if things went wrong, he had to have access to the outside world.

He searched for the nearest doctor's surgery. What day was it? That was the problem with living off the grid. You let it all go by and didn't even know what day of the week it was. Hating the outside world, he'd chosen to live in his own ecosystem. Growing fruit and vegetables. Butchering their own meat. Being responsible for building and repairing within the station, and relying on resilience and imagination more than outside resources, meant they only went to town every couple of weeks.

Just before Iris grew ill, they'd bought this thousand-acre property outright, after a particularly lucrative contract, where he'd helped build a stone mini-castle for a billionaire. He'd been less averse to the outside world then, and they'd enjoyed the concept of creating their own paradise. The golden valley of grasslands and timber called Luna Downs had piles of glorious rock he could work with, though the land was still black from the fires. He'd just needed to ensure they could secure their water supply in times of drought. They'd had such plans.

Halfway between Armidale and Dorrigo, the parcel had been vacant since the drought. It was run-down, and had been left with a habitable shearing shed and stumps of the old burnt farmhouse. He, Iris and Leo had moved in.

At night, there'd been magic in the moonlight, enchantment falling with the stunning sunsets, and they'd all loved the freedom and pride in their own valley as it grew more self-sufficient.

Until their world had gone crazy with pain, anguish and desperation. It seemed the hounds of hell had moved in with them, too, when Iris became sick.

Modern-day medicine battled and tried, but it couldn't help Iris. The love of his heart had withered and twisted until one day she had begged him to help her die. That was the worst day of his life.

Then Iris was gone. For Jude, finding purpose – a reason to get up every day – had been hard.

And now Leo was sick.

Chapter Six

Hannah

Hannah's first day as Featherwood's new GP dawned cloudy and wet with an early wind that felt way colder in March than anything she'd experienced in Queensland. Pulling her scarf closer, Hannah decided she'd get used to it.

The rain had continued unabated over the weekend, while Hannah stayed snug and warm in her new home with the fireplace crackling and her consulting rooms ready, thanks to hard work, dear friends and her new super-secretary, Nell.

It was all so different to those horrendous weekends when she'd tried to keep the labile and unstable Porter happy. Where had the funny, sexy guy she'd first met gone? He'd been ripped away by drugs and the quest for more money and minions. Well, she would never be a minion. Right up until she'd seen the calculating, callous and controlling man he'd become, she'd hoped he would change back. But deep down, she had suspected that most of the man she'd first met had been lost forever.

Except that when she'd left him, he'd stalked her. He'd shocked her with threats if she didn't come back, so she'd told the police what he'd done and asked for a restraining order. Then he'd been caught and detained for distribution of drugs, and she, someone seen often in the past with him, had been shown as a dupe. Naive. A doctor who dated a drug lord.

But that was over now, she reminded herself. He was in custody and she could start afresh, in Featherwood. *Let it go*, she begged. *Let the baggage go*.

This place sat as a very small blip in a different state's map. It was safe. Much safer than Roma. But inside, a tiny voice whispered, *You hope . . .*

This was an adventure with the opportunity to break free of the constraints she'd built around herself. *Protection*, she'd called it, but *isolation* and *withdrawal* were the real words. Here, hopefully, she could find herself again.

In an upswing of luck, real estate prices in Featherwood had proved so reasonable compared to Roma, that Hannah's small treatment room held an array of only slightly second-hand, good-quality medical equipment with the change from her savings.

She was here, and it felt right, like home. Sitting on top of the rise above the church with the town spread below, it felt like an eyrie. A safe eyrie.

From the front porch, she could see the creek, Gracie's house and the school, Jed's store and the street going both ways. Inside, she had open fireplaces, high ceilings and gorgeous cornice work that gave space and light and welcome vibes. Right at this moment, a pink row of sunlight shone on the polished wooden floor across from her, making her smile.

In the new waiting room sat the polished pew from the crazy-big shed, running all the way along one wall. She'd put it there for families, thinking they could squish up together. And the rest could have the chairs that lined the other wall.

Hannah caught the swing of the front door as she fired up her computer for day one, and her new secretary, tall and elegant in a buttoned white blouse and black jacket, raised dark brows at her.

Nell carried her satchel and a plastic container through the waiting room to her new reception desk. Nell Truman was a star. Nurse, midwife, receptionist, bookkeeper, unlikely farmer, and now good friend. Hannah had struck it rich when she arrived in Featherwood.

'Morning, Boss. Excited?' Nell's well-modulated voice carried the same private-school tones as Hannah's.

Hannah shook her head. 'Nervous.'

Nell slow-blinked in mock censure. 'Nope. That's unacceptable. Try again.'

Maybe *excited* carried a more positive vibe, with an element of truth. Hannah tried again. 'Nervous and excited. It's a new start.'

'It is. And Molly sent butterfly cakes for morning tea.'

Of course she did. Molly, a 42-year-old frustrated mother without kids, was kindness personified, and she loved to cook and spoil people. And she had decided that Hannah needed spoiling.

Hannah's first four patients were booked to begin arriving in ten minutes. The last three were check-ups, though she suspected they were checking out the new doctor more than vice versa. But that was fine.

The phone rang and Nell raised her brows with a demure smile as she picked it up. 'Featherwood Medical Centre. This is Nell. How may I help you?' She listened then said, 'There's an appointment at three this afternoon.'

This is going to work, Hannah thought, and then Nell said, 'I'm sorry. We have no appointments this morning,' before she paused. Then she said, 'I'll just put you through to the doctor.'

The phone on her desk rang. She looked out through the door to Nell, who held out her hands in the universal question mark. Something Hannah needed to deal with.

'Dr Rogan,' she said into the phone.

'Jude Waugh.' The voice, which was brusque like gravel underfoot, growled. 'My son, Leo, is sick. He's twelve. He's thirsty, tired, has lost weight. His mother died of cancer a little over a year ago. He needs to be seen this morning. I'm worried.'

Clearly, he was a man used to shooting orders – *possibly shooting anything*. Hannah stiffened. Where had that thought come from?

She stared at the phone. 'Then you should take him straight to the hospital.'

'No.' The word, aimed like a frozen bullet, was fired from the phone with a bang.

Extreme concern, and a voice dripping ice. Did she need to see this man? Hannah chewed her lip. There was a story there, one that worried her, but she wouldn't risk a child by saying no.

'You can bring him in, Mr Waugh, though it's likely you'll have to wait.'

'Fine. The nurse can check him out while we're waiting.'

'Certainly. Nell would be happy to. Come in when you're ready.' She put the phone down because he'd already hung up. Looking at Nell, she raised her brows in question. 'A worried father?'

'Very.' Nell tapped her lip with a finger. 'Agitated. Abrupt. Angry, even? That's why I passed him to you.'

'You can do that at any time. Your instincts are good. He said the boy's mother died last year and now his son's sick.' Their eyes met. 'That would be terrifying.'

Silence fell as they both thought about that and then, simultaneously, they glanced at the clock. They could hear voices outside.

'That's for later.' Hannah drew a deep breath and plastered on a smile. 'Right. It's time. Let's do this.'

Nell stepped out of Hannah's consulting room as a familiar elderly woman in dark-red trousers and a maroon football jersey stomped in towing a reluctant teenager. The boy, gangly and teen awkward, with messy blond hair and long, freckled legs, was limping. He also wore a football jersey, though this one had *New South Wales* stamped on it in blue, and his face looked stamped in trepidation.

Chapter Seven

Mavis

'Mavis. How are you?'

Nell's smile really is a delight, Mavis thought. Like a China doll she used to have as a kid. The girl had really come on since she'd sold her that dog on her first day in town. And now she was working for the new doc.

Mavis wondered if the new doc needed a dog? She had a litter of new puppies, the cutest things, and the twelve-month-old bitch she needed to find a home for before she started to breed.

'And Archie.' Nell's voice broke into her thoughts. 'Here for your tetanus shot.'

Mavis Maloney heard her great-grandson suck in a breath beside her. The kid had worked himself up. Well, too bad. She'd seen someone with tetanus once and she didn't want to see it again.

She'd dragged Archie to Gracie yesterday for an opinion on a rusty nail injury, and Gracie, as a midwife and previously the village-nominated first-aid officer, had gladly referred him on to Hannah, who had been visiting too. Since they had a doctor now, it was only sensible.

Hannah had cleaned and bandaged his foot with Gracie's supplies and slipped him into first spot this morning for this tetanus injection. The kid had been thinking up excuses ever since.

By the time they both answered all the questions for that new file in Nell's computer, the doctor was ready for them.

Mavis followed a reluctant Archie inside the consulting room and scrutinised her surroundings with obvious satisfaction. Bookshelves, medical equipment, a computer and even an examination table behind a curtain. She felt her eyes widen in approval.

'It's like a real doctor's surgery.' Mavis nodded her appreciation. 'In Featherwood.' She relished something she'd felt the town had needed for a long time. 'It's good to see you here, Doc.'

'Thanks, Mavis.'

The doc was another good-looking woman, one who spoke and dressed with the confidence Mavis always thought of as city dressing, like Nell. Unlike Nell, though, the doc stood medium height, all curves and shiny, bouncy blonde hair and clever eyes that glowed with what Mavis suspected could be too much kindness for her own good.

She glanced at the kid. Archie wasn't seeing the doc's reassuring smile. He was staring at the injection in the small silver tray with morbid horror – and possibly limited vision, as his fringe seemed to cover most of his face.

Mavis grimaced. She was still working on getting him to cut that hairy thing.

The doc said, 'Are you allergic to anything, Archie?'

He shook his head, fringe flying, though the movement resembled a shudder more than a denial. Terrified. Jerky. Poor kid.

'You don't like needles?' the doc asked.

A rapid head shake emerged from the boy, and Mavis tried not to smile. The attempt at controlling her features didn't work, and she ended up snorting and grinning.

Hannah looked at Mavis. 'At the end of next month, your gran will probably have her flu injection. Is that right, Mavis?'

Oh, wasn't that sneaky. Mavis had resisted those flu needles for years. She wrinkled her forehead, but she grunted in consent. 'Could do.'

The doc looked back at Archie. 'Reckon you can be braver than her?'

Archie stilled and narrowed his eyes at Mavis. Then he moistened his lips and swallowed, with a slight lift of his chin. 'Maybe.'

The doc leaned over and wiped his upper arm with a swab, and Archie flinched. And that wasn't even the needle! *She might have to wrestle him yet*, Mavis thought.

'It's going there.' The doc tapped the spot with the swab. 'Are you ready?'

Archie's wide eyes stared helplessly at Mavis, and she held his gaze with amusement. 'Braver than me, you reckon?' she scoffed.

Archie's eyes narrowed.

'And done.' The doc dumped the empty syringe in the sharps container.

Archie swivelled his face away from Mavis and turned his elbow out to look at the spot. 'It didn't hurt.'

'Told you,' Mavis murmured, but she was pleased, anyway.

'Good,' the doc said. 'You have to stay for fifteen minutes, but I've got a couple of questions to ask before you go. And I want to look at that wound. Okay?'

'Okay.'

Ten minutes later, Archie was pronounced healthy and released from the doc's office after being weighed, measured, his immunisations confirmed by a tattered book Mavis had brought with her, and medical file commenced. Mavis had an appointment for a month's time for her first check-up and the flu injection. Tricky young doc.

Now she'd have to take the kid for the burger she'd promised him at the shop. She wasn't running him into Dorrigo for anything flashier. She didn't fancy anywhere further than town. Driving the car was becoming more of an effort every week, and soon she'd have to drive to Armidale for that specialist's appointment. She couldn't wait for Archie to get his licence. He had today off school since he'd missed the bus to attend the medical centre.

She eased into the new chair, a surprisingly comfortable seat for a doctor's waiting room, for the last five minutes they had to kill after the needle. *That creek paddock needs slashing anyway*, she thought, *he'll enjoy that*.

Someone opened the door and Mavis watched from where she sat. A big bloke, who looked like he had muscles in his breath, came in with a kid around Archie's age. A kid who looked unwell, Mavis figured, and she settled back to see what happened.

Chapter Eight

Hannah

First patient done.

Hannah wondered briefly how long it would take to create histories and update the medical files for all of the inhabitants of Featherwood who might visit her, let alone those from the valleys beyond. Quite a while, she imagined.

With the consulting room door still open, she sat in prime position to see the darkness fill the outside door as it opened, and a tall, grim-visaged man ushered in an obviously unwell teenager. This had to be Leo and his worried dad.

The scheduled next patient hadn't arrived yet, so Hannah stood and walked to the door of her office. 'You can come straight in, Leo.'

His dad's piercing eyes, the colour and temperature of sunlit grey ice, raked her as he turned his son towards the consulting room.

Hannah resisted the urge to step back. This guy was running on high emotion with iron control. A scary combo. 'Mr Waugh? Perhaps you could fill in the details of Leo's full name and date of birth with Nell, please, before you come in, so I can create a medical file?'

The boy shuffled in, giving the impression that he could barely place one foot in front of the other. He was tall, gangly, too thin and pale. His father was right. Leo was seriously unwell. She should have pushed the hospital more.

Leo flopped into the chair with a heaviness that spoke of bone-deep weariness and gusted out a relieved breath.

Hannah breathed in. *Phew.* Acetone. Her suspicions grew more solid. Even from the brief symptoms gleaned during the phone call, she'd had her fears that it could be this. They were lucky he hadn't gone into a diabetic coma. She'd bet his sugars were through the roof.

'I'm Dr Rogan, Leo, and I'm glad your dad brought you in today. I suspect you're starting to feel worse and worse. Is that right?'

'Pretty much,' the boy said and closed his eyes. Long lashes settled on his pale cheeks, and it made something inside Hannah ache at the thought of this boy having no mother.

'I have an idea why. I'd like to check, but to do that it involves me sticking a small needle into your finger for a drop of blood. Do you think you could manage that?'

The boy shrugged, without looking up at her. 'Go on. Don't care. Do it.' His dark head drooped along with his shoulders as he slumped in the chair.

'Before I do, can I get you to pee in this urinal for me, please. To rule out infections in your wee that could also make you feel like this.'

Wearily, Leo rose and took the plastic 'bottle' towards the door she gestured to. 'There's a three-way bathroom that opens off here and the reception area. Just lock the door on the other side and nobody will be able to get in, but don't lock this one.' The last thing she needed was an unconscious patient behind a locked door.

The boy nodded and disappeared.

Two minutes later he returned. Handed her the specimen and slumped down in the chair.

Hannah took the receptacle over to the sink, poured urine into a red-topped specimen bottle to send away to the lab, and tested the remainder with a dipstick. The stick held varied coloured litmus patches to highlight any other reasons for Leo's illness. The ketones and the glucose on the stick flared instantly to the darkest reading.

Crikey, as she'd suspected. She washed her hands, but she could feel her heart pitter-patter into overdrive. The kid's sugars were off the chart. He could crash at any moment.

Hannah opened a drawer in her desk and pulled out a disposable lancet and one of her glucometers. She slid the test strip in one side.

Leo's eyes remained shut, but he was still sitting upright. That was good. 'Do you want me to wait for your dad?'

He shrugged. She probably should. The boy was a minor, but time was of the essence. The problem was made redundant when the looming figure of Jude Waugh filled the doorway.

'Please sit down, Mr Waugh. I'm Dr Hannah Rogan. I agree, Leo is unwell. I'd like to check his blood-sugar levels and that requires a drop of his blood. Leo said that's fine with him. Are you okay with that, as well?'

'You're the doctor.' His voice was like crunching through a creek bed when the water was cold. More biting control. More disquiet on Hannah's part.

Delightful, Hannah thought, but she was more interested in Leo than his boor of a father. 'Thank you,' she said politely and pricked Leo's middle finger pad. He didn't flinch and a bead of bright blood bloomed like a small red rose.

She positioned the test strip into the blood bead and watched it darken as it absorbed the blood into the machine. They waited. The machine beeped to say it was done. They all saw the word *HI*. So, too high for the machine to record. Judging by the clinical condition of Leo, Hannah could believe it.

She looked at his father. 'Did you know that your son is a diabetic?'

'He's not.'

'Your son's sugars are dangerously high and he's at risk of going into a diabetic coma. He needs emergency fluid replacement and insulin for the extreme sugar in his blood. Which we'll do now, before he deteriorates further.'

She held his cold gaze with one of her own. 'But this is an emergency and he'll need assessment in a major centre by a specialist endocrinologist. I'm going to call the ambulance, and hopefully, by the time they arrive he'll be stable enough to travel.'

They stared at each other for several long seconds as the words hung between them. 'Which hospital?'

She had no idea. The two hospitals were equally distant. It had to be Armidale or Coffs Harbour. 'The one the ambulance will take him to,' she said.

Hannah picked up the phone. 'Can you come in, Nell? Bring a wheelchair to transfer Leo to the treatment room, please.'

Jude held up his hand. 'I've got him.' The man reached over and pulled his son's arm over his neck and lifted him as if the boy was half his age and weight. 'You're right, mate. I've got you.' The words were quiet and gentle, and totally unexpected from so big and tough-looking a man.

'Cancel that,' Hannah said into the phone. 'Ring an ambulance for Leo. Diabetic emergency for transfer.'

She put down the phone and hurried to open the door, but Jude Waugh managed it easily as he held his son, so she went first. 'This way.'

Chapter Nine

Jude

Leo was a diabetic? Hell. The echoing words – *coma, ambulance, hospital* – ran around in his head as Jude carried his son into another room after the doctor.

He placed Leo along the narrow bed with his head gently on the pillow, but Leo's eyes didn't open. 'You still with us, mate?'

Grey eyes flickered open. 'Still here,' but the words were slurred and faint now. He sucked in a breath. Fear punched Jude in all the sore places it had already punched, places that were still so raw it only took a finger tap to inflict agony.

He forced himself to step back from the bed, while the doctor washed her hands at the sink and the nurse started opening packets onto a stainless-steel trolley with noisy speed. She was tipping the contents like missiles onto the surface, with rattles and clangs against the steel.

The urgency rang unmistakably, and his own heart rate rose with the noise. He took another step back and pushed his shoulders into the cold wall. To distract himself, he glanced around. It was a small area and there were four in here – one of them taking up space on a bed. He wouldn't have even known this medical centre was here if it wasn't for the website. Lucky for Leo, it seemed.

Later, he'd worry about which hospital they'd have to go to, but if it was that desperate, he didn't care. Still, he wished he was anywhere else but here, and that he and Leo were still at Luna Downs having a normal day.

He watched the doc. Small, blonde, nicely rounded, she looked confident. Efficient. Lucky, that. She'd already inserted a cannula and was taping it in. The nurse had connected the tubing to a bottle over the bed and joined it to the cannula. The doc's words interrupted his thoughts.

'I'm going to give him a rapid-acting insulin to bring his sugars down, but not too far because we don't want him to swing the other way and go into a "hypo". The intravenous fluids are to correct his dehydration and they contain sodium and potassium to help his cells start working again.'

Suddenly, Jude's legs felt weak. A diabetic coma. Coma. Leo could have died in the car if he hadn't been quick enough.

She went on. 'Treatment for type-one diabetes involves insulin injections or the use of an insulin pump, frequent blood-sugar checks, which you'll have to ensure Leo does, and carbohydrate counting to keep him stable. They'll explain the ramifications at the hospital.'

'Give me the "why it happened 101" now.'

She paused, lifted her determined little chin and held his gaze. Her eyes were baby-bell blue, big and bold and fierce with intelligence. 'Basically, I don't know why it happened. It could be genetic. Or it could be that he had a viral infection that wiped out his pancreas. Nobody knows why. But Leo's natural insulin management has stopped and now he's at risk of having too much sugar in his blood or not enough. Both are life-threatening and require huge changes of lifestyle. When a child gets diabetes, his whole family is impacted. That's you, I gather. The endocrinologist will explain it to both of you. Leo will have to manage it strictly for the rest of his life.'

He suspected as much. 'Thank you, sunshine.' She obviously felt he didn't need it sugar-coated.

'You're welcome.'

Chapter Ten

Hannah

By the time Hannah had stabilised Leo and the boy had woken up, much to everyone's relief, the ambulance arrived. She scurried back to her office and hurriedly created patient notes and a transfer form.

As she printed them off and handed the referral to Nell for the paramedics, an influx of patients had trickled through the front door and settled into the chairs. Nell was explaining there was an emergency, but Hannah suspected her new clients were happy to relax and watch the excitement. Bless a village gossip opportunity.

Silence fell as the chattering women stopped to watch. Nell stepped back to reopen the door for the paramedics, who pushed the ambulance trolley through to the waiting vehicle. Right behind them, big and grim-faced, Jude Waugh turned her way and his silver-grey gaze met hers and held. He nodded his head once in acknowledgement while towering over them all, slightly menacing in protection mode, then he followed the paramedics out the door. As he left, it felt as though the air was sucked out with him and then rushed back in again when he was gone.

Hannah tried not to compare Jude Waugh to another man who had been not quite as big and tough but had turned out to be terrifying. She tried not to acknowledge that despite his almost aggressive abrasiveness, Jude Waugh had intrigued her. He would be hard to forget.

His vibe came across as hard-nosed, but thank goodness there was none of that 'look at me, I'm the man of your dreams' air Porter had given off.

When Leo had woken up, this man had taken her hand in his strong fingers and clasped it once; a fast, fierce thanks. Something unexpected had vibrated between them and both had pulled away. He'd frowned and then cleared his throat to say, 'Thank you.' There'd been such depth of emotion in the gravel of the man's voice, Hannah had had to swallow her own emotional throat prickles.

She needed to stop thinking about that. About the strength in his hand. The emotion in his eyes. The obvious love of a father for his son. Because she couldn't help the suspicion that, despite all the positives there, he just might be everything that had ruined her life before. Trouble was, after that one long look, she had the feeling he could be a major disruption for the peaceful life she aimed to build here.

Once she was out of sight in her office, the quiet void was filled with a babble of exclamations and murmurs from the waiting-room ladies, and she heard the words *closed community, alcohol, criminals.*

Her chest tightened and she shut her ears to the gossip. Or tried to. At least they hadn't said *drugs.*

Hannah scanned her patient list. An 'expecting' mother and two small children were next. Audrey from Oliver's first birthday party. She needed to focus on her new life, which centred on meeting and helping people from a small village. She'd soon know them all. Know them well. She sincerely hoped they'd get past the gossip and rumours and let her enjoy her new start.

Moving to the door, she smiled at the very pregnant woman she'd already met at Gracie's. 'Audrey Peroni? Nice to see you again. Please, come in.' She'd make sure she had an obstetric history as well before they were done.

By the end of the day, Hannah had seen twelve patients and Nell had almost filled the next day's appointments, except the small spaces Hannah had instructed her to keep for emergencies.

On the whole, her clientele appeared healthy, though Audrey's hyperactive four-year-old twin boys both had hearing issues that would need to be addressed by the ENT specialist she'd referred them to. Mikey and Mitch would turn out to be red-headed hellions, Hannah had no doubt, and their mother was not helped by the fortnightly absence of her fly-in fly-out miner husband.

Inquisitive boys meant Hannah had trouble keeping anything on the bookshelves in her office during the visit. The thought made her smile, though. Luckily, Audrey had the calm of a Zen monk as she had gently chided and pulled the boys back into line.

The other patients she'd seen had needed little assistance apart from prescriptions and health checks, and she reassured herself that the idea of creating medical records was something she was better to do earlier, rather than later, when a medical crisis appeared.

Her new patients' oft-repeated appreciation for her opening a surgery in Featherwood warmed her heart, and as she and Nell closed up for the day, they grinned at each other.

'A successful start, I think.' Nell's beaming face broadcasted her pleasure.

Hannah wriggled her shoulders to release the tension that still pulled her neck. 'It did feel a little like being the new girl in school.' Mainly because she had to ease herself away from the questions of why she'd moved here.

Her fingers rubbed tight shoulder muscles loose and let the satisfaction of achievement curl in her belly. This moment felt good. 'But it was better than I expected.' Or even hoped. 'You're a star, Nell. We make a good team.'

'Absolutely. And we get to do it all again tomorrow.' She glanced at the treatment room and raised her brows. 'Have you heard how Leo is?'

She'd just put down the phone from the consultant. Would have phoned the hospital if she hadn't heard. 'The endocrinologist said we'd done everything right in the crisis, which is nice to know. Leo's condition is satisfactory now, but they'll keep him a few days for stabilisation and education.'

'I wonder if his dad will stay.' Nell pursed her lips. 'The ladies-in-waiting were agog. Did you hear what they were saying?'

'No.' Not clearly. In fact, she'd tried very hard not to eavesdrop.

'I wouldn't worry. There was an awful lot of speculation, not many facts.' Nell wrinkled her nose. 'Wonder what Mr Waugh's story really is?'

To Hannah's ears, it didn't sound like Nell took much store in village gossip, which was another bonus she really appreciated.

'He's a bit of a looker, don't you think?' Nell added as she shut down her computer.

'I didn't notice.' But she couldn't keep a straight face and they both laughed. 'He could be.' Hannah sobered. 'But I'm trying to avoid the dark and dangerous type.' Hopefully, that wasn't an attraction she was doomed to suffer from for the rest of her life.

'He could just be dark and protective, without the danger? It's obvious he cares about his son.'

Hannah had to agree with that. She'd seen his fierce but caring behaviour. 'He'll need to learn about diabetes now, so I guess he'll stay with Leo for a few days.'

Hannah did not want to be curious about Jude Waugh. She was, but she could shut that down. Learn her lesson. 'Great job on getting everything set up so fast when we needed it, by the way. Let me know if you think of anything else we should keep in emergency stock.'

Nell nodded. 'I've set up an electronic pharmacy system, so we automatically reorder when we use emergency drugs. But I'll have another scroll through the medical practice sites tomorrow, with an eye on diabetes.'

'You are my clever practice nurse.' Hannah was still bowing to the stars in gratitude for Nell.

'Thanks, Boss.' Nell glanced at her watch. 'Which reminds me, it's weekly date night tonight and it's Liam's turn to cook. I've emptied the bins, and the rooms are ready for tomorrow.'

'What are you still doing here, then? Go, scoot.' She made a shooing gesture with her hands.

The knock on the front door came at seven pm. It wasn't dark outside, but Hannah had showered, and the sun had set. She glanced ruefully at her bright-yellow flannelette PJs with bumblebees and the word *beezy* printed randomly on the fabric in rainbow-coloured bubbles. Comfort clothes for a rainy evening in a lonely house.

It could be Gracie visiting, but hey, it was unlikely, because her friend would be busy feeding Jed's enormous appetite and putting their son to bed. It could be a patient with a medical emergency, in which case she should throw on a white coat before opening the door. But somehow, she didn't think so. It hadn't been that kind of knock.

It was very, very weird that she decided it had sounded like a Jude Waugh, come-to-the-door-now knock. Confident. Brief. To the point. *Dammit*. She'd just stopped thinking about him.

She needed a surveillance camera. Or a chain with a bolt. Or a dog.

She eased open the door a hand's width. A man in the shadow with familiar shoulders and a strong profile stared away to the side of the house. 'Mr Waugh, is there a problem? How's Leo?'

His chiselled features turned her way. 'Leo's condition is stable. And he's a diabetic. Forever.'

'Huge life changes, then. But he's smart. He'll stabilise and he has his dad.'

'Lucky him.' His hard mouth curled in disgust. It still looked sexy, though. Cripes, she did not just think that.

Think something else, she commanded herself. Okay. The guy was beating himself up that he'd missed the early signs. 'The onset of the disease can be insidious, Mr Waugh.'

'It's just Jude. Or Waugh. Not Mr.'

Nope. This was not a social relationship, though she could meet him halfway. 'Jude Waugh,' she said, with just a hint of exasperation in the words, though whether that was for herself or for him she didn't know. 'What can I do for you? The surgery's shut.'

She was still holding the half-closed door and his black brows drew together. 'Is there a Mr Rogan?'

She raised her brows.

He grimaced. 'I thought not. You need a surveillance camera. Or a chain with a bolt. Or a dog.'

Hannah murmured under her breath, 'Great minds think alike.' She'd get right on that. One day. 'What can I do for you?'

'Nothing. I just wanted to say thank you.' He lifted something from near his hip; she hadn't seen it hanging there in the gloom. He was offering her a grocery bag. 'Your surgery bulk-bills your fees, so you being here to save Leo's life didn't cost me a thing. The specialist said you did. Save his life. I brought you a thankyou.'

She reached out and took the bag. She hadn't intended to, but such was the man's authority that she found herself obeying the unspoken command. When it clinked, she frowned.

'I live in a dry community, so I can't take it home and give it to you at a reasonable hour.'

And with that, he turned and left, covering the ground to the back of the rear parking area in long strides until his shape disappeared into a large, all-terrain vehicle that lit up with a very distinctive roar. Like its owner. She watched him rumble away, and gradually, the weight of the bag reminded her that she needed to bring it in. Or leave it outside.

The illusive words of the women in the waiting room whispered, *Be careful.* She thought of Porter. God, she hoped whatever was in there was legal.

She backed into the house and pulled the door shut. Locking it one-handed, she went through to the kitchen and put the bag on the table. It clinked again.

She looked in at what was obviously not contraband. 'Now I feel bad,' she muttered, and pulled out a bottle of very expensive French champagne, a second, smaller bottle and two boxes of chocolates. Handwritten notes attached to the chocolates said, *For Nurse Nell* and *For Dr Rogan.*

Sweet. And that wasn't going to make him any easier to forget.

Chapter Eleven

Jude

Jude accelerated away from the doctor's house, but his mouth twitched at the first amusing thing he'd seen all day. All year, really.

The efficient and excellent Dr Rogan in neck-to-toes yellow flannos with pretty polka dots and bee motifs. She'd looked cute, her big, blue eyes startled, and far too vulnerable. His brows drew together. She shouldn't have opened the door at night.

Still, the sight had left him with a memory snapshot that seared itself into a hollow space in his brain – along with the feel of her small, capable hand in his from earlier in the day. What was it with that connection?

It was too soon, too dangerous for his already broken heart. He could not risk losing anyone else – today had shown him that. And he was a man who'd been to jail for killing his wife. Though he hadn't done what they'd accused him of.

In shock, he'd said yes to Iris's pleas at first, but inside, he'd known that he couldn't. She had asked him again every day until she had passed.

'It's illegal,' he'd told Iris, in defence of his denial.

'I know,' she'd whispered. 'But you're my hero. A leader. If anyone can survive in jail, you could. Let me die. Now. If that happens, Mum will take Leo.'

Losing Iris had been worse than seeing Leo taken away by his grandparents. But those moments had been bad when he'd been accused of causing Iris's death after the event. He almost understood why her grieving parents believed he'd agreed. Because they had needed someone to blame for their loss.

He hadn't been in custody for long, but his grief had made him impatient with the baby lawyer the court had appointed him, and he'd been so bitter at the accusation he hadn't done himself any favours to make bail. Eventually, the conviction had been overturned with lack of proof on appeal, but when he'd come out of prison, he'd wanted nothing more than to jump on a dirt bike and disappear into the depths of the desert.

His anger and grief had ridden like a pillion, resentment hanging about him like red outback dust. But he'd simply picked up his shattered son from the hostile in-laws, who had brought the charges against him, and returned to Luna Downs.

At Luna Downs, where they were kilometres from the nearest neighbour, Jude had struggled with his anger. And Leo had been silent, doing what he was told and waiting for Jude to come out of it.

Until that day in Dorrigo when he'd seen a drunk camped on the corner with the icy wind turning him blue.

The vagrant had been stoned as a skunk. And smelled like one, too. Reminding Jude of the down-and-outs he'd met too recently inside the prison. This vagrant's spirit had been even lower than

Jude's and he'd wondered if he needed to change someone else's life and stop feeling sorry for himself.

He'd talked it over with Leo, who'd been struggling with the isolation and Jude's silences, and they'd started there with Ben, the lost soul. Red-bearded Ben, who'd turned into a rock they both could rely on.

It had been a tough two months as Ben had battled his addiction and demons, but once the big man had taken on the cooking and challenge of finding recipes with what they could grow, his focus had changed from the past to his future on Luna Downs. And they were always busy, working on that future.

Somehow over the next year, Jude had collected five blokes a little older than the youth services catered for, men who needed a corner to turn. He'd offered warm beds, hard work, plain food, and a place that was dry in more ways than one. A place that was safe, stern, solid. Jude's word was law or they left.

Jude and the newcomers had built another room. Most had some talents they'd lost with the drink, and now the carrot of learning stonework from a master mason – with farm work on the side – gave them purpose. As a bonus Jude hadn't expected, three had some experience labouring for tradesmen, though they hadn't practised for years, and imparting those skills became their focus.

He and the men, and Leo, kept extending the shearing shed with felled timber and stone. Ben, an ex-plumber among them, led the group in this space. Xavier, the son of a carpenter, revealed his long-dead dad's secrets. And they all worked together to build dams and expand the shearing shed into a long house. The group's aim had been to drought-proof Luna Downs before next summer, which of course had become a joke with this bloody rain that wouldn't go away.

But the shearing shed had grown, room by room, like the house that Jack built, using stone and cut timber from the station, until their long shed stood more like a rough-hewn convention centre, with separate studios and common areas, and Jude and Leo's private wing.

The growing kinship they all needed had happened. Sure, it was rough and ready, but it was also real. And it had a solid future away from the world, which was how Jude preferred it. But now with Leo sick, he would have to re-enter said world.

He hadn't wanted to leave Coffs Harbour tonight. He'd wanted to stay at the hospital with Leo, but both he and Leo knew he had to go home and watch the guys, even if he just checked in every night at Luna Downs and left the next morning to return to the hospital.

He'd promised rules, after all, and it took just one weakness to bring the others down. Although he felt pretty confident they'd be fine, he wasn't confident enough to stay away. Even if Ben had morphed into a sensible man.

But the new guy – Tesla, they were calling him, because his hair stood on end and he reckoned he had electrical experience but nobody believed him – was shorting out. They all knew that the first month was the tricky one coming down from drugs and alcohol. He'd find out soon enough if Tesla had the guts to stay.

But most of all, Jude was thinking about how sick Leo had looked this morning. His son shaking, weak, unsteady, practically delirious before he, the kid's father for crikey's sake, had even noticed. Surely, that made him the worst parent in the world. He could have lost him – the idea gnawed at him like a bad tooth.

Iris would never have missed those symptoms, Jude knew. And

now Leo was a diabetic for life, with insulin needles and finger pricks half-a-dozen or more times a day. Poor kid.

In a tragic irony, it was lucky they'd all been practising control and routines because this was the biggest AA of all. Eat the wrong food, miss some symptoms and his son could die.

God, his life was a mess.

As quickly as he'd thought it, an internal voice insisted, *No, it's not.* He needed to remember what the doc said: Leo was a smart kid who had his dad by his side. Him. And he wasn't leaving him anytime soon.

Rain splattered against the windshield, and Jude switched on the wipers. He was driving more carefully because his safety was now Leo's safety.

Someone in the hospital cafeteria today had been talking about an east coast low, and he wouldn't have taken much notice except that Coffs Harbour Hospital was on the coast. With luck, the rain wouldn't set in because the trip down the mountain from Dorrigo to Bellingen got tricky in the wet. One of his blokes reckoned half the mountain could slide down sometimes.

Hopefully Leo wouldn't need to stay in Coffs too long, and there'd been some talk of setting up an online chat with a diabetic nurse for the first few weeks if they could find one. Jude himself might hate technology, but it was going to come in damn handy for his and Leo's new education.

The consultant had suggested he call on Dr Rogan if they had worries. Unexpectedly, some of the tension seemed to slip away as his mouth curved into what felt like a rusty, creaking smile — a bit like an old windmill stirring in a paddock with a bit of traction. *Creak. Creak. Grin.*

Dr Rogan and her flanno bee pyjamas.

Dr Rogan, who had opened her door to him.

Dr Rogan, who was too cute for words.

Chapter Twelve

Mavis

Mavis muttered, 'I don't like the look of that paddock. It's soaked in about as much as it will take with this rain, Archie. And there's more coming.'

The boy lifted his droopy, dripping Akubra, and stared up into the dark clouds overhead. 'Looks like an ordinary storm to me, Gran.'

'It's a storm all right. A front, more likely. They said on the telly last night we might get an east coast low over the next week or so.'

'What's an eastcoastlow?' He ran the words together as one and Mavis smiled.

'Wild weather. Stormy seas. Torrential rain. Each low doesn't last long, but they can be very violent and dump hundreds of mils of rain. You're probably too young to remember that Sydney to Hobart race a couple of years ago, when they lost all those lives in the crazy storm. That was an east coast low.'

'But we're not near the coast.'

'True.' Mavis glanced in the direction of Dorrigo, which was too far east to catch a glimpse of. 'There's a big mountain between us and the ocean, but that might not stop a bunch of gully rushers causing a flood if it rains hard enough.'

Archie nodded sagely. 'Bet you've seen a lot of weather patterns over the years, Gran.'

'I have. And only a few of them cause me a second glance. There isn't much you can do about the weather. Droughts and floods are supposed to be dished up every now and then.'

'And fires,' Archie said, a poignant maturity on his young face as he glanced over his shoulder at the new building they'd moved into six months ago. The one that had replaced Mavis's razed family farmhouse.

'Yeah. Well, good years make a person not complain.'

She turned up her face and glared at the big, black clouds coming in from the coast. Had she turned into a skittish old lady? A worry wart? The kind of person she didn't have time for?

As if he'd read her thoughts, Archie said quietly, 'You always tell me to listen to my instincts, Gran.'

Mavis squinted up at him. The kid was growing, and not just like a young sapling, but he was becoming wise to the wind. There, in his eyes right now, was that little old man he often became.

'We'll have that second bottom flat slashed as soon as we can, but for now, get the quad bikes out and we'll shift the cattle into a higher paddock.'

Chapter Thirteen

Hannah

A week later, the impish twins were back in Hannah's office. Mikey stood cuddled up to the shredding basket and was rifling through Hannah's crumpled papers and tossing the most interesting-looking ones onto the floor, before placing them in a circle. Mitch had backed up against the bookshelf and was carefully pulling books out one at a time, running his fingers around the edges of the covers and stacking them in a tower.

When Audrey gave her a questioning look, Hannah shook her head. 'There's nothing he can harm there. What can I do for you all?'

'Mikey's just started wetting the bed again,' Audrey murmured, as she stood and gently disentangled tiny hands from the waste-paper basket and lifted the pilferer onto her knees because her big belly stopped him from sitting in her lap.

'How recent?'

'Just this last week. I thought he might have an infection.'

'What about Mitch?'

'No, not Mitch, thankfully. They've both been in dry training pants since they were two. It's a shock to be back into nappies and wet beds again even with just one. Especially with the baby comin' soon.'

Mikey wriggled and tried to escape. Audrey whispered, 'Sit for a minute, honey,' and the child sagged against her. He reached up and pulled a strand of Audrey's long red hair into his fingers and began to tug softly, but he didn't try to escape. His other hand began to stroke her belly.

Audrey kissed the top of his head. 'I'm worried that he'll have trouble staying dry when he goes to pre-school this year. I thought I'd check if there's anything you can recommend that would help him get back into his normal night-time routine.'

Hannah had done extra study on this one for another worried mum in Roma and felt she could help a little. 'There are two types of bedwetting. Primary enuresis, or night-time incontinence, when children have never been dry at night. That's usually caused by a delay in the maturity of nerves in the bladder that slow the message through to the brain. You have to wait till it's grown enough to tell the child, "You need to get up and go to the toilet." Children usually mature out of that one.'

'Nope. It's not that. They've been so easy.'

Hannah smiled, because although she'd only met the little ones three times, the word 'easy' had never sprung to mind.

'The second type is the one you're describing, which is usually caused by change or stress. It can be a minor or major stress, like a new baby'—she added ruefully—'moving house, or even tension in the home. One of the most common reasons is the worry about starting school. Have you been talking about pre-school?'

Audrey's shoulders drooped. 'Yes. They're just old enough to go, and with the baby coming it would be easier. But if that's it, why wouldn't Mitch get nervy?' Audrey glanced across at the builder of towers.

Hannah shook her head. 'That's not uncommon. They may be twins, but they're also individuals who may have different reactions to the same stimuli. Or it could have nothing to do with new worries and Mikey has picked up a bladder bug.'

'They were playing with some puppies over at Mavis's a couple of days ago. Maybe there?' Audrey chewed her lip.

'It's probably not related to the puppies,' Hannah said. 'And the issue of when to send them to school is a tough one, and it's really up to you.' While she appreciated this perennially worrying question for parents, she didn't feel qualified to comment as a childless woman. 'So let's focus on the medical possibility that it could be an infection or a simple problem of constipation, as you suggested. We'll check those two things first, even if just to rule them out.'

They talked about the signs and symptoms, none of which they found, and Hannah reached into her drawer and pulled out a yellow-topped jar. 'Let's start with the simple things like cutting fluid down after four pm. You'll need a calm bedtime routine, with a wee at the beginning and a wee at the end of the story if you're reading to them, just before lights out.'

'We can do that.' Audrey looked at the twins and smiled.

'Remember, bedwetting is the problem, not Mikey. He can't help it, so keep telling him it will get better. And having easy bed changes helps everyone.'

Audrey nodded. 'So, dry pads in the bed and waterproof pants?'

'Yep. And I'll need a urine sample to check for infection. See if you can get him to pee in that jar before you leave, to save you from having to drop it back here later. But it's fine to do it later if he gets stage fright.'

Audrey laughed. 'If there's one thing my boys can do it's find a reason to watch themselves pee.'

They both laughed and Audrey slipped Mikey to the floor, where he hurried over to his brother. Mitch's tower had made its way book by book back into the bookshelf, which was unexpected but charming, Hannah felt, as she'd anticipated she'd have to sort it after they left.

'Good boy, Mitch,' Audrey said as she stood and hung out her hands for her boys to grab.

For the first time in a long time, Hannah felt a wistful longing for children and a family of her own. Audrey was so calm and content, somehow mixing *serene* and *twins* in the one sentence, despite her part-time husband. And her boys were seriously cute.

But children? No. She did not just think that.

Hannah stood up. 'Chat with Mikey about going to pre-school this year. If he is feeling anxious, you'll suss it out. I'll phone when the results are back.' She gestured to the bathroom door. 'Go that way and you can give the specimen to Nell when you go out through the other door. She'll test it before you go.'

As she watched the door to the three-way bathroom close, Hannah thought that another cause of bedwetting was early-onset diabetes in children. She might be hyperalert after Leo last week, or the fact that she'd seen who was coming in next, but what it boiled down to was that young Mikey would be checked for sugar, too.

She cleared her desk for the next patient.

Thinking of Leo: he'd missed his appointment in Coffs Harbour because the roads were blocked. The Waterfall Way between

Dorrigo and Bellingen had a landslip and would stay shut until the workers could clear the dirt and rocks.

No one knew how long that would take with the rain still coming down, so the endocrinologist had arranged for Leo and his father to meet at Hannah's office for the consultation via video link. She could keep herself up to date with Leo's treatment and give the boy and his father a chance to ask any questions afterwards. Everyone knew when you saw the doctor, and especially a specialist, it was easy to miss something in the pressure of a timed consult.

Of course, they were the only reasons she looked forward to it. Leo's name had been highlighted on her screen as waiting, and she stamped down a tiny flicker of awareness of who else would be outside in the waiting room.

Hannah finished Mikey's notes, unconsciously moistened dry lips and stood to open her door.

Yep, it was Jude Waugh she saw first, tall and towering over his son, inscrutable and wearing a two-day growth that looked far too fabulous. His big arms were folded across his chest, biceps straining the material of his rolled-up sleeves. His chin lifted as she stood in her doorway, speechless and gawping. But, *oh my*, she felt incapable of doing anything else.

Jude was not whom she needed to greet.

Gathering her professional self together, she turned her gaze sideways to Leo – a much stronger and more alert Leo – and smiled. 'Come in, you two. Nice to see you looking so well, Leo.'

Chapter Fourteen

Jude

Jude had almost forgotten how cute the doc was. Almost. A sudden memory flash of yellow pyjamas made the side of his mouth kick up. *No, get out*, he told the teasing image. He needed to concentrate.

She was talking, her soft voice matter-of-fact yet warm, with all her attention on Leo. Which was where his should be.

'How are you managing the injections, Leo? You've probably given more than I have by now. Bet you're good at it.'

Jude liked the way she offered sympathy but not pity.

Leo ducked his head and smiled shyly back at her. 'I don't like them, but the injections aren't as bad as the finger-prick thing. I hate that with a passion.'

Jude looked at his son. He hadn't known that. And if he hadn't known, why hadn't he asked?

Dr Rogan nodded. 'They are nasty little suckers, and they do hurt. Although, if you use the side of your finger, it's not quite as bad as the pad.'

Her eyes slid his way and Jude met her baby blues and saw the laughter in them. That jolted him. Laughter? 'Have you done one for Dad yet? So he knows how much of a pain it is?'

Her eyes sparkled and he had no doubt she'd enjoy seeing that. Jude lowered his brows at her, but his lips twitched. 'No, thank you.'

She smiled, joking with his son but all aimed at him. 'We've probably got time to do one before the professor rings.'

Leo grinned and turned to look at him, and Jude unconsciously leaned back. 'You're teasing, right?'

'You reckon? Should I?' The side of his son's mouth lifted into a cheeky grin, which wasn't something he'd seen over the past weeks. Leo amused was a good thing and he relaxed into the easy atmosphere. Bonus points for the doc.

Hannah checked her watch and feigned disappointment. 'Rats, Leo, we're going to have to raincheck that for another time. I'll turn on the screen.'

Jude was enjoying the banter and Leo's amusement, but then, he wasn't adding anything useful. The screen flickered on and he found himself saying, 'The last time I was here, I thought it was strange to have a television in your consulting room.'

'It's only just come online,' she answered, but he was hearing the cadences in her voice more than the words. She sounded like the weather girl, with her round vowels and full words. *Proper*, his mother would have said. He liked it.

She went on, 'It's a Telehealth screen. Hopefully, I won't ever need it for a medical emergency that needs backup online, but that's why I installed it.' She chewed her lip, maybe considering the potential disasters that could happen in a country practice, while he watched her white teeth nibble down on soft flesh and had to drag his eyes away.

'But it is great for this, too,' she said, and he snapped back to the present. 'After we practise today, I'll start offering it to many of the older patients or those with disabilities. Some find it a struggle to drive to see their consultants a long way away. And this'—she waved a hand to indicate the screen—'is much more cost effective for everyone.'

Jude nodded. 'I can imagine that. It's quite a way to town, and this is easy.'

'Online consultations have taken off.' Hannah waved to the screen again. 'In a big country like Australia, they should be used more. I know that remote nurses use them. Doctors dealing with COVID patients just bumped the awareness along.'

'Um,' Leo said diffidently, 'before the professor comes on . . .' He stopped, fizzled out, then started again. 'I wondered . . .' He looked at Jude, then back at Hannah. 'One of the other kids in the hospital mentioned a continuous glucose monitor – CGM? Does that mean I could just wear it, like a patch, and wouldn't have to prick my finger?'

Jude sat forward. This was the first he'd heard of it. Leo could get whatever he needed.

Hannah shifted in her chair, pulling his eyes to her, and pushed her fringe aside. She did that a lot, Jude had noticed. She had thick, bouncy hair – bit of a blonde bombshell, really – and she shoved it aside as if it annoyed her. It didn't annoy him. He liked her hair, Jude realised, as he watched her mouth form the words his son was eager to hear.

He gave himself a mental shake, forcing his brain to concentrate on what mattered here.

'I can understand why you'd ask,' Hannah said, compressing her mouth. *Sad, that*, Jude thought. 'The monitors sound good and do give an ongoing indication of how your sugar levels are tracking – maybe too much information available on your smart phone – but you still have to calibrate them twice a day, which means two finger pricks as well as having another monitor taped to your body that can fail.'

'Oh. Okay. I thought it sounded too good.' Leo sank back. Back to looking like the despondent kid he'd had at home all week, and Jude ground his teeth. It was all so unfair.

His chest hurt again for his son. Why Leo? Hadn't the kid been through enough? It had been a tough couple of years, Iris sick and Iris gone, for all of them.

'We could find out more information,' Jude said. 'Find the money if needed.'

Lines crossed the doc's forehead, and he had the feeling he'd said something she wasn't happy with. *What?* he wanted to ask. 'We can ask the specialist about it,' he added.

Hannah nodded. 'The financial cost shouldn't be a problem. Between four and five thousand dollars a year, but'—she gestured to the screen—'it is fully government-funded if you're under twenty-one and your specialist agrees it would benefit Leo's care. He probably will at some stage, but I'd like to see Leo settled with his insulin pump first, which is a totally different thing and to my mind more important to spend the adjustment time on.'

The screen flickered and the face of a surprisingly youthful man with wire glasses appeared. The professor still looked way younger than Jude expected, even after last week's meeting, and he could see Hannah's jerk of surprise, too.

Hannah pointed the remote control at the screen and unmuted the call.

'Hello, I see you're all there. Can you see me?' the professor asked.

'Professor Bligh? Yes.'

'Dr Rogan, I presume. Thank you for arranging this.'

'It works well with the road blocked, at the moment. As you can see, Leo and his dad made it through from their end. I'll step back and let Leo tell you about his week.'

The consult went for forty minutes, Leo being surprisingly articulate, Jude mused with pride. And it seemed they had to do this again next week, as well. And possibly the week after.

To his surprise, and not a good one, he discovered his son had several concerns that Jude had no idea about after some subtle prompting from Hannah. The woman seemed to have an uncanny insight into teenagers that he lacked. He needed to work on that shortfall, but it annoyed him that she could pick up on issues that he couldn't. The last thing he needed was a perky little GP who absolutely pushed his buttons and made him feel like even more of a loser. Or maybe that was his imagination.

The fact was, he did need her. With Leo's diabetes, Jude had to keep coming back to this village and the doctor if he wanted to keep his son's health stable.

By the time the online chat ended, they had clear instructions for the next week, as well as a bevy of safeguards and contingency plans for fluctuations in Leo's blood-sugar levels. New information had been emailed for Leo to read on pumps and continuous glucose monitors and they'd check those out when they got home.

She was saying, 'You can phone me, Leo, anytime, if you come up with new questions.'

She didn't say Jude could phone her, but he would if he was worried. That was when he realised he would look forward to the next visit in the coming week. It wasn't all because he'd learned so much at this one. There was something wholesome and attractive about this woman; it slid under his guard. Her genuine caring for his son was a beautiful thing. Truth be told, *she* was a beautiful thing. And he needed to stop looking.

Chapter Fifteen

Hannah

Hannah watched the tight line of Jude's mouth compress. She suspected he'd heard some things he'd been unaware of during the consult. She'd been too conscious of the tightening of his jaw and that little tic over his right eyebrow, which he did when he was surprised or annoyed. Not to mention the white line that formed across his cheek as he held back. These were considerable movements for a guy carved from granite. Of course, his chiselled features were soon stilled and back under rigid control.

What happened to this man? she wondered. Such movements suggested he hadn't been reading the subtext at home as well as he thought he had. And because she'd been watching him too closely, she saw every subtle shift of emotion.

She wondered what home with Jude and Leo looked like. Was it fun or fraught? Easygoing or disciplined? Then she pulled herself away from that thought. *No. Noooooo.* She didn't wonder at all. No wondering. Or only in a medical capacity.

The rain drummed on the roof and she hoped the road stayed open long enough for them to return to their station. There'd been washaways when different creeks had created a log jam that suddenly freed. Dangerous weather. Then she looked at Jude, who was tough, obviously resourceful, built like a brick dunny with the door shut. He was expressionless now.

They'd be fine, she decided. She didn't need to worry about Leo because she got the sense that Jude could handle anything. And besides, she had patients waiting.

At the end of the day, Nell and Hannah had their first meeting about the running of the surgery. They'd been too pooped by Friday last week and had blocked out the final appointment of Monday afternoon to talk about glitches and improvements they could make in the ongoing running of the medical centre.

'We need a third incoming phone line for when I'm on hold to arrange appointments,' Nell started.

'Agreed. Are you happy to apply for that with the telephone company tomorrow?'

'Yep.'

'The flu-injection clinic for next month. As soon as the new batch of this year's immunisations are available, I'd like to make a date for that. Let's start booking people in. Mavis offered to lead the patient list,' she said with a smile.

'Not how I heard it happened, but she did agree.' Nell smirked. 'I can create flyers to place around town. At Jed and Gracie's store and anywhere else I can think of, to encourage people from the village to book.'

'Sounds good. The other thing I wondered about was antenatal appointments. I know we're not having babies here, but the midwifery clinics are a long way away for pregnant women to travel to. Would some of those women like to do some appointments here, do you think?'

Nell sat back. 'Gracie had a small antenatal class when she first came, but we haven't started it up again since Oliver was born.'

'Of course she did.' Gracie would love that. 'I should have suspected as much. She's such a champion. I thought the village might be too small for a class.'

Nell thought for a moment. 'She had half-a-dozen women when she ran them, I think.'

'Okay. If I encourage antenatal appointments here, liaising with the two different hospital clinics so we share medical records, would you be interested in doing the midwifery pre-visit? That way, you could be the one sharing the info they'd usually get from the midwives at the hospital.'

'I think that would be a great service. Not sure how it would work, though.'

Hannah had used this model before with one of Gracie's Roma colleagues. 'I'm thinking two appointments in the one. First with you, and then they come through to me for test results and anything you flag. We could trial it. Sound good?'

'Sounds amazing,' Nell said, though her voice was strained. 'I am missing the antenatal mums. I have been since Gracie's baby last year.' She looked down at the floor and rolled her shoulders, as if shrugging off a weight.

Now Hannah wondered if despite her yes, Nell wasn't keen. 'Are you sure?'

Nell nodded. Firmly. 'Yes. I'm keeping up the CPD points for my registration with online courses, so that will give me hours in face-to-face midwifery as well as the ones I'm getting in general nursing here at the clinic. So it's good by me.'

Her eyes met Hannah's. A small silence stretched until she offered, 'I had a bad experience in a home birth a couple of years ago. Before I moved here. I'll tell you about it one day.'

Ouch. Hannah knew about bad experiences in medicine. They scarred you. 'Okay. Anytime you need to debrief, I'm here. Or not. That is entirely up to you.'

Nell's face softened. 'Thanks, Hannah. Gracie's already heard it all. You should too, one day soon.'

Chapter Sixteen

Mavis

A week later, Mavis cursed as much as a good Catholic girl could as she drove home. She disliked driving from Armidale on a sunny day, let alone when rain pelted the car so hard the wipers couldn't keep up. And the news from the specialist hadn't been something to smile about.

No way was she going to the city for some risky – even the doctor had said risky – operation. Imagine if she died there. *Nope. Not happening.* But she had to get home first before she could rant about it.

She guessed returning from Armidale was better than coming back from Coffs Harbour in this maelstrom, because she couldn't imagine winding up the mountain to Dorrigo in a freak rainstorm. Darn right she couldn't wait for the boy to get his licence, and darned if she wouldn't just hand over her ignition keys to him now. They didn't have traffic cops in Featherwood. He could drive from tomorrow. She'd been driving since she was twelve, and Archie was almost thirteen.

The car rocked as a gust hit her. And Mavis wished Archie was with her this moment. His phone glowed from where she was charging it on the seat beside her, and for the first time, it felt good to have it there. He had nagged her into taking it when she drove, but the stupid thing was always flat. For some reason, she'd plugged it in coming back from Armidale today, and strangely, the dratted thing was giving her comfort, as if a piece of the boy was sitting beside her.

Mavis snorted. 'Getting fanciful in your old age, woman,' she muttered out loud, but she couldn't hear her voice through the drumming on the roof.

The rushing creeks at the side of the road seemed way higher than when she had left this morning. They didn't cross the road, however, so she was sure she'd be fine. As if to challenge her belief, the deluge increased, but she knew the way blindfolded and only had this final stretch to get through. It was half past two. She'd be home soon and the boy would be back from school in an hour.

The rain increased and Mavis slowed to a crawl, seriously considering pulling over at the side of the road until it lessened. The problem was, she doubted she'd be visible if someone else came up behind her, and the road was narrow here between the creek and gully on the other side.

Her headlights bounced back at her, switched on even though it was mid-afternoon, the wipers swiping valiantly with no difference to visibility. Peering through the windshield on the last bend before her gate, she thought she heard a roar, and swung her head to glimpse a low wall of foam and sticks coming. She had no time for anything before a viciously turbulent, muddy wall of water smashed against the side of her vehicle. As if a giant's hand had picked her car up like a leaf, she was washed off the road on the wave that shoved her sideways into the rushing creek.

'What the . . .!' Mavis twisted her head, trying to comprehend the events as her heart leaped and thumped and she white-knuckled the wheel as the car spun and twisted and clunked against rocks. Everything was so noisy and fast and deadly powerful.

Her passenger door slammed against the cliffside and tangled in the silky oaks, branches smashing against the side window, and she thought for a moment that the glass would break. The wave pushed her up the trunk and into the lower branches, and began to subside as it carried on.

Mavis's breath puffed in quick pants and she forced her breathing to slow as the wild water ride settled to a jostle and bump and the wave rushed past her stranded vehicle to surge away.

A landslide? A gully rusher? She had absolutely no idea what had happened. She realised her hands were aching from the strength of her grip and she eased them slightly – she couldn't force herself to let go. Yet. Not that she'd be driving anywhere now. Shakily, she pried one hand free and let both windows down before the electrics failed, in case the car sank. No matter what happened, she'd be getting wet, anyway.

Around her, the torrent of the creek level dropped as the wall of water receded, but more insidiously, the level in the creek under her now began to steadily rise again.

Still panicked, she realised that she wasn't sinking and her seat, for now, was still high enough above the water to be mostly dry. But even as she thought this, her shoes filled with the water seeping through the floor, and as the creek height increased the water covered her ankles.

She was in trouble, serious trouble, and she didn't have much time. With the car absurdly still running, she shakily pressed the horn as the interior tilted and shifted in its precarious perch.

Trying to block out the roar of the water and the instability of her position, Mavis squeezed her eyes shut and tried to reason. The trouble was, all she could think of was what would happen to the boy if she died.

He'd be returned to his mother. Why hadn't she planned for this? She should have protected him with a back-up family.

Drugs and the city.

His pleading eyes asking if he could stay with Gran.

Hell no, she thought, and unclipped her seatbelt, trying to push open the driver's door. It was jammed by the swirling water or maybe the tree she was wedged against. Maybe she could crawl out of the driver's window . . . and what? Tumble into the fast-flowing stream? She'd never been much of a swimmer.

She darted a look to her left. The passenger's window, perhaps? Could she cling onto the tree on that side? Was there even room to get through the window to the tree with the vehicle slammed up against it?

She twisted her head, checking the car for something that would float in case she ended up in the water. Nothing. Her gaze slid past the phone and jerked back. She had a phone! Bless the boy.

For the first time in her life, Mavis Maloney dialled triple zero on a mobile phone. She closed her eyes as the call went through and almost instantly a woman answered.

'Emergency services. Which service do you require?'

Lord save us, she didn't care. 'Any. Police? I'm Mavis Maloney. I'm in my car. I was swept off the road into the Featherwood Creek two miles west of Featherwood.'

'Which state is that?'

The car bumped and shifted, and the water rose. 'New South Wales. The closest large town is Armidale.' How could the woman not know which state?

'I'll put you through now.'

She'd have been better calling Jed at the store. She didn't have time for police from Armidale. But what if Jed tried to help and something happened to him? No. She couldn't ask that.

When the police dispatcher answered, she recited it all again. Something hard crashed against the side of her car, rocking it. She gasped and her seat tilted sideways towards the water and then bumped back up again, almost level.

Mavis's free hand, which again had crept onto the steering wheel, tightened. The dispatcher's voice cut through the chaos. 'Are you okay?'

'Been better,' Mavis muttered grimly. 'The car slipped down the tree a little and the water's up to my waist now.'

'We have a vehicle coming for you. Twenty minutes. Hold on.'

Hold on? Mavis looked at her white fingers, clawing like bleached skeletal bones against the steering wheel, and snorted shakily. 'I'll be here.' Though she'd probably be holding her breath under water by then.

Chapter Seventeen

Jude

'I'm glad we didn't have to drive to Coffs,' Leo said as he and Jude splashed back through the torrential rain after their third doctor's visit in Featherwood.

Amen to that, Jude thought, and not just because he was growing fond of his visits to Dr Hannah Rogan more than he should. Hannah had a quirky wit he hadn't expected, and finding humour in a situation that was less than ideal had become a habit. Not that he smiled – he didn't want her to think he was a fun guy – but he could admit to himself that he liked her bouncy hair and her delightful walk, and, despite his distress and concern over Leo's diabetes, the world wasn't so dire when Dr Rogan was in it.

They climbed in his all-terrain vehicle and headed out of town as Jude swerved to miss a pothole that hid the depth of its sides. The tricky bugger of a thing – which was probably deeper than his axle – could have swallowed a smaller car. His heavy vehicle didn't shift much as they ground out of Featherwood towards Luna Downs, and he felt confident they'd get through even if his driveway had a washaway section by the time he got there.

'Heavy rain,' Leo said, and if there hadn't been a slight hitch of nervousness in his son's voice, he would have ribbed him for stating the obvious.

'Heavy indeed,' he started to agree, only to stop as something flashed up ahead through the curtain of water. A horn sounded just over the roar of the rain. Headlights? A reflection? It was swinging an arc, or was it actually swirling in a circle?

The lights disappeared to the side behind the bush and he slowed even more. There was a creek to the left there somewhere, but he couldn't see it through the scrub and the pounding rain. He knew about the dip in the road around here, and with the amount of water coming off the gullies into that creek, he wanted to be prepared for unexpected depth when he hit it.

'Did you see that?' Leo leaned forward to peer through the front window.

Jude doubted it would help his vision, but he tried it, too. The water continued to fall in such a thick curtain, they could have been staring through the bottom of a glass bottle.

'Are those lights in the trees?' Leo had his seatbelt off and his nose on the windscreen.

'Yeah, mate. It might be someone in trouble. Put your belt back on. I'm looking for somewhere safe I can pull over to have a proper look.'

He eased onto the edge of the road on the high side, just past where he'd seen the lights, with no hesitation at the thought of stepping out into the deluge. If it was a vehicle, then they didn't have much time. Still, there was the possibility that it could be something light-coloured and not lights. It could even be a pale horse or roo. But it could also be a car. 'Stay here,' he told Leo, 'so

I know where you are. I might need you to phone someone.' He handed Leo his mobile.

The last thing he saw as he pushed open the door was Leo's white face bobbing up and down as he nodded. The poor kid had had enough shocks this month.

'I'll be careful,' he reassured his son. 'Promise. Back soon.'

He stepped out and pushed the door shut behind him. Instantly, the rain splattered into his shirt like machine gunfire and he was soaked in seconds, but as he trudged back to the part of the road that gave him a line of sight to the creek, the deluge slowed to a shower.

It only took a second to spot the car jammed into the trees across the torrent; the water was almost halfway up the doors, already. Something moved inside. He could see the driver.

He sprinted back to the truck and poked his head in the door. 'Dial emergency services. Tell the police there's a car half-submerged in the river about two kilometres west of Featherwood.'

In his gut, he winced at the idea of asking for police help – a hangover from his time in custody – but what choice did he have? This wasn't about him. He could ask the fellas at home to bring the other truck; however, Ben was the only one with a licence and he was fencing out the back with Tesla. There wasn't time. They didn't need another run-in with the law. Boys wouldn't be happy that he'd left them out when they could've helped, but he'd deal with their complaints later.

'Stay in the car as long as you can,' he told Leo. 'Run the engine and put the heater on because the driver will be chilled. I'll use the winch just as a safety line and wave when I need you to wind it back in.'

Leo nodded his understanding and concentrated on the phone, already starting to dial.

'Good man.' Jude ran a tight ship on Luna Downs, and everyone knew when he wanted orders followed without question.

Grabbing a thin blanket they kept in the truck, he tied the ends around his neck with a tight knot to make a big sling and jammed it down the front of his shirt. Just in case the person was unconscious or there was a child or animal. He shut the door and unclipped the winch hook from the bull bar. The high-tension wire spooled out behind him as he pushed through the short scrub at the side of the torrent, moving steadily away from the car.

He needed to start higher up the creek than the stranded vehicle, because with the water around his waist, it would push him downstream. And it was getting higher all the time. Jude had enough experience to know that he shouldn't go into flowing water deeper than his knees, but he had zero choice here.

When he looked at the stranded car now, the water was past midway up the side, so getting upstream again if he was swept with the current would be impossible. And deadly. He fisted the hook of the winch wire and stepped carefully into the torrent.

Chapter Eighteen

Mavis

Mavis gripped the phone in one hand and the steering wheel in the other. Her fingers had cramped a while ago, but she couldn't seem to let go of either one. The time on the screen said it was only ten minutes since she'd phoned, and yet the car had become half-filled with water in that short time. At least the rain had eased down to a light sprinkle, as if it had done what it needed to and was sitting back to watch the fun.

She could make out the broken branches around her more clearly now. Even though the creek was higher, it didn't seem to be running as fast. Rather, it was slyly powerful, as if the wave had taken the speed but left the power.

Still, her teeth made tiny clicking chatter sounds from the bitter cold seeping into her bones with the water. Every time she shifted a little in her seat to reach towards the window, the car slid deeper and closer to the flow, and the level inside the cabin rose to wash her waist. She wanted out. Now. She had to make it happen.

'Move, you old goat,' she growled, but her cold limbs refused.

Although she didn't want to wait for help, every time she tried moving again the car shifted and turned slightly. She didn't want it to lose its hold and swirl away and maybe sink to the bottom, so she stopped. At least she had the windows open, and she knew that a rescue was on the way – they said they were coming. The problem was, she had too much flippin' time to think.

Something caught her attention – lights. A dark four-wheel drive had stopped across the road on the other side of the creek and someone big got out and was now peering across the water. She saw the man run back to the car and finally he bent to what she prayed was a winch on the front.

He must have seen her. Lord, she hoped he'd seen her. Please.

'Help.' The tiny sound like a pitiful bird noise inside the car, and the tinny sound mocked her with just how helpless she was. Mavis hated being helpless, but she'd never been so frightened in her life. 'Help,' she cheeped again.

The man walked upstream and eased into the flow. She saw his body sway with the pull of the water, but he kept coming, one step at a time, absorbing the force. The big man seemed to have power in his body, yet suddenly Mavis wanted to tell him to go back. She didn't want anyone dying because of her, even if it meant Archie had to live with his mother until he could inherit the farm.

The man didn't stop. Mavis felt the breath tight in her throat and remembered to breathe. She realised that because she was facing backwards, which had seemed like a curse moments ago, she could watch him come down the stream towards her.

It looked deeper than his waist now, which made sense because the water was lapping around hers and she was in a tree. Her heart thumped with the fear and adrenaline as the cold sapped what energy she had left, making her limbs feel strangely sluggish. It would be ironic if he made it at the same time as the water went over her head.

No. Not happening, she vowed. She wasn't going to die today.

As the man edged closer, Mavis saw his face and recognition tickled. Had she seen him recently? Then she remembered the doctor's surgery with his son.

Ah, hell, he had a boy, too. She began to pray that they both would make it out safely.

The water was lapping her boobs now and she heard the chink of metal on metal as the hook he held touched the car. And then he was wrapping the wire from the winch once around the tree and back onto her steering wheel through the window.

It wouldn't spin away if she climbed out, she realised. Except that she was so cold and stiff she doubted she would be able to move at all. She slid the boy's phone down her shirt and into her bra. She'd just have to try.

Massive arms reached in, and before she knew what was happening, she was out, her hands clinging to his neck. He slid something down her back and over her butt, and she felt herself caught in some kind of wet, cloth cradle.

'No one else in the car?'

'No . . . no . . . no.' She had the stutters now.

'I'll unhook the winch,' he said, 'and my son will wind it in.'

There was a struggle as he untangled the wire from the tree one-handed, but within seconds he had it around his waist again and they began to push through the water to the bank.

Chapter Nineteen

Hannah

Hannah had an early mark. The last four appointments after lunch had cancelled because of the torrential rain, roads and bridges going under, so they'd closed the practice for the day. Nell had smiled with delight as she had swanned out the door.

Hannah was looking forward to her first hot bath in her new bathroom. 'New' as in circa 1950s with tiny tiles everywhere and a rectangular deep step up into the enormous, long-sided bath. The rectory must have had ten kids to bathe to create this indulgence. It had a wide shelf at the back where she could rest candles, a glass of wine and a book well clear of the water. Utopia. With all the rain, she had the tank water to spare, and soft piano music was drifting through from the Bluetooth speaker connected to her phone.

Steam floated out of the bathroom door as she stood in the kitchen and tried to decide which shaped glass she'd use for that special French champagne. *Decisions, decisions.* She refused to feel guilty. She had to have a glass of wine sometimes without worrying that someone would knock on the door.

Which was precisely when she heard the growling of a large vehicle grinding up her driveway.

Speak of the devil who brought wine, she thought. She knew that sound and Hannah wasn't happy. There was no reason for Jude Waugh to interfere with her hedonistic afternoon.

'At least you're still dressed in clothes and not PJs,' she grumbled to herself as she opened the back door. Maybe they just forgot something.

When he climbed out, she was surprised to see Jude's shirt moulded wetly against solid abs, like an armour-bound action figure. *Man, oh man.* And the way his soaked jeans clung to his muscled thighs in a second shiny skin – it was eye candy she should not be enjoying. But then he opened the rear door and lifted a small woman into his arms, and she stared.

Good grief. 'Mavis, is that you? What happened?'

Jude crunched swiftly through the gravel, striding across the drive with Mavis nestled in his arms like a small bird. Belatedly, Hannah noticed that Leo was still sitting in the car and she waved. 'Come in. Come in,' she told the boy. Leo's door swung open, and he climbed out and dashed across to them.

She could hear Mavis's teeth chattering, and her face and arms looked mottled with a shade of blue Hannah didn't like.

Jude answered for her as they all rushed inside. 'Her car got washed into the river. I brought her here so you could warm her while she waited for the ambulance.'

'Don't need an ambulance,' a querulous voice complained. 'Just need a hot bath.' She held out a damp mobile phone to Leo. 'Hold this.'

Ignoring her, Jude said, 'She's freezing and probably in shock.'

'Come in. All of you. Oh, Mavis. I've got the bath running. How about we just pop you in clothes and all and I can help you sort the rest later.'

'He should get in, too,' Mavis said around the shudders and shivers. 'It's been a while since a handsome man carried me into a bath. He's cold, too.'

Hannah bit back a grin and shot a sideways glance at Jude. 'It's a big bath.' Without waiting for a response, she said over her shoulder, 'Pop the jug on, Leo. We'll need hot tea.'

Really, she just wanted the young boy safe in the kitchen and not in the bathroom, where Mavis might do something crazy like have a cardiac arrest. Hannah grabbed her medical bag, which always sat in the hallway.

Jude and Hannah eased through to the bathroom as Mavis's teeth clicked and clacked like castanets on crack. The tough old bird had to be freezing.

Hannah hurriedly blew out the candles and swept away the book, not looking at the large man in the doorway as she slid them onto the old-fashioned vanity. Dipping her fingers into the water, she checked it wouldn't burn the older lady. She found it a little cool, which was probably a good thing. She could increase the temperature when Mavis was used to the change.

'Lower her in. I can add hot. But stay handy in case she needs retrieval.' Hannah didn't want Mavis to go into shock because she couldn't resuscitate someone in the bath.

Jude did as asked, kneeling with ridiculous ease with his burden, one knee on the step and the other strong leg outstretched. His powerful shoulder muscles and biceps bunched as he swung Mavis over the lip of the tub and gently lowered her into the water.

Mavis gasped, whimpered, and then closed her eyes as she sighed out. Jude sat back but stayed close, hovering in protective mode again.

Rustling through her bag, Hannah found the thermometer and took Mavis's temperature, which was low but not critical. Then she slipped the blood-pressure cuff around her wet sleeve. It read high, which wasn't surprising with the stress and cold that would have narrowed Mavis's arteries and veins. There'd be a whole lot more pressure needed to force the blood through the narrowed lumen.

She'd see how fast the water heated Mavis before she thought about a warmed IV infusion. They both watched as her small body shook in tiny seismic waves until the severity of her rigors lessened and finally stilled. After only a few minutes, the heat visibly eased the tightness from her pinched face.

Hannah turned on the hot tap. 'I think she'll be fine, Jude, thank you. I couldn't have managed that.'

'You're welcome.' When he stood, wet clothes plastered to his impressive slabs of muscle, the bathroom shrank, becoming cramped and airless.

Funny that, she thought, trying to block out her reaction and concentrate.

Jude said, 'The ambulance should be here soon. I want to get Leo home.'

She eased past him to the door. She needed something warm for Mavis to wear. 'Can you stay for a sec while I put some of my clothes in the drier for her to warm them up? Then I'll take her temperature again.'

'Sure.'

Hannah escaped – no, she eased – from the room on a task. It only took a minute, and when she returned Mavis was lying quietly with her eyes closed, face peaceful. The tap had been shut off. The distant sound of the clothes rotating in the drier bumped oddly in time to the music Hannah hadn't had a chance to stop.

'She looks better,' Jude said quietly when she came up behind him. 'Not so blue now. I was worried.'

'I'm tougher than I look,' Mavis muttered from the bath, eyes still closed. 'You should be in here with me.'

Jude's mouth quirked. 'Indeed, you are. And thank you. But I'm shy.' He looked at Hannah. 'You right if I leave?'

'You don't want a shower?'

He raised one black brow and his too-darn-sexy mouth flicked in a tight, lopsided smile. It was the first time she'd seen anything like that from him, and her insides sloshed into mush.

He shook his head. 'Not this time. Ask me another day.'

She turned her face up at him, trying to project irritation, not the sudden slash of heat in her cheeks, as she imagined him in her shower. Maybe with her. Skin to skin.

Stop this, she told herself, and turned her back on him to grab a towel. 'At least dry off,' she said, handing it to him.

He took the Turkish wrap and towelled his hair and the back of his neck. Then swiped his hard chest once and down to his abs, before giving it back to her. 'Done.'

Was it odd to wish *she* was a towel? she wondered.

Gesturing to the puddles along the polished wood of the floor, he took the towel back and swiped a particularly big puddle. 'Sorry about the mess.'

Hannah brushed that away. 'Will you get through on the roads if you leave?'

'The rain's eased off. Mavis caught the gully rusher. She said she was hit by a wave from the side. It's gone now. We've had some freak rainfall, but most of it's probably calmed down. I need to get back to Luna Downs.'

'In this?'

'They need me there.'

He still didn't give a reason as to why. But this wasn't the time to push for answers. She needed to get Mavis sorted. 'If you get blocked, come back. There's room here for you and Leo.'

He didn't say he would, or wouldn't, but he nodded and left.

Hannah shifted her attention back to Mavis. When she turned on the hot water again, Mavis groaned in pleasure. 'He's gone. Let's get these wet clothes off you. How're you feeling?'

'Stupid,' Mavis grumbled. 'I couldn't get out myself. I should have climbed out the window, but every time I shifted the car moved and I thought I'd get swept away.'

It sounded terribly frightening to Hannah. 'You made the sensible choice, because you didn't get washed away.'

'Hmph. The boy makes me take his phone when I drive. Lucky that. So I knew the police were coming. Just not how fast the water would rise.'

'Then you weren't stupid at all.'

'If it wasn't for that man,' she jerked her head towards the empty doorway, 'I'd be dead. The water was up to my boobs by the time he came.'

'Oh, Mavis.' Hannah leaned in and touched the older woman's shoulder. 'It's a miracle you weren't screaming when he brought you in.'

'No good screaming when no one can hear you. Although . . .'

She closed her eyes again. 'Can't say I've ever felt more alone in my life.' Then she opened them resolutely, wiped her hand across her nose and sat up. 'I want to be dressed by the time the ambulance gets here, but I'm not going with them.'

'I think you are.'

'I got dunked for less than half an hour. I'm fine now. I'm not going with them.' Mavis's chin stuck out stubbornly. 'The boy will be home from school soon. I need to be there for him.'

Ah, Hannah understood. Mavis needed to see Archie, as well. To reassure herself he was fine. Hannah had no doubt the afternoon's fright had really rocked the older woman. 'I'll ask if Molly can meet Archie off the bus and bring him here, okay? Then there's no rush. We can make sure you're warmed and stable before we decide what's next.'

Mavis nodded.

'But when the ambulance gets here, I'll be the one to say if you need to go. I'm the doctor.'

Mavis suddenly looked stricken. 'The man. I didn't even thank him before he left.'

'Jude Waugh? You'll see him again. His son, Leo, visits me weekly. Leo's the same age as Archie. Maybe they know each other?'

They had Mavis's clothes off now, and Hannah floated another towel in the water to cover her and keep the warmth in. The bath was steaming and she was glad to see pink in Mavis's pale cheeks.

Maybe her patient wouldn't have to go with the ambulance. Of course, another factor was if she did go, there'd be the problem of getting her home again. In this weather, she doubted Mavis would be in any hurry to travel back on the roads to Featherwood.

Chapter Twenty

Molly

Molly arrived as soon as the school bus dropped off Archie and brought him to Hannah's, but her heart still pounded in sympathy with Mavis's close escape.

Hearing of his great-gran's escapades, Archie had nudged his chair at the kitchen table very close to Mavis, as if he wasn't letting her out of his sight. And now the two of them were talking quietly about what they needed to do at the farm.

The police had been to interview Mavis, and when the rain settled, a tow truck would come to winch her vehicle out of the creek if it was still there. Either way, it would probably never recover.

The ambulance officers hadn't stayed long once Hannah had agreed that Mavis didn't need to go with them. They had another call close by and left quickly.

Molly had washed the wet clothes and now they were bumping around in the tumble dryer. Mavis sat dressed in pink woolly socks and a fluffy dressing gown that covered the floor-length nightie she'd borrowed from Hannah. There were spots of red in her cheeks and she was sipping from a large mug of homemade, home-grown tomato soup Molly had brought with her. Molly decided the world was crazy because it was still only four-thirty in the afternoon.

'It feels like it should be eight o'clock at night,' Hannah murmured as she sipped her own soup.

'I was just thinking that,' Molly said with a shiver. She'd had a phobia about being swept into a creek and trapped in a car for as long as she could remember, and she kept imagining worse scenarios.

She'd used Hannah's hair dryer on Mavis's short hair, and Hannah had taken Mavis's temperature. She was happy to hear that the older lady's body heat had returned to almost normal.

It seemed that Mavis had bounced back faster than anyone else any age would have. Typical. The woman was as tough as that old red cedar tree outside the back door. The one standing in the teeming rain, now that the heavens had decided to open again.

Hannah had moved to the kitchen window to stare out at the curtain of rain that was running down the pane.

Molly nodded at the streaming glass. 'We've had a flood warning for the creek. Haven't had one of those for a long time. Jed's moving the floor stock in the store up to the top of the pallet racks with the forklift, and Nell's helping Gracie pack the shop shelves into boxes to move upstairs into the office.'

Hannah said, 'I can't imagine water that high. Maybe they should bring them up here? I have a big shed.'

'There's all the big hardware stuff still to move. I'll let Jed know. In case.'

'Do you think a flood will come? Maybe flow down the main street?'

'I've seen it once before.' Molly had, when she was a kid, and all her life old-timers had mentioned that flood. But she was more worried about Jed's store than the road. 'The shop's lower than the street, though, and so is Gracie's house. The creek's backing up and spreading. It could get really bad.'

'And you were helping them move stuff when I called? Extra thanks for dropping Archie, then. If Mavis wants me to run her home instead of staying here, I'll come down and help.'

Of course she would. Hannah was good people. 'The more hands the better.'

'What about your house?'

'It's off the ground on pylons and I don't have a creek running past like Gracie and Nell. Local lore says in the forty-nine flood the water only reached the floorboards, so it should be fine.'

'We're talking about floods,' Hannah said. 'I come from sun-baked Roma, though, even there they were inundated in two thousand and ten.'

'Crazy times,' Molly said.

Hannah shook her head. 'I can't believe a road I arrived on washed Mavis into a creek.'

'It's terrifying.' Molly shivered. 'Mavis said Leo's dad pulled the winch across the river. And he just lifted her up out of the car.' Molly could imagine that. She so could. 'Like Rambo.' She could hear the little bit of awe in her voice, but really, she wished she'd seen it.

Hannah laughed, but her eyes went wide as if she, too, could imagine it, maybe in technicolour. Molly watched her. Hannah's face looked a little dreamy. Molly smiled. *Well. Well.*

Nobody minded looking at a muscled male body. Some days, Molly wished she could find one for herself. An older one, of course. She didn't want a toy boy even if he looked like Jude Waugh. She wanted someone who was her other half, like her husband had been. He hadn't been a romantic man, but they had talked in bed at night, and she missed that.

Maybe she was just a little tired of watching Liam and Nell skirt around their future plans, because Molly knew time was ticking away.

Hannah was saying, 'He carried Mavis into the house like she was a wet kitten and not an adult weighed down with wet clothes.' Then she muttered softly, 'I have to stop remembering that.'

But Molly heard and she bit back a grin. 'I bet he looked good in wet clothes.'

'That he did.' Hannah actually blushed and her eyes took on that faraway look again. Seconds ticked by. Then more seconds.

'Earth to Hannah?' Molly gave a knowing smile. 'Nell says you've both seen the elusive Mr Waugh several times in the last month. Most of us haven't seen him ever.'

Hannah stared at her in surprise. 'Not even at Jed's store?'

'No. Gracie said she hadn't met him at all. Apparently, Jed said he must buy his rural supplies out of town. They have no idea if they run cattle or horses or anything out at Luna Downs.' Molly shrugged. 'Or maybe he just doesn't need the things Jed sells.'

'Luna Downs.' Hannah nodded. 'I remember that place from when I drove in. He's only said they were on land out of town. I didn't notice the address on the records.'

This was a good way for Molly to get her mind off the possible disaster of a flood. It was much more fun to gently tease Hannah. 'The gossips,' Molly lowered her voice, but she was smiling; she didn't believe gossips that much, 'have their own ideas on the possibly nefarious activities the high fences are hiding.' She shrugged. 'Nobody knows for sure.'

Hannah frowned and shook her head. 'Jude told me it's a dry community at home,' she said decisively. 'When he dropped off that bottle of wine after Leo's first visit.' The good doctor blushed again. Molly had heard about that wine from Nell. 'Anyway, that doesn't sound nefarious to me.'

'It could still be a sect. With polygamy or nudity and all sorts.' Molly tried to keep a straight face as Hannah's darkened.

Yep. Hannah compressed her mouth tightly. 'Maybe we should just mind our own business.'

Instead of being put down, Molly laughed. 'I knew it. She's attracted to him, so she defends him.'

Before Hannah could complain, Molly held up her hand. 'Sorry. I'm teasing, that's all. And I've gotta go. Hope you get your bath, Hannah. You deserve it after all the drama.'

Chapter Twenty-one

Jude

Jude and Leo carried the last of the groceries into the long kitchen, and Jude glanced out the window at the rain pelting down. He turned to watch Leo place the fish and frozen vegetables in vertical stacks across the bottom of the empty freezer. The freezer he'd just powered up and hoped would stay on.

If the power went out, they had a full tank for the generator, which should keep the freezer going for a couple of days while the rain continued. He doubted any problems would last longer than that, but he'd gone into Featherwood's store before Leo's appointment and stocked up on flour, sugar and other staples just in case.

'That was crazy.' Leo glanced up at him. 'Mrs Maloney must have been scared, Dad.'

'Mavis looks tough to me,' Jude said. 'The doc will sort her. And . . .' He slid the bulk tin of coffee on the top shelf with the dozen cartons of long-life milk. 'She didn't panic. Lots would have.'

'I'd be terrified.' His son's eyes widened at the memory.

'You're not eighty-one. I'd hope you would have shimmied out of the window before the car slid down the tree.'

Leo thought about that and nodded. 'I know her great-grandson, Archie, from school. He's in my year. He's quiet but friendly.' Leo's hand paused on the bread as if the loaf suddenly became very interesting. 'They live on a farm near where it happened.'

Leo didn't usually talk about school, and Jude didn't ask. After the scare of missing Leo's illness, however, Jude had vowed to himself that he'd have at least one long conversation with his son every day. Learn stuff. Keep up to date. 'Have you got many mates at school?'

'Not really.' Leo gave more of a mumble than an answer. 'Archie spoke to me a couple of times. I keep to myself.'

Sadly, his son probably had learned that from him. He looked across and Leo was staring at his hands. 'Make an effort if this Archie speaks to you again. At your age, you should have a bunch of mates.' And Jude didn't want his son to end up a loner like his dad was now.

'It's not like I can ask him to come back here,' Leo muttered.

Jude thought about that. He had discouraged outsiders because he hated people knowing his business. This was left over from his brief time in custody, when he'd felt watched every minute. Nobody except those who lived on Luna Downs came onto his land. Deliveries were left at the gate and the mail at the road in the big box. They tried to be as self-sufficient as possible. 'There's no reason you can't ask him,' he told Leo.

Leo swung his head and stared at him. 'Do you mean that?'

'I said it, didn't I?'

'And if he does come here . . . can I go to his place, too?'

There was no logical reason why he couldn't, but Jude didn't like that, either. What if something happened to Leo? 'I'll let you know after I talk to his grandmother.'

'Cool.' Leo started laying bread again in another layer. 'We could ride the quad bikes.'

'Not until I make sure he knows what he's doing. And his grandmother agrees. I'll phone her tomorrow to check how she is and ask her then.'

Ah hell, Jude thought. What had he done? Whatever it was, well, maybe it was about time he did it. He'd have to give Leo the spare phone if he was out from under his scrutiny. And put it in another military container in case he dropped it.

Chapter Twenty-two

Hannah

The next day, Tuesday, Hannah watched the rain fall from her office window. The deluge from the sky hadn't stopped.

'Flood rain,' Mavis said darkly, when she came for her check-up. The older lady had been determined to go home with Archie last night, and Hannah had dropped her there, but the conditional agreement hung on Mavis returning the next day for a thorough check.

In Featherwood itself, the post office and shop were dry on Hannah's side of the street, which was higher than Gracie and Jed's house and store. But the water had begun to flow a few inches over the road along the whole street, which meant it was flowing down Jed's driveway and through his drive-through at the shop. He had spent much of the day with Liam shifting stuff up to Hannah's shed on the hill.

From the rectory, Hannah watched the level rise and widen behind Gracie's house as her friend's previously ambling creek became a torrent. Dark pools gathered in wait like doorways to another dimension, as they lapped around the edges of trees and crept towards Jed's store from the back as well.

The main road from Dorrigo to the east had been cut at the Waterfall Way with a surge pouring over the mountain waterfalls and another landslide. That wasn't unusual, she was told, but to the west, two kilometres past Luna Downs, Mavis told her the road had been cut off from Armidale by rushing tides from the gullies through the hills.

'Hmm,' said Mavis. 'I've heard of it doing this, but I'd never seen it myself till yesterday. I could have done without that, let me tell you. I'm glad the boy and I moved those cattle.'

'And Archie's off school now until the road's open, then?'

'I'm happy with that. I know he's here and not stuck on some bus goodness knows where.'

'Archie looks pretty happy, too.' Mavis had left him in the waiting room talking to Nell. There'd been a message from Leo for him.

'The boy would leave school yesterday if I let him and work the farm seven days a week.'

'He's too young, surely.'

'I told him to get his Year Twelve certificate and we'll talk about it then.'

'Did you walk here in the rain this morning?' Hannah had had a flurry of early patients, so she hadn't seen Mavis's mode of arrival.

'Jed dropped off his small delivery truck last night. He said he wouldn't be delivering anything for a few days now with the rain and the flooding.'

'That was good of him.'

Mavis harrumphed. 'That's Jed. He wouldn't take no. He'd give you the shirt off his back. But I won't be driving anywhere except from here to the farm.'

Hannah unrolled the blood-pressure cuff from Mavis's arm, but she still heard the whisper of reactional emotion from yesterday's adventure. Hannah would be remembering too, if it had been her. She'd still be shaking, in fact. 'Your blood pressure is normal. You're a marvel, Mavis. Did you sleep?'

'Not bad, considering. I've always been lucky like that. All that church-going has kept me safe.'

Hannah didn't think Mavis losing her house in a fire and being washed into a creek were blessings, but who was she to dispute the woman's faith. Neither had killed Mavis when others might have died. A personal angel protector didn't seem too far-fetched an idea. 'You must be blessed,' she agreed.

They both stood and Hannah opened the door to the waiting room. As soon as Mavis stepped outside, Archie cast hopeful eyes her way.

Hannah heard him say, 'Can Leo come to our place if his dad drops him off?'

So Jude was coming into town?

Mavis rolled eyes. 'Yes. He rang to see how I was. Didn't mention it then?'

'My idea. Leo said his dad would pick him up in a couple of hours?'

'Of course.' Mavis straightened with an almost militant look in her posture. 'I want to thank that man face to face, anyway.'

Archie's grin grew even brighter. 'Thanks, Gran.'

'It'll be good for you to have a friend.' She studied her grandson hopping from foot to foot, then narrowed her eyes at him. 'Though isn't that boy a diabetic?' She turned back to Hannah. 'What do I feed him?'

Hannah, a spectator of Mavis's skill at handling her grandson, smiled. 'Good pick-up, Mavis, but he's a sensible kid. He knows what he can eat. Just remind him that you're relying on him to let you know. If you get worried about him whenever he visits, just phone me.'

The worried look on Mavis's face receded and she nodded decisively. 'Right, then.' She turned back to Archie. 'Let's get home. I want to make a box with some of those pumpkins and a few jars of pickles and marmalade for his dad as a thankyou.'

Hannah watched them go and considered the empty waiting room. 'Another quiet afternoon in the rain, do you think?'

'When it stops soaking everything, the appointments will fill fast,' Nell said. 'Folks are being sensible and staying in.'

Hannah looked at her friend and then at the streams of water running down the window, thinking about the sensible folk. 'What about you? Are you safe coming in from your place? I keep thinking about what happened to Mavis yesterday.'

'Me too. I did feel wary this morning, so I asked Liam to drive me.' She shrugged and smiled. 'I felt as safe as houses then.'

Liam adored Nell. Hannah had seen that. No way would he let anything happen to his love. It was a shame that Hannah didn't have someone like that who cared what happened to her. But as soon as she had the thought, she frowned at herself.

Pathetic. She didn't need a man. Or a minder. Or a Jude Waugh man-of-steel type. And how had he popped into that thought?

'Mavis mentioned that spot where she had her scare is running six inches over the road now,' she said, to redirect her thoughts.

'Liam thinks something's happened upstream to change the course of the creek. As well as super-heavy rain up further.'

Hannah furrowed her brows. 'Like a tree falling and diverting, do you think?'

'Maybe. Or a boulder. Or even a landslide.'

'Is your house safe?' She'd been up to Nell's farm once. It was an idyllic valley a few kilometres past Mavis's, with cows and a creek ambling through the middle from a waterfall. The new house was on a slight rise, so Nell's place should be safe, but she'd been another who had lost her house in the fires and devastation twice would surely be too much.

'My place used to back up almost to the waterfall. I'm glad we moved the house site now because that water's pouring off the mountain there like a torrent.'

Torrents were dangerous, and they washed over roads. 'You don't need to come in until this is over.' She did not want to be responsible for Nell being washed away. 'I think I'll shut the surgery for a few days. This flood should all be over soon. I don't want anyone pushing through water to get here for an appointment. Can you reschedule everyone who has a booking? I'll just be here for emergencies until the rain stops.'

'I think that's sensible.' Nell chewed her lip then nodded. 'They appreciate you. People are saying they feel safer, just having you here, especially while we're blocked off from the big towns.'

Hannah felt herself warm at the praise, and the rightness of her move to Featherwood settled deeper. Yes, she was glad she had come, glad she'd begun to feel a part of the community. Even if she was going to be flooded in for the first time in her life, this was her home now, and it felt good to be here with everyone.

Nell said, 'Tomorrow I'll get Liam to bring me into town to help Gracie and Jed with packing up Gracie's house. Just in case.'

'I'll come down, too. I can divert the phone. Many hands and all that.'

'Good thinking. She could probably use all the hands she can get.'

Chapter Twenty-three

Nell

Nell listened to the drum of the rain on her new roof. Her little bush chalet, as she liked to think of her replacement house, had settled into its spot on the hill overlooking the sodden paddocks and didn't feel so much like a substitute but her true home, now.

Pre-fab and low-maintenance, the house contained two bedrooms, a study, lounge and combined dining/kitchen, which were all surrounded by the verandah.

She knew that behind her, out of sight, back where the waterfall raged against the cliff, water lapped around the burnt stumps of her first house. The house where she'd sought refuge after the emotional devastation of her midwifery career in Sydney and her father's death. The haven where she'd found herself, and Liam.

Now, life had settled to contentedness, and her home was hers again. Liam – apart from the dilemma of whose house they'd move to if they permanently lived together – was everything she wanted in a life partner. And she had her new job. All of which were wonderful, affirming things, so why did this new drama have to creep up and threaten everything. Because, despite trying to believe everything would be fine, this rain was a worry.

Nell stared over the verandah rail towards the raging creek that roared across her lower paddock and had begun to creep towards the cattle yards like a shallow black hole closing in. The other cattle were up the hill in the far paddock, but one mother and calf were in the yards. Moo, the big white Brahman matriarch, had her sharp, curved horns over the top of the wooden fence and was looking towards the house. Looking for Nell to come and release her before the water rose any higher.

The man who'd been supposed to pick them up in his cattle truck yesterday had bogged in the mud and couldn't get out to her house. She couldn't leave Moo and her calf there. What had seemed like a sensible idea – having them where she could handfeed in the few days after birth – had backfired with the incessant rain, and her brilliant idea was now a problem.

'Rightio, Moo. I'm on my way.'

Nell considered tucking her phone into her jeans, decided against risking it dropping into the pools of water, and stashed it in the kitchen before she pulled on her heavy, high-sided gumboots.

'Grin! Here, boy,' she called. The blue cattle pup she'd bought from Mavis when she'd first arrived had matured well and learned to heel. Grin eagerly came at her command, and stayed to heel, instead of chasing the cattle into the distance like he used to, with Nell screaming from behind with frustration.

'I'm not happy with the way that water's swirling, Grin,' she said and grabbed the long walking stick Liam had sanded back for her. It had proved a boon when the ground was so wet.

Moo's new calf looks tiny and miserable in the rain, she thought as she trudged through the mud. Grin seemed to glide over the top of the squelching mire, tail wagging, mouth wide in his usual toothy smile.

Moo bellowed unexpectedly and stepped back from the fence as if she'd seen a snake, or perhaps something even more dangerous, which made the hair on the back of Nell's neck stand up. She hurriedly took an extra step forward until she heard the rumble and roar, behind not in front, and spun to look.

A wave of water had shot from the top of the mountain. It had been flowing strongly, but nothing like this. A massive spume flew out from the waterfall, as if something had held a dam back and now let go.

The water hit the ground, arched and creamed and swirled between her and the house in a whirlpool of debris, and all she could do was run for the cattle yards.

Nell smacked into the rail and climbed up the fence in her awkward rubber boots. Hurriedly, she shuffled along the bars to unclip the gate so at least Moo could get away if the water kept rising. Then she scrambled up on top of the cattle crush, which was another arm's length higher, until she was precariously balanced across the top of the horizontal bars.

The cresting wave smashed against the side of the steel structure, causing the rails to wobble before they settled again as the water poured through them. The wave pushed the gate open and hit Moo, then foamed up the sides of the yards and pushed her calf into the corner of the fence, while sweeping Moo out of the gate. She bellowed but was swept sideways, her big-horned head swivelling and eyes wild.

Nell cried out in horror because she'd thought she'd gathered them to safety, but instead she'd put them in the gravest danger.

The level of the water dropped as the wave rolled on down the paddock, carrying Moo towards the creek, but there the flow spread out over the whole of the lower field. The wave surged away. And yet, slowly, inexorably, the water level started to inch up again.

Now she'd blown it. She was stuck in the middle of a lake when she should have been safe in the house across the paddock. She needed to climb down now before the water level in the paddock rose past her boots, but she couldn't leave the calf to drown.

It all had happened so fast and so powerfully, and the way it swept a five-hundred-kilo Brahman away meant if she hadn't made it to the yards in time she'd have been washed away like a twig on top of that wave.

There was nothing she could do for Moo except hope she'd be washed onto a bank somewhere down the creek.

She pushed that horror away because for the moment she needed to save the calf. She had to rescue her up to the house on the rise before she could save herself. Hopefully, it wouldn't be too long before she could retrieve Moo back to feed her.

Gingerly, she climbed down from her precarious position and onto the side rails then into the water. Unexpectedly, the level of the water poured in over the top of her boots, filling them instantly. The calf tilted her head up, flaring nostrils above the water as she panicked and gulped, and Nell had no idea how she could grab her and get her across to the house.

She checked her feet, suddenly realising that Grin was nowhere to be seen, and her throat closed in horror that Grin had been swept away, as well. She couldn't think about that now, Grin or Moo, or anything else except not getting swept away herself. Then work out how to get the calf to the house.

She patted her pockets, but there was no rope, of course – she hadn't thought to bring any. Her fingers brushed the hard leather around her waist. Her belt! The beautiful western leather Liam had bought her, laughingly telling her that she was 'a real jillaroo' when he gave it to her.

She unbuckled the stiff band and sloshed towards the calf, sliding the leather strap around her neck and looping it back through the buckle so that she had a hand's width gap between the calf's neck to pull her along. She was a baby but probably weighed more than thirty kilos. Lucky she had been swept into the corner and not out the gate.

The calf bucked and reared, almost forcing her off balance, not helped by her water-filled boots dragging like sandbags on her feet.

'It's okay, baby. I'm not trying to hurt you. I'll get your mummy back.' She hoped. Nell winced as that horrid photo-bomb of Moo being swept away reappeared in her mind.

Her shoulder jerked again. The calf wasn't listening. She was in full panic mode now, fighting against Nell's pull and trying to dislocate her arm from its socket. Nell strained back, elbow and shoulder and wrist already painful from the battle, but she dug her chin into her chest and leaned her body towards the house to pull the little calf forward through the water.

Sturdy calf legs dog-paddled in distress as the baby searched for ground purchase and didn't find it. Black ears jerked back and forth while Nell dragged her towards the house, one agonising step at a time.

The water level climbed to Nell's waist. Fatigue pulled as the rising flow pushed against her, and the calf wriggled less frantically as she too grew tired.

She heard a familiar bark and suddenly ahead there was Grin, prancing at the edge of the water. Barking, anxious, dripping wet, he must have swum his way back to the house.

'Thank goodness, Grin. Stay there. You're such a good boy!'

Panting with the effort, she waded waist deep towards the bank. The slope should have been lifting her out of the water, but the water level continued to rise. She glanced back towards the cattle yards and the flow was almost up to the cattle crush she'd perched upon. Unbelievable. And was that wall of water rushing towards town?

The calf must have found her feet, but she didn't pull away. Obviously, she had exhausted herself and was barely lifting her head above the water now and was sluggishly trotting behind Nell, which made everything so much easier.

Nell's shoulders dropped as she found the steps of the house and then realised the driveway was under and she was marooned. But she pushed that selfish fear aside and rushed forward.

She needed to warn Gracie that the water was coming.

Chapter Twenty-four

Molly

Molly picked up the phone and instead of hello she heard a gasp.

'Molly? Thank God,' the caller wheezed. A pause, then, 'Hang on,' as the person on the other end panted again with a strangled breath. Deep, ragged breathing sounded. Seconds ticked by.

'Audrey?'

More deep breaths and Molly suspected a contraction, or a bunch of contractions were causing the problem.

'Nearly.' Audrey sounded like she forced the word out and finally she sighed into the phone. 'Oh, my goodness.'

'I thought it was you, Audrey.' Molly decided her voice sounded calm. That was good. 'And you're in labour, right? Want me to come?' Still calm. Excellent. *Stay that way, Mol*, she admonished herself.

'Yesss.' Audrey's voice hissed with relief. Knowing Molly would help. Of course. She and Audrey had become close since Audrey's husband had started his fly-in fly-out job. She'd begun to babysit the twins for those times Audrey needed to do things that taking two hyperactive twin boys didn't help with.

And her man was away. 'Who's with you?'

'Nobody. Well, the babies are. They're staring up at me with wide blue eyes.' Audrey blew out another breath. 'It's okay, babies. Aunty Molly is coming.'

'Yes, she is,' Molly said. 'I'll phone Hannah too.'

Audrey whispered, 'They won't be the babies for much longer,' and if Molly wasn't mistaken Audrey was crying. She sniffed as if pulling herself together. 'I don't know why that makes me want to cry. It's okay. They're reorganising my kitchen cupboard.'

'Of course they are. I'm on my way. I'll hang up and ring Hannah.'

Molly ended the call and tapped in Hannah's name in her address book. She answered on the first ring.

'*This is a recording. The doctor's surgery is closed for the next few days to keep everyone safe. Please ring back on Monday to make any non-urgent appointments.*' Molly's heart sank. Then, '*For emergencies, please hold.*'

Molly held her breath and squeezed the phone until her fingers turned white.

'This is Hannah.'

'Hannah, it's Molly. Audrey just phoned me. She's in labour. It sounds like it's strong labour. I'm on my way there, now.'

'Okay.' Hannah sounded as calm as Molly was trying to be. 'I'll get some equipment and meet you there. Hopefully, she can be transferred up here to my surgery before she has her baby. We won't be able to get her out in time unless it's a false start.'

'It didn't sound false. Do you know where she lives?'

'Yes,' she answered matter-of-factly. As if this was all fine. 'See you soon.'

Molly nodded, which was dumb when Hannah couldn't see her, but she felt a lot better knowing Hannah would arrive and take control.

Molly had been in Jed's house when Gracie had her baby, but Nell was a midwife and she'd been there then. Otherwise, Molly had no experience with birth. This was probably the most exciting thing that had happened to her in years. Except for the fires. But the fires were not exciting, they'd been terrifying.

Molly forced herself to calm down and looked around for her keys. They were on the hook where she always hung them. She tore out the door to the big shed where they parked the cars, wrenched the door open and jumped into hers.

'Hang on, Audrey,' she whispered and floored it in reverse, handbrake-turned it in a slew of gravel into the drive and headed for the road.

She hadn't driven recklessly for years. Not since she was twenty and a newly married woman. It felt unashamedly good.

Audrey met her just inside the squeaky front door, clearly aiming to keep the boys inside. Leaning against it, she looked to be wincing between pursed lips, as if willing the tension in her body to ease.

As Molly edged open the noisy door to let herself past, she saw that both boys were staring up at their mother, worry creasing pinched faces.

'Everything's fine, babies, Mummy's fine. Aunty Molly is here.' The gentleness in Audrey's voice sounded like a lullaby. Until she gasped and her fingers whitened on the edge of the door.

They all stood there while Audrey closed her eyes and breathed. Nobody said anything. After a minute, she blew out a breath and sagged a little. 'Thank you for coming.'

'Wouldn't miss it for the world,' Molly teased just as gently as Audrey had spoken to her boys.

Audrey smiled. A real smile. 'I've been having those practice pains for a week or two now. I should have paid more attention when the water rose beside the bridge into Featherwood.'

'I thought you were going into Armidale to your mother-in-law's house?'

Audrey scrunched up her face at the thought, then glanced at her boys with wry amusement. 'Nana Lyn likes her house tidy. And I won't have Steve as buffer between them and her while he's away. He's not back till next week.'

Molly understood. Looked at the deceptively angelic twins. 'They can cause chaos.'

Audrey nodded. 'The last time we stayed at Nana Lyn's, she felt a migraine coming on. I thought I'd leave it to the last minute, to cause as little disturbance as possible with her, when I went into hospital for the baby.'

Another shudder from Audrey and this time she squeezed her hand against the tightness in her belly with a gasp.

Molly mused that perhaps dear Audrey should've left last week, but she didn't say it. When the contraction had passed, they moved through to the kitchen, and the boys wandered back to the plastics cupboard.

Audrey said in almost a whisper, 'I don't like to admit I preferred the idea of having my baby in Featherwood to leaving the boys with my mother-in-law. But right now, I've changed my mind.'

'That's understandable,' Molly said, with no hint of scolding. Audrey had been between two tough places. Trouble was, her uterus said she'd left it too late, now, to choose.

The next contraction rolled through and Audrey steepled her fingers, nail edge down on the hard lip of the kitchen bench, the twins under her feet combing through the bowls and lids in the cupboard.

It's not fair that Audrey's Steve isn't here, Molly thought. That's what husbands were for. But she knew they'd changed his holidays so he could be here for the due date.

It could be worse. They had a doctor coming. Audrey's house could have been cut off in the flood.

Gracie had mentioned that Hannah delivered babies all the time in Roma at the hospital. Featherwood didn't have a hospital, but they did have a doctor. And two midwives. And Gracie had had her baby in Featherwood.

Molly glanced back towards the front of the house, hoping that Hannah would be here soon.

Chapter Twenty-five

Mavis

'What does diabetic mean?' Archie asked the question in a low voice, but Mavis heard through the open window. She leaned her good ear closer.

'It means I get an insulin needle at breakfast, lunch, dinner, bed and whenever I want a snack. Otherwise, my body can't convert the sugar. Or I get really sick.'

'That's five needles a day?'

'I wish.' Leo's voice held quiet disgust. 'There are at least five finger pricks to check the sugar levels, as well.'

'Ten stabs?' She heard the horrified incredulity in Archie's voice. *That did suck for the kid*, Mavis thought glumly. Archie had panicked over one tetanus shot.

The boys were out on the front porch, hanging their feet over the edge as Mavis washed up. The rain had stopped again, and her hero, the new boy's surprisingly pleasant dad, had just left. He really was a big bloke, which was lucky for her since he'd carried her across a swollen creek. But he was also quietly spoken, particularly when he'd said he'd return in two hours.

Mavis had the feeling it would be on the dot.

It was funny how people turned up in your life just when you needed them. Jude had turned up for Mavis, so maybe Leo was here for Archie?

Leo was taller than Archie, would probably grow up to be as tall as his dad, and he had big bones and the same dark hair as Jude. Even as a teen, Leo's cheekbones and jaw promised a man's face in the not-too-distant future.

Her boy was changing too, she'd noticed lately, and she thanked God again for depositing him on her doorstep for the time she'd had of his company. If keeping Archie meant she had to host other boys her great-grandson's age, then she'd do it, no problem. For as long as she was here. And that was before the flood. She bit her lip, not wanting to delve too deeply into her recent specialist appointment. And Leo seemed like a good kid.

'What do people who don't have diabetes need to know about it?'

She heard a huff of disgust from the visitor. 'That you can't catch it from me, I guess.'

'Someone asked you that?' Archie sounded incredulous. 'What an idiot.'

'Yeah. As if I didn't already feel abnormal.'

'You're not too abnormal,' Archie murmured, and gazed off into the rain.

There was a slight growl from Leo. 'Great. Thanks. That makes me feel better.'

'You're welcome.'

Mavis smiled. He did like to tease, her boy. She suspected things were a bit more serious at Leo's house and it might take him a bit to get used to being stirred.

'Anyway,' with just a touch of impatience, Leo went on. 'Too much sugar or not enough in my blood makes me feel weird.'

'Weird?' Archie shrugged his shoulder, not understanding.

The answer came flatly. 'If I have too much insulin or not enough food, I get shaky and sleepy. And I slur my words. That's dangerous, so if that happens, you tell someone.'

'Okay. I can do that.' Archie sounded serious this time.

'Thanks.' There was something odd or even shocked in Leo's one word, as if he hadn't expected the answer he got. Lord knew what the other kids had been saying to him.

Archie, still musing, asked, 'What helps if that happens?'

'Something sweet. I carry jelly beans in case the blood sugar levels drop really low. And I have needles and stuff if it gets too high.'

'Oh. Okay. Let me know.' Archie hopped up and Mavis stepped back from the window. 'The rain's stopped. Did you want to ask Gran if we can take the quad bikes for a run? Seeing as your dad said it's okay? We only have a couple of hours.'

'Are you kidding?' There was delight in the voice that had just been clinically detailing his depressing new life.

Mavis pretended she was busy when the boys came in.

'Hey, Gran?' Archie sidled up to her with a big smile. His please-may-I-have smile that made her laugh because he didn't do it often enough.

'I've got a job for you,' she said before he could ask. Two could tease.

His smile faded, but he squared his shoulders. Bless him. Her grin grew. 'Could you boys move those horses off the bottom paddock and in with the cows in the top pasture? If you want, you can take the quad bikes.'

Archie's grin bounced back. 'Sure.'

'And wear your helmets.'

'Will do, Mrs Maloney.' Leo saluted. She suspected it was something he did with his dad. Cute.

'See that, Archie. You should salute me too.' She'd have to see if Archie would do it.

Archie grinned and flicked up his hand to his forehead. 'Yes, sir, Gran.'

'Back by twelve. Yes?' Mavis added with a pretend frown.

Both boys nodded and Archie checked his watch. Leo did as well. Then they were gone.

Chapter Twenty-six

Hannah

Hannah slid into her car, thankful for the brief lull in the rain. She'd called Gracie and Nell for backup on their mobiles, but neither had answered. She left a message for each to return her call or meet her at the surgery. At least Molly would be waiting with Audrey.

She'd do a swoop and scoop. Audrey and the boys had to come to her house. Lucky she knew where the young mum lived, between Nell and Mavis, because Gracie had pointed it out as the home of the cutest twins, on the day she'd visited Nell's place.

The Peronis lived on a small farm on the same side of the creek as Gracie, but on a decent mound at the top of the paddock. Their little dwelling had been one of the few spared during that black day of fires last year.

The gate hung open, which was another bonus since she didn't have to get out in the sprinkling rain to gain access. And as she braked at the front steps behind Molly's car, she could see the screen door was shut but the front door stood ajar.

'Hello,' she called when she climbed onto the verandah. 'It's Hannah. You there, Audrey? Molly?'

'Come through,' a tense reply drifted from within. 'Molly's just packing the boys' clothes.'

Hannah pulled open the squeaky door and stepped along the thin carpet runner towards the back of the house. It was dark inside without the lights on, and suddenly the rain returned to pelt on the tin roof like a bucket full of nails dropped from overhead.

Outside the house, she could hear the creek rushing even more loudly than it had been at Gracie's when she'd gone over to help yesterday evening, and she wondered just how safe they all were from being isolated in this house on a hill. They were still on the low side of the road.

The sooner she shifted Audrey and the boys to her place, the better.

Audrey stood hunched in a small bedroom with twin beds. A large duffle bag open on one of the coverlets. Molly was rifling through the drawers. The contents – small shorts, coloured shirts and nappies – spilled out, and one of the young mum's hands gripped the edge of a chest of drawers with white-knuckled strength, while the other gripped the bag. Her breathing huffed in and out. Not good.

Hannah used her most soothing voice. 'Great job. Let's just take what you've got now and get you up to the surgery. Nell and Gracie will meet us there. Molly can sort this.'

Audrey turned, her eyes wide and guilt stricken. 'I wasn't supposed to go into labour. My husband's home next week. We thought we'd left enough time!' She turned tormented eyes to the window. 'I should have gone earlier.'

'Not worth the brain space now.' Hannah eased the bag from Audrey's other hand and zipped it closed. 'Where are the boys?'

Audrey's head jerked. 'In the kitchen. The cupboards.'

'I've got a cupboard like that, too. We'll get them. Do you have a bag for yourself?'

'Molly put it beside the front door.'

'Okay. I'll put both bags in the car and come back for you and the boys. Molly can follow.' *Darn.* Hannah grimaced at a thought. 'I haven't got child seats, but you can't drive. Can we strap them in the back of my car with just seat belts?' She didn't fancy driving a strange car in this weather.

'That's fine. We do that around the farm. They know not to move.' It was an attempt at a joke.

What a champion, Hannah thought. But she could see Audrey's tears were there, ready to flood, her eyes glistening with wetness like the leaves outside. Hannah touched her arm. 'We'll sort this, Audrey. Let's make it a happy day.'

Audrey sniffed and nodded, then plastered a smile on. 'I'll get the boys while Molly grabs their toys.'

Hannah swept up the duffle. 'Back in a minute.' She turned and moved quickly to the front door, where she grabbed the second bag and whisked down the wet steps to throw them into the boot and slam it shut. The rain had eased again. It seemed to come in waves of heavy fall and then barely any.

A howling wail rose from the house, and Hannah spun and jogged up the steps and through the door towards the sound. 'Audrey? Where are you? You okay?'

In the kitchen, the back door stood open, rain obscuring the backyard. Audrey stood in the opening, swivelling her head. Molly leaned beside her. Audrey leaned precariously out over the steps and Molly was holding her back.

Hannah rushed to her side and took over. 'What are you doing?'

Audrey swept her arm out at the paddock that dipped down towards the swollen creek. 'I think the boys are out there.' She waved her hand wildly. 'Outside.'

Hannah's stomach dropped. 'Are you sure they're not hiding somewhere?' Her gaze darted around the small kitchen as she turned her head, jerky with wild hope that she'd see a small figure crouching somewhere. Molly had spun and dropped to the floor and was looking in the cupboards. Only plastic containers sat in a tidy line on the floor. Chairs and table, kitchen detritus, but no boys.

Audrey kneaded her stomach as she bowed over with a gasp. 'I closed the back door, but I didn't latch it. I found it open.' Tears tunnelled down her face as she swept her hand again around the room. 'And they're not here.'

'They could still be in here,' Molly was saying desperately. 'I'll look in the rest of the house.' She took off down the hallway.

Audrey gasped and clutched her stomach as another contraction gripped her. Her fingers clawed like talons on the doorframe, she muttered fiercely, 'Not now, uterus, not now. I don't have time for this.' She lurched for the stairs and somehow Hannah caught her before she made it onto the top step.

'No. Stay here.' She held Audrey's arm. 'You can't have a baby in the paddock. I'll go. Get Molly to phone Gracie and Jed. Get them to come. Nell will get Liam.'

Hannah dashed into the rain, down the steps in the direction Audrey had pointed, but as she reached the soggy ground, she heard the roar of a vehicle over the downpour as it drove past on the road. She knew that sound. It was Jude's car. Hope flared within her.

Grabbing at her phone with one hand and wiping the rain away from her eyes with the other, she searched for his number. She had it for Leo's results. She tapped his name as fast as she could, praying he would answer.

The call opened. 'Jude.'

'Stop the car. It's Hannah. I'm in the house to the left of you with the open gate. Audrey's twin boys have gone missing and she's afraid they're heading for the creek. She's in labour and I need help.'

'On it,' he said. 'Where are you?'

'Around the back of the house.' She saw the car brake, turn in a tight circle and then cruise slowly down the driveway. He was going too slow . . . *No.* She thought of the boys and realised he needed to go slow in case the little ones had walked that way. Lucky one of them was thinking.

She headed back to Audrey, who was calling the boys' names between gasps. 'Jude Waugh is coming to help,' she told her. 'His four-wheel drive can cover the paddock faster than we can run. Any ideas where they'd go?'

'To the fence, maybe. There's a rabbit hole under that tree.' She pointed. 'But that's so close to the creek now.'

Hannah stared in the direction Audrey pointed and saw the swirling water, the rush of branches and flotsam tumbling in the race. If she left to search for the boys, Audrey would be in the house with only Molly. She couldn't leave her.

As Jude pulled up next to her and the side window came down, she said urgently, 'We need to take Audrey as we search. I can't leave her here alone in case she births.' Then she called up the steps, 'Audrey, you have to come with us.'

Molly appeared at the door. 'I'll check the front yard.'

Hannah nodded and said to Jude, 'I don't know if Audrey is capable of climbing in.'

'Fine.' His door opened and he loped past her up the steps so fast she called out, 'Let Jude help you into the car and we'll search together.'

Jude got to the top of the stairs, said something to Audrey that made her shoulders ease, and then he scooped her up in his arms and came back down the stairs.

Hannah opened the door and he placed her gently on the back seat. Then he was behind the wheel and Hannah had to scramble into the front before he drove off. 'Towards that tree down there first,' she told him.

Audrey croaked through her tears, 'They're wearing green and yellow.'

'Put the windows down if you need to see better. The car won't melt with the rain.' He glanced into the rear-vision mirror. 'Who owns next door?'

'Mavis,' Audrey was sobbing now.

'Ah,' he said and pressed a number on the Bluetooth. The number rang in the car as Jude turned the vehicle and began to roll slowly down the paddock towards the creek. The speakers kept ringing, then a boy's voice answered.

'Yes, Dad.'

'Leo. You boys on the quads?'

'Just putting them away.'

'Tell Archie's grandmother that the twins next door have wandered off. I need you boys to search along the adjoining fence down to the creek. Take the quad bikes. Go slow. They're little kids. Don't run over them. And don't get too close to the creek. Phone me if you see anything.'

'Right.'

That was two search parties, Hannah realised. She swivelled in the seat towards Audrey. 'Did you get onto Gracie or Jed?'

'Molly got Jed,' she puffed as a contraction eased away. 'He's on his way.'

Three search parties, then. And Jed would know who else to call. She spun to the front, her eyes searching the recently slashed grass for little figures. 'The little blighters can move fast.'

'Too fast,' Jude murmured beside her, but she caught the words.

'Though why would they go out in the rain?' Hannah thought out loud.

'They love the rain. I usually let them splash.' A sob escaped Audrey. 'I wish I hadn't now.'

'Kids will be kids,' Jude said. 'We'll find them.' There was certainty in his voice.

Hannah had wanted to say those words, but she'd learned a long time ago not to promise what she couldn't give. A flash of white down near the creek caught her eye.

'What's that?' The white thing bobbed past in the distant creek.

'There goes a cow,' Jude said, 'and we don't have time to help.'

Watching the thrashing beast fly past around the bend of the creek made Hannah feel sick. 'Has it got any chance?' She glanced at Jude.

He shook his head. 'Doubt it.' When he looked back at her face, he said in a softer voice, 'But stranger things have happened.'

There was another flash, this time khaki, moving along the fence line coming down the slight hill towards the creek. The boys had arrived on the quadbikes.

Jude drove towards the corner of the fence, to where it disappeared under the creek. There were no demarcation dividers between the properties once you hit the wash. All the creek-crossing fences were either gone or deep underwater. The rain eased back to a sprinkle again, and their field of vision widened.

The two older boys wore Driza-Bone coats and black helmets, and water streamed down their faces and chests, sluicing the mud on their legs towards their boots.

'Stay here,' Jude said. 'I just want a quick word with the boys and then we'll drive back along the creek's edge towards the opposite fence line.'

Before she could answer, he jumped out of the vehicle and slammed the door, before jogging over to the fence, where Leo had skidded his bike up against a post. Father and son had a brief conversation and then the boys turned their bikes and crawled off parallel to the creek, but a car length back at least. Hannah had seen the stabbing two fingers of Jude's hand giving them the parallel to work from.

Audrey puffed and hissed in the back seat and Hannah spun around to look at her. Audrey's face shone white in the poor light, with red spots of colour on her cheeks and terror in her eyes. Some fear might have been for herself in labour, but definitely most of the panic was for the boys. Hannah couldn't even imagine the agony the young mum was going through in her mind. As soon as Jude climbed back in the car she said, 'We have to get Audrey to the surgery.'

'We'll do that. We need more help.' As he said that, a decrepit small vehicle angled down towards them. Hannah recognised it as Jed's latest reinvented second-hand vehicle, an old Suzuki Vitara – the man changed cars like hats, restoring and selling to make extra money. He came around the side of the house and drove towards them down the paddock. His smaller and lighter ride was more manoeuvrable than Jude's heavy vehicle.

As Jed drew closer, she could see another man in the car – Liam. Excellent. The ex-soldier would be another strong resource to the search party's manpower.

Jude's car drew up next to them and Liam slid out lithely and crossed to Jude's door, where he'd lowered the window.

'Liam. You're Jude?'

'Right.' Jude jerked his head towards the back of the car. 'Audrey thinks they might have come down to look for a rabbit hole near that tree. Archie and my son, Leo, are crawling on quad bikes along the creek next door in the direction of the flow. I was about to go along this side of the creek upstream, but if you do that'—he jerked his head again towards the rear of the vehicle—'I'll run the women to Hannah's car so she can get Audrey to the surgery. Then I'll come back.'

Liam gave an assessing glance at Jude laying out what to do, but only nodded his head. 'Fair call. Give me your phone number,' he said, and pulled out his own phone to enter Jude's number into his own hard case. Then Liam texted his name quickly in a message and sent it through to Jude.

When Jude's phone pinged, Liam nodded and jogged back to the smaller vehicle and climbed in. The car began to follow the creek upstream.

Jude turned his car, leaving deep tyre marks in the wet ground, and headed back towards the house.

'No,' Audrey cried. 'I have to stay. To be here.'

'No. You have to keep your new baby safe and let others search.' Jude's voice was calm and emphatic. 'I've got Liam's number and Hannah's. Any news at all, I'll ring her straightaway.'

He pulled up next to Hannah's car. As he'd done before, he came around to the back, picked up Audrey, and put her in the rear seat of Hannah's car like she was a fragile parcel.

Hannah climbed in and turned to hear him say to Audrey, 'I promise. Any news at all. Plus, I'll phone every half an hour to let you know where we're searching.'

Audrey said in a whisper, 'What if I missed them in the house? What if they're hiding somewhere I didn't look?'

At that moment, Molly hurried down the front steps. 'Molly's here,' Hannah said quickly, before Audrey tried to get out again. 'Molly, can you stay here until they find the boys and then come with them to the surgery?'

'Of course,' Molly replied, leaning in to Audrey. 'You have that baby and we'll find the boys. You'll see them soon.'

Hannah winced. Again. Was she the only one who hated tempting fate with promises?

Jude nodded. 'Go. Now. Get Audrey up to the surgery.'

Yes, Jude. Thank you, Hannah thought, because Audrey sank back against the seat, beaten for now.

Hannah didn't wait for anything else. She wanted Audrey out of the car and into the surgery, too. But one thing continued to niggle at the back of her mind.

Why hadn't Nell or Gracie phoned?

Chapter Twenty-seven

Hannah

In the rear-view mirror, Hannah watched Audrey twist her neck awkwardly to see out the back window as they drove away from her house. 'Nooo,' she whispered in denial as the distance between them and the paddocks widened. 'What if they're out there somewhere and they can see I'm leaving them?'

Hannah suggested quietly, 'You've got good men looking. And Molly will make sure the boys aren't hiding in the house.'

Audrey sobbed once. 'God, if only it was that easy. If they'd just be somewhere in the house, hiding. They like hiding.' Her eyes met Hannah's in the mirror, then glanced up to the roof of the car. 'Please, God, just put them in the house,' Audrey whispered, but Hannah suspected strongly they weren't there.

'You can't help them while you're giving birth.'

Audrey's face contorted as if another contraction had grabbed and twisted. Oh yes. Her labour was powering. She grunted and Hannah guessed this time the first inkling of pressure had begun to build. 'No,' she grunted again. 'I won't be any help until I have this baby.'

Hannah's eyes flitted between the road ahead and Audrey in the mirror. She saw the young woman grit her teeth and breathe through the pain. Saw her eyes narrow as if she'd said out loud, *Be fast, then*.

Tears trickled down Audrey's face. 'Come on, Baby. The quicker you come, the quicker Mummy can get back to look for her boys.'

Her other babies. Hannah felt her own throat close up. She couldn't imagine the turmoil Audrey suffered. She shook her head in awe at the determination in Audrey's face. Those gorgeous baby boys with their big, blue eyes would be looking for their mummy. They had to find them. Jude had to find them.

Audrey's husband should be here, beside her. Or searching. Hannah knew the boys had been born on their due date, when everyone said twins came early. So the couple hadn't thought she'd have the baby so early or in the middle of a flood.

For Hannah, the horror image of that empty paddock and the raging creek made tears burn her eyes. It would be a hundred times worse for Audrey. And for the husband who couldn't be here.

Where were those boys? Surely not . . . She shied away from the thought of the river as Audrey gasped from the back, in the grip of another pain wave.

Their eyes met as Audrey moistened her lips and raised her voice over the noise of the rain. 'We might have to hurry if you don't want me to birth here.'

No. No, no, no. 'Got it.' Hannah's foot pressed harder on the accelerator.

'Feels like barbed wire dragging through,' Audrey ground out through gritted teeth and then she moaned. Hannah's car jumped forward in another lurch of speed. Audrey swayed.

'Hang on,' Hannah hoped her voice infiltrated Audrey's wall of pain.

When Hannah's phone rang, Audrey gasped, 'Is it Jed?'

Instead, it was Gracie's voice that came through. 'Have they found the boys?'

Audrey slumped back and Hannah thought she heard her retch with the disappointment.

'Not yet,' Hannah spoke quietly. 'Audrey's with me.'

A pause and she imagined Gracie biting back words.

'Sorry it took me so long to get back to you,' Gracie said. 'I didn't have my phone with me. I've been moving the house contents up higher because the water's surrounding us. I'm just leaving with Oliver now. How's Audrey?'

'Almost ready to push. Have you heard from Nell?'

'No. I'll try again on the way.'

'We're almost back to the surgery. See you there.' Hannah paused. 'Is it safe for you to drive through the water?'

'For the moment.'

'Okay. See you soon.'

Hannah's car slipped and slid up the driveway to the house. A detached part of her brain thought she might have to get an all-wheel drive or put more gravel on the driveway, because it looked like half of that had washed away.

The car jerked to a halt. 'Okay, Audrey, let's get you into the house and comfortable to have this baby.'

Although, Hannah mused wryly, she doubted there was anything comfortable about having a baby. Audrey's eyes were wide and wild. *Nope. Not comfortable.*

'I wish Jude was here to just pick you up and carry you,'

Hannah said as she opened the door. Wistfully, she could so imagine that.

'I'll get there.' Audrey heaved herself to the edge of the seat with one hand low on her stomach and the other on the door for purchase. 'I'll have this baby and then look for my boys. Baby first and then I'm going back.'

Hannah didn't say that wasn't going to happen, but she suspected Audrey saw it in her face. Hannah would have to watch that Audrey didn't slip away, before she could be sure her patient was stable after the birth. Who would have thought all this could happen in a quiet country town?

But first, she had to get Audrey inside. As Hannah opened the door, Audrey hoisted herself out and took off at almost a jog towards the surgery entrance, as if she needed to get inside fast, before the next contraction. Hannah could understand that. And was grateful.

'Bathroom?' Audrey searched the doorways ahead.

'Second on the right. You don't want to be on a bed?'

'God no. The shower's best now. There's no time for a bath.'

Bath. Hannah's stomach sank. She did not feel comfortable with the idea of waterbirth. But Audrey had said there wasn't time and Hannah breathed again. 'I'm glad about that,' she said. 'Gracie's not here and that's not my expertise. Let's get you in the shower and warm. I've caught babies with the mum standing up before.'

Gracie arrived at the same time as Hannah saw the first strands of the baby's hair on view. 'I've brought a birthing kit,' she said by way of greeting.

'Excellent. I have emergency equipment, towels and disposables,' Hannah said absently, her whole attention on the action in front of her. The baby was coming.

That overwhelming, unmistakable, unstoppable expulsive force took hold of Audrey, and the miracle of birth, which Hannah felt privileged to witness every single time, began.

Audrey's baby eased gently towards Hannah's waiting hands.

Chapter Twenty-eight

Jude

After dropping the women at Hannah's car, Jude drove slowly across the top paddock, checking the twins weren't near, or past, the house towards the road. He scanned along the top fence and down the sides. They weren't anywhere. The rain had stopped, but through his open window the creek in the background resonated as a dull roar. This wasn't looking good. He'd been involved in searching for a lost child before, not anyone he knew, but he still had nightmares about the little body he'd found in the old cattle trough.

Liam called to say they were coming back along the creek with Liam walking the edge looking for footprints. They hadn't found any, and Jude decided he'd go down to Mavis's fence and start back that way.

When his phone vibrated in his pocket, he pulled it out and glanced at the screen. Leo. 'What have you got?' There was too much snap in that, so he forced out a breath. 'Sorry.'

'Dad. Best news. We found them. They're safe.'

Jude felt relief expand and grow into a gust of pride and release of tension. 'Great job. Where are they now?'

'They were in the paddock headed for Mrs Maloney's barn and the new puppies. We're taking them to Mrs Maloney. Archie said she'll put them in the bath.'

'Right. Put the bikes away and I'll be there soon.' He hung up and dialled Liam's number.

'The boys have them,' he said without preamble, and relayed that Mavis would put them in the bath.

'You beauty. I'll ask Molly to take some clothes over to Mavis and give her a hand. Then we'll take them up to the doctor's surgery.'

'I'll ring Hannah.' Yes, he realised. He wanted to do that. Then he'd butt out. The locals had it now and they'd sort it out. He wasn't needed. His job was to pick up the supplies he'd ordered and take Leo home.

After hanging up, he dialled Hannah's number. It rang four times before she answered, and he wondered if she was busy delivering a baby. The woman was incredible in what she could do. *Remember that*, his inner voice said. *She's wayyyyyy out of your league.* But right now, he was glad she'd called him to help with the search. Very glad.

'Jude? Have you got them?' she asked, as if she half-expected him to say yes. Was that blind faith or the mistaken illusion that he would save the day? *Whoa there*, he thought. It was definitely the latter, which as far as he was concerned right now, was a dangerous hope for her to hold.

'Yes. They're safe.' He repeated what he'd told Liam, thinking gruffly that he'd learned more names of the townsfolk in the last three days than he had in the last year.

'Thank goodness.' Relief streamed from the phone and his chest warmed. 'Thank you. Thank you so much.' If he wasn't mistaken, Hannah's voice had tears in it. She cared about everyone. This didn't surprise him, because he'd witnessed firsthand her care of Leo. Of Mavis. She'd even asked him if he wanted a shower. Even him.

She cleared her throat. 'That's wonderful news.' Her voice became faint, as if she'd pulled the phone away from her face. 'They've got them.' He heard someone shout in the distance. Then Hannah's voice came back. 'And we've got a baby girl here.'

'It's all happening,' Jude said softly, soaking in the joy in her voice. Soaking in how wonderful she was. And trying desperately not to soak in how out of reach she was for him.

'It is. Thank you so much for your help this morning.' She paused and added softly, 'I saw your car. I've never been so pleased to see anyone in my life.'

His chest warmed even more. *Quit it*, that brutal voice sounded again. *Out of your league.* 'I'll talk to you later,' he said brusquely and hung up.

His phone pinged with a text before he could put it away. *Please drop in on your way home. I'll have something for you. Hannah.*

He knew what he wanted. And that wasn't likely to be something she'd want to give him.

Chapter Twenty-nine

Mavis

Mavis twisted her work-worn hands together as she heard the boys' bikes getting closer. She hurried to the tiny back porch, wishing she had the old farmhouse verandah so she could pace while she waited. But the new place did have modern extras like air conditioning, so the house would be warm for them when they came in.

They hadn't been away long, and she tried to stifle the simultaneous hope that they had good news, and the dread that the news could be horrible. Old people should die, she felt – that was normal, the circle of life – but not young ones. Especially not babies.

One of Mavis's joys was watching the kids play down at the old playground between the church and the racetrack after service on Sundays. Her husband had been one of the men who'd built the first playground many years ago. It was old and worn now, but she still found joy in the watching. She'd seen Audrey's young twins get up to mischief there on more than one occasion. It didn't bear thinking they might never do so again.

Two moving bikes popped into view down the paddock. There they were. She could see the boys, and what was that at the front of the bikes? Two spots of colour. They were going slow, but Mavis's hand crept up to her throat and she huffed out a huge sigh. She almost couldn't believe what she was seeing. The green and yellow specks were lads in front.

Her boys were coming back with the little lost twins.

As they drew closer, she could see that all four of them were covered in mud and completely drenched. She could also discern the wide grins on every face. Instead of crying at being lost, the tiny ones were delighted by the ride on the quad bikes.

Typical boys, she thought, swallowing the happy tears in her throat and wiping her eyes. This wasn't something she would have given Archie permission to do, doubling preschoolers, but it would have been stupid to walk the babies back instead of riding.

Her shoulders relaxed and her brain started thinking again. There'd be another couple of minutes before they got here, so she slipped inside to put the plug in the small fibreglass bath – she missed her old clawfoot – and turned on the warm water.

It was funny how it was her turn to run a bath for someone, when two days ago the doc had run one for her. Times were certainly interesting, but if they kept having these good outcomes, she was okay with that.

She heard the bikes' motors die outside, and she hurried to the back door with an armful of towels.

'Come in, all of you.' The grins had faded from the wee ones' faces. They looked nervous now, but Archie and Leo looked like happy cattle dogs at a barbecue. If they had tails, they'd be wagging.

'Good job, you fellas,' she said gruffly, as she looked at Archie. 'I'm proud of you.' Then she glanced at the other boy. 'And you, too, Leo. Good job. I'll get these babies into the bath. You boys can take turns in the shower.'

Archie looked horrified because there was only one small bathroom, and Mavis waved away his pulled face. 'You can leave your undies on, not that I'm gonna look.'

Leo snickered at his new mate's embarrassment. 'Reckon I could do with warming up, thanks, Mrs Maloney.'

Ten minutes later, the teens were dry and dressed and the little ones were still splashing in the bath. Mavis heard a car pull up and she slipped away from the door to let Molly in with the twins' clothes.

Molly was another with sunshine smiles on her face. She whispered through the sunbeams, 'Audrey had a baby girl at the doctor's surgery.'

'Both well?' Molly nodded, grinning. *What lovely news*, Mavis thought. 'The doc's proving handy.'

'Gracie was there, too. We can't find Nell, but Liam's going back to her place to see where she is. It's odd that she hasn't answered any of the messages.'

Mavis felt the warmth from the good news dim. Nell was a sensible girl, but times were wild. She sent up a prayer. *Keep her safe, Lord*. To Molly she said, 'Let me know when she turns up.'

Chapter Thirty

Hannah

Hannah heard Jude's big vehicle rumble up the driveway and a small spurt of uneasy energy lifted her chin. It had been a busy morning, and it was going to get busier with people moving into her house like a stream towards Noah's ark.

Jude was here and she wasn't sure why she'd invited him, except she wanted to see him, to thank him, because he'd come when she had asked him to. She wanted to thank him face to face before he disappeared into the hills once more.

She'd settled Audrey into one of the front rooms and notified Armidale hospital that their expectant mum wouldn't be coming. For Audrey to leave Featherwood in this weather, a chopper flight retrieval would be required, and the emergency services had enough on their plate. Audrey and her baby had both been checked by a midwife and a doctor and pronounced healthy.

Which meant Hannah had a mother and her baby and two mischievous twins moved into her house until the water went down and everybody could safely return home.

Molly, who thought she could still come and go to her own

house because her farm was on the high side of the road just out of town, had said she'd stay for an hour or two to keep an eye on the twins. For the moment, and understandably, their mother didn't want them out of her sight.

Gracie and little Oliver were staying too. When Gracie had tried to go home, she'd found the water almost up to the floorboards of her house, and she, Hannah and Jed all agreed that she and Oliver should stay put until the water receded.

Jed would come back to sleep in Hannah's house, but he was busy in the meantime rearranging house furniture and the stock in the roof space of his rural store, as well as helping others.

By the time Jude stepped out of his vehicle, Hannah could admit to feeling stretched emotionally from all the people and the drama. Yet here she was, suddenly buzzing, smiling shyly at the man before her and wanting to hug him for his rapid and efficient help when she had been at her neediest.

'How's the mother and baby?' he asked by way of greeting, and she suspected he wasn't staying long because Leo raised his hand in a wave from the cabin of the vehicle but didn't open his door.

'They're both well. I've a house full. Now Gracie is staying here, as well.'

'I don't know Gracie.' Jude glanced towards the house.

'My friend. Would you like to come in and meet her? Both of you, I mean.'

'No. I need to get home.' His response was short, clipped, letting her know that she was holding him up. She nodded. 'Well, you met Gracie's husband, Jed. He was with Liam at Audrey's place looking for the twins. They own the produce store.'

'Ah.' Jude nodded. 'Got it.'

'She's the friend I came down to visit from Roma and I ended up moving here because of her.' She was gabbling. *Ease off the accelerator*, she told her wayward mouth. *Just, slow down. Maybe even stop rabbiting on.*

His stern face lightened, and he said quietly, 'Then I like her already.'

Hannah blushed. An honest-to-goodness teenage flush. She felt the warmth creeping up her face, the heat in her chest and belly, just from the compliment that wasn't really about her. Or was it? Even though her move here was more because of the idiot she'd left in Roma, but she wasn't saying that. No way.

Instead, she said, 'You're probably sensible for not coming in. We have the twins, a newborn and a one-year-old, and five adults counting Molly, who's running the house like the champion she is.'

He stepped back and held up his hands in mock surrender. 'You have enough here without me arriving, then.'

She could tell by his tone that he'd be gone before she could blink, which was fine, of course. Except she didn't want him to. 'Molly made a batch of scones. It would please everyone if you'd take some, especially Audrey, who's so thankful that you and the boys helped in the search.'

He frowned, looking at her with hooded eyes and a stern but still, *darn it*, too-sensual mouth, that she should not be thinking about. He interrupted her thoughts. 'Is that what you had for me?'

That wasn't all, if she was honest. She had a sudden, overwhelming urge to hug him. To put her head on his chest and say thank you with all her heart. Because, in one of the few times of her life, apart from her friendship with Gracie, someone had come immediately with no reservations to help her. She valued that more than he could possibly know. But how did you tell someone that?

Just woman-up and say it, her brain urged. 'The scones are for you, yes, but mostly I wanted to say thank you. In person.' She shrugged, a little embarrassed now, feeling foolish and stupid. But oh, how she meant it. 'So . . .' She smiled shyly. 'Thank you.'

Then, before she could doublethink anything else, she stepped forward and kissed his cheek, and then put her arms around his broad back to hug him quickly.

Just as quickly, she took a jerky step back. 'Because you were there for me. When I needed you . . . when I needed help.' Her throat scratched and jammed. So many people hadn't been there for her, and the words thickened more than she would have liked as they left her mouth. Tears stung but didn't fall. They just made everything blurry. 'It means a lot.'

The harsh lines around his eyes softened, his rigid shoulders dropping a little and his beautiful mouth quirking up. Her muscles loosened in response, as fierce attraction curled in her belly. *Oh my.*

To her surprise, he leaned in, slipped one firm arm around her shoulders and pulled her back in against his chest. He smelled like pine and ginger and damp male. His other arm circled her, too, until her face was pressed into the hard muscles over his buttoned shirt. He hugged her gently but comprehensively. 'You're very welcome, delightful Dr Rogan. You just call anytime you need me.'

He released her, took the bag of scones from her left hand and crossed the distance between her and the truck in a few long strides. The vehicle started and then he was gone.

Strangely, she didn't feel so stupid, now. She felt a little bit brave and a little bit proud that she'd pushed through the embarrassment and hugged him. Because she knew that he understood she meant it.

Chapter Thirty-one

Jude

'So how come you hugged the doc?'

Leo's curious voice greeted Jude as he shut the door and started the engine. His brain still felt foggy from the scent and softness of her. The warmth of holding her against him. Her lips on his cheek.

'She hugged me first.' *Great job, mouth*, he thought dourly.

His son gave him a long look that someone his age shouldn't know how to give. 'I haven't seen you hug anyone since Mum.'

And douse went the guilt, like standing under one of those rain gutters drenching with cold water. 'She needed a hug,' he said. 'It's been a big morning for her. She was there when the twins went missing, and then the mother had a baby in her surgery. All during a flood.'

'It just seems strange she wanted it from you. You don't know her that well.'

'Women are strange,' he quipped, then quickly changed the subject. 'How'd you go with Archie and his grandmother?'

Leo straightened and his mouth broke out into a grin. Jude hadn't seen that for a while. 'Awesome. Mavis is his great-grandmother, but he calls her Gran 'cause it's easier. His mum lives in Sydney. He said she does drugs.'

Jude opened his mouth and shut it. Which was lucky, because Leo went on. 'His gran's house on the farm burned down last year. Archie had to drive the tractor into town with the fire behind them. He said that was pretty wild.'

He thought of Leo driving away from an oncoming fire front on a tractor by himself and shuddered. 'Sounds . . . wild.'

'Archie said not as wild as when he lived with his mum in Sydney.'

Hell, thought Jude. 'Maybe that's why Archie and his gran are pretty resilient, then.' Jude guessed he'd be hearing a lot of 'Archie said' in the near future, which wasn't a bad thing, he decided.

Leo's brows furrowed.

Jude glanced his way. 'Problem?'

'What's *resilient*?'

'Resilience is when you pick yourself up when you get knocked down. Some people can't.'

'Can't what?'

Recover, Jude thought. Like he'd had trouble doing from the loss of Iris. 'Can't lift their chin. Live their life. Get on with it.'

'Like we had to after Mum?' asked Leo.

Hell again, thought Jude. 'Maybe. We're beginning to, though, right?' he said. Maybe he'd go back one day soon and give Dr Rogan a kiss. Just to show he was getting on with life. Or just because he wanted to. 'Like the guys on Luna Downs. They're learning about resilience instead of hiding inside a bottle.'

'You reckon Tesla is getting on with it?' Leo cocked an eyebrow at him, looking older than his years.

Tesla was a problem, Jude admitted, and he was trying hard not to blame the man's high maintenance for Jude missing Leo's symptoms. But the bloke was struggling with abstinence, and the other men were getting sick of his moaning.

They'd been so fortunate that Ben, the first test case they'd taken on, had turned out to be so steady. He'd been a rock for the others as each went through withdrawal and found their place in the hierarchy of the station. It was a simple order. Jude made all the decisions, and Ben backed him and made sure everyone ate and didn't drink. But even Ben had been side-tracked by Tesla's fits and moaning. Ben had felt almost as bad as Jude had, when Leo got sick without them noticing.

Jude pressed the remote on the gate and drove up the now rutted drive. The run-off water had washed away both sides of the gravel and it was rough and wet, but still passable. Both new dams were overflowing and he'd bet the tanks at the house were too. There were new shoots of grass coming through in the paddocks and the cattle were looking sleek.

It was good that they'd all come in out of the rain, but it meant the men were mostly inside and going stir-crazy. He couldn't blame them, though. Which brought him back to Tesla.

They pulled up at the long, extended house and maybe what they needed was a verandah that ran the length. Somewhere to get away, outside, if he spread it all the way along the exterior of everyone's rooms. They had enough wood from the sawmill they'd started last year, and a fair bit of it was ready to be used.

But it didn't feel right to be holing up safely at the house. People were going under in town, and some would be stranded. He had strong men who could help. But would the town want them?

Chapter Thirty-two

Nell

Nell splashed through the water to the front steps in her sodden gumboots, leading the now docile calf. Grin leaped up beside her and wagged his tail, then sat and waited at the top. As she climbed past, she patted him. 'Good boy,' she said on autopilot, because her brain was racing with scenarios, and none of them were good.

There was a dog lead on the verandah tied to a post. She usually used it when she was going down the paddock and didn't want Grin to follow. When she snapped the clip onto the belt around the calf's neck, it half-heartedly pulled away and then relinquished. She gave the poor wet thing another pat, before she plopped down on the chair to take off her boots. Water spilled everywhere and she also removed her sodden socks.

She felt the weight of the task that now needed sorting and the weight of responsibility because she had to do this alone. It was too daunting, and she wished Liam was here. He'd been coming later to take her into town, but there was a definite chance he wouldn't get through.

In fact, now that her brain had started to work again, she should phone Liam because he'd be with Jed. Then Jed would keep Gracie safe if the wave came. She jumped up and found her phone in the kitchen, where she'd left it. Her fingers shook as she tapped Liam's name on the screen.

'Nell?'

'Liam.' Even she could hear the relief in her voice when he answered.

'Are you okay?' He must have heard it too.

Suddenly, she didn't have enough air to speak and forced herself to take a breath. 'There's a flood coming. A big wash down the river, if it hasn't hit you yet. Pouring off the waterfall like Niagara. It's flooded the paddocks and halfway up the posts on the cattle yards. The house is surrounded.'

'You okay?' he repeated, his voice calm – battle calm, the tone she heard when things were dire.

Her voice broke. 'Moo washed away. I'm hoping she'll just climb out somewhere.'

'Right. I'll keep an eye out for her. What about Grin?'

'He's fine, he's with me. I've got Moo's new calf on the verandah. I won't be driving anywhere.'

'Is the water still rising?'

She looked down at the lake in front of her house. It was only one step from the verandah. She swallowed, suddenly very, very scared. 'Yes. I think it will go into the house soon.' Her house. Her beautiful new house. New rugs. New curtains. She'd lose everything again. *Again.* How could she survive that?

Liam's voice remained calm with a serve of implacable. 'Pack a bag. Now. I'll come get you.'

And that was when she knew it was too late. 'I don't think you can. The driveway's flooded. There has to be half a metre of water over it.'

'I'm not leaving you there.'

He didn't understand. He couldn't get to her. No one could. Her blood ran as cold as her frozen, wet feet.

'I'll work something out,' Liam went on. 'See you soon.' And such was the conviction in his voice she had to believe, too.

'Okay, not sure how. But yes.'

'Pack a bag,' he said again, and hung up.

Where did she begin? She looked back at the water, which had risen another couple of centimetres. She didn't have time to think about what to save. It was like the fires all over again.

You have to save the people, she reminded herself. *Everything else can be replaced.*

So she went to the bedroom. Saw the antique writing desk Liam had bought her and lovingly restored. The carved chair that matched. She allowed herself one sob and then pulled it together. They were just *things*.

Picking up her new duffel, she threw in the phone charger and computer. Bathroom bag. Purse. Underwear. A set of clothes. She paused momentarily at the irony. These were the same clothes she'd saved before, because she'd been wearing them on the day of the fires, and here she was again.

There was no use in taking much. They'd have to walk with the bags over their heads. Hopefully, they wouldn't have to swim with them. And where would they go? Hannah's, of course. Because the surgery would be high and dry. Or the church. Any of the buildings up the hill on the right side of the street in Featherwood.

She suspected Gracie's house would be inundated with water, too. *Poor Gracie.* And the store. *Poor Jed.* Both places would be damaged. At least Gracie had Jed. Nell couldn't worry about anyone else until she could help them.

On the verandah, the water lapped against the top floorboards. She dumped her belongings on the chair and the calf shuffled and mewled with distress and cold.

'I know, baby. Everything is scary. Maybe Liam will find your mummy.' Her eyes filled with tears and she dashed them away. There was no time for crying. 'Please be safe, Moo,' she whispered.

But for now, she could stack things up higher while she waited for Liam. Her writing desk on the bed. Her lovely chair, too. She could pull up the rugs and knot the curtains higher. It was probably all useless to do, but she might as well while she waited.

When Liam arrived, he came in Jed's big, blue truck. The one with the white sign writing of *Farmer's Friend* emblazoned on the door and the enormous wheels that kept it high above ground. Grinding through the water, the truck forced a brown bow wave to peel from the high sides in a frothy wash. He drove straight to the verandah over the top of the submerged garden beds, and parked parallel. Opening the driver's door right above the verandah, he climbed down to splash across towards her. There was ten centimetres of water running through the middle of the house.

She'd turned off the power at the fuse box and managed to put all their small electrical items on top of the wardrobe. Also, she had collected a plastic bag of sheets and blankets to take to Hannah's. They'd just get ruined here, and maybe Hannah would need them for unexpected visitors. Hannah might receive many guests if the rain didn't stop.

'Let's move,' said Liam. 'It's touch and go if we'll get back to town.'

'Throw in the blankets, pillows and sheets, as well.' He nodded and gathered the enormous armful and leaned over to push it behind the driver's seat in the truck cab. She handed across her own bag and three soft, cold bags of food she'd emptied from the fridge and stripped from the cupboards.

Liam pulled back. 'Climb in.'

She squeezed past the steering wheel as Liam disappeared again. When she turned, he was clipping Grin's collar to a chain already fastened to the back of the truck, and then he scooped up the calf and secured her, too.

He urged her to buckle up. 'Do we have time for any furniture on the back?'

'No. Sorry.'

'Okay.'

Then they were driving through water. As the house increased in distance behind them, she didn't want to look back across the paddock. To the new house she'd just started to love. Like she'd loved the old one. *They were just possessions*, she repeated silently.

When they reached the driveway, the cab sat high above the water until they reached the end of her property. The road below her gate ran awash with muddy water and they splashed down into it. If it wasn't for the tops of the posts, they wouldn't know where the road was.

'Most of the way it's not too bad,' Liam said.

'What happens when we reach the area where Mavis was washed off?'

'We don't stop. And we hang on.'

'So we're high enough?' It was half-question, half-hopeful expectation because he would say yes, of course, to reassure her.

'Should be. No guarantees. It was on the way out.'

Did that count as reassurance, she wondered. 'Thanks, Liam.'

He looked genuinely perplexed. 'For what?'

'Coming to save me. The truck. Being my hero.'

He turned his head and smiled at her, his strong features softening in something she rarely saw. His heart. There in his eyes. Her own heart melted. 'That's my job. My aim in life. You are my love.'

She blinked. They didn't speak of love. They spoke of respect and caring, if they spoke at all. And she was as much to blame as he was for the lack of words. But he was laying it out there. Verbally spouting romantic. It was as unexpected as it was wonderful.

Nell put her head down, but she was smiling. She said softly, barely audible over the splashing of water outside and the rumble of the big engine, 'You are my hero and my love. And I'm glad you came to save me.'

They smiled at each other, back to normal.

Silence fell between them. The water rose. They had to survive the journey back to town first.

Chapter Thirty-three

Molly

Molly watched, rapt, as Audrey's gaze fixed on the tiny face at her breast. The rose-petal skin that glowed the palest pink with dark-blue eyes stared back, then blinked slowly as the baby grew sleepy. Molly marvelled again at the wonder of birth and babies.

She'd missed being here, but she'd been where she needed to be. Thank God for the search parties that had found the twins. Thank God for those young boys on quad bikes. Thank God for all the people who came to help when Audrey and the boys had needed them.

Molly gazed down at the sleeping boys and her heart ached for something she would never have. But she felt filled with gratitude that these babies were safe. The twins were curled together like edgy puppies in the corner of the room on a small pile of blankets Molly had folded as a makeshift mattress for them, holding hands in their sleep.

She'd read them a story about a wombat, and they'd liked that. So had she. Molly often read to them when she babysat, and there was normality for them in that, she figured. There was normality in that for Molly, too, because the world looked a little crazy at the moment, and she felt strangely isolated among the dramas of others.

She noticed Audrey's eyes grow heavy until she shifted herself in the bed as if to get up. Shuffling her way to the edge of the mattress, she leaned to tuck Adella into her makeshift crib. Adella Rose. *A beautiful name*, Molly thought.

'I'll do that,' Molly whispered, lifting the precious bundle from her mother's arms and tucking her gently into the drawer bed she'd made. She smiled at a memory. 'My mother made one just like this for Gracie's baby last year.' Molly stroked her finger gently across Adella's cheek.

Audrey's eyes were shadowed by the blue of exhaustion. 'Rest,' Molly whispered. She was here and could help. Other people were out there in the rain and the rising water doing it tough. But in this house, they were safe and dry. The sound of the rain drifted through the only just-cracked-open window.

Molly pulled the blinds on the weather outside, all safe in here, and she backed out the door and shut it quietly.

Chapter Thirty-four

Hannah

Molly had slipped away with Gracie as soon as Oliver had gone to sleep. Gracie said he'd sleep for hours, and Hannah had instructions to ring when he woke if she wasn't back in time. She and Molly would try to salvage belongings from Gracie's house.

Hannah nodded but winced at the dangers, because going back out into the heavy rain felt like a disaster waiting to happen. So here she was. Custodian of a new mother and a baby, plus reunited twins, in one room. And a one-year-old who barely knew Hannah's face in the other. At least she didn't have ill patients.

Outside, the rain deluged as if God had pointed a fire hose at the rectory. The solid wall of water cascaded off the roof and the hill behind her in thick brown snakes, carrying mud and everything else to meld with the torrent that used to be a road below.

In the cacophony, she heard the recognisable rumble of Jude's vehicle. Was that him? Again? She had no idea why he would come back, but all she could think was *how wonderful*. No other adults were here, except for Audrey, and for some reason that made her cheeks grow warm.

Stop it, she told herself. Being attracted to Jude Waugh was not a sensible action. He was as unknown a factor as the guy who broke her heart the last time.

That thought was cut off when she heard the sound of a second vehicle, a deeper engine and a grinding roar on her driveway, and now she was totally confused. She peered out the window. Who was this?

Jude's car came into view. He had an inverted, flat-bottomed tin boat up on the roof and three other people sat in the vehicle, their faces unrecognisable through the rain. He pulled over where he always did – across the yard from the rear of the house – and she could barely see him through the sheets of water, even when she opened the back door.

A big, blue rumbling truck – one of Jed's, she realised – drove past him and parked the passenger's side close to the edge of her house, which seemed more sensible with the downpour. Brakes squealed and the engine quietened down to a rumble as it paused. Inside the cab she could make out Nell and probably Liam, and at the back a calf bleated miserably beside Grin, who was also tied to the cab. Grin, teeth exposed, wagged a bedraggled tail when he saw Hannah.

Hannah opened one of the big, black umbrellas that had come with the rectory, and Nell wound down her window. 'Can you take another lodger?'

Hannah waved her hand. 'Of course. Anytime. Come in out of the rain.'

'What about my dog and my calf?' There was a crack in Nell's usually calm voice. 'Maybe the carport?'

'Sure.' Hannah found she was smirking to herself because she had originally wondered why the rectory had all this parking. Right now, it looked like she needed a place for tents, as well. 'Everyone is welcome at the rectory, especially you and yours. Do you want the brolly?'

'I've got bags to bring inside. We'll use the umbrella for those. I can't get any wetter.'

Nell jumped down with a splash and reached across for the umbrella. Then Liam passed her a big plastic bag, which she juggled with the brolly across the short space between the truck and back verandah. She transferred the bundle into Hannah's arms.

'Did you pick up Jude on the way?' Hannah asked, nodding towards Jude's car. 'He's just sitting there with the motor running . . .'

'He's talking to Liam on the phone. More people are flooded in their homes. They're discussing rescue logistics.'

'More people?' Which people? 'Who's already been rescued?'

'Liam rescued me.' Nell chewed her lip. 'The flood's gone through my house.' She brushed water off her face. 'Anyway, Jude and his friends rescued our truck with his winch – a deep hole, long story. Luckily, Liam had Jude's number, or we mightn't have made it.' There was that wobble in Nell's voice again, but she turned away and reached up for more bags from Liam.

Hannah thought, *Jude's getting around, being handy. He even has friends with him.* She pushed the thought away and replaced it with, *Nell needs a hug.* Spinning around, she stepped inside with the bundle, put it down and went back for the bags Nell was waiting to give her.

Hannah said, 'I've got Audrey and her children asleep in one room, and Oliver asleep in the other. Take the fourth bedroom, it's the only one with the door open.'

Liam handed the last duffel to Nell, who passed it on to Hannah. Then he swung out of the truck door above the ground and around, ignoring the torrential rain, until he was standing on the back of the truck. He untied Grin, who jumped off the back with a smaller splash than Nell and trotted over to the porch and Hannah, to sit out of the rain.

Liam then untied the calf and scooped her up and handed her down to Nell, whose knees buckled a bit with the weight until she put her down. There was a dog lead and western belt around the bedraggled creature's neck as she found her feet. *Lucky Jed has half the rural store in her shed*, Hannah thought. There was bound to be something to feed a calf on in there.

As Liam climbed into the truck again, Nell stepped back and shut the door and waved him off. The truck splashed noisily away.

'I'll take the calf and Grin to the carport,' Nell said as she urged the woebegone little Brahman towards the side of the house. *There is a lot happening, yet not much discussion between those two*, Hannah thought with amusement, but it wasn't her business. More importantly, Nell would need a hot shower very soon.

Jude's car turned in a circle and drove to the spot where the truck had just been. He wound down his window and she saw the three men inside more closely. All about thirty years old; she didn't recognise any of them. 'Looks like Gracie and Molly can't get out. Liam's going to pick up another tinny in the truck. When we put the boat in, we'll bring the women here?'

'Of course. I have her son, anyway. Can we do anything else to help?' Hannah asked.

'You're doing it. Looks like your house is the ark and everyone's coming in two by two.'

They did think alike. She smiled at him. 'That's what happens when you buy a rectory on a hill.'

'You might need more bedrooms.'

'I can always make up the waiting room and consulting room into places to sleep.'

'Maybe keep your emergency room.' Their eyes met and held, filled with their shared history with Leo and the direness of medical crises between them.

'I will.'

He said, 'I'll be back soon. Hopefully.' Then he too splattered away through the rain.

Hannah turned and went back into the kitchen, looking at the bags and duffel and the bundle in plastic. She carried the duffel through to the bathroom. Nell's skin had been pebbled with cold. She put out a towel and hair wrap and dryer on the bench for Nell, and then went back into the kitchen to put on the kettle and make tea. She needed to sort out the calf, too. And maybe start a huge pot of soup. That was more Molly's department, but she could use tins.

Twenty minutes later Nell stood in the kitchen, showered, hair blow-dried, sipping hot tea after she'd been hugged. She was saying, 'The water just kept rising. It happened so fast. Within an hour of looking out the window, it had come up the steps of the house and just flooded through. Must be heavy falls up the valley for that volume of water to come down the creek. A flash flood. If the rain doesn't stop, half of our town will go.'

Our town? Did she feel that way? *Yes*, Hannah realised. This was her town, too. But she had never expected to hear those words. Although everyone talked about the chance of flooding, it was different to hear of the water just washing through Nell's lovely house.

'Have you heard from Gracie or Molly?' She knew what Jude had said, but she needed more. Hannah hadn't liked to call and be a nuisance just to satisfy her own concerns.

'No. Liam tried to ring Molly back, but it dropped out.'

'Let's hope Oliver stays asleep, then, he's my godson but at least he knows you.'

Nell waved that away. 'He'll be fine. Just feed him. He's like his dad, loves his food. Though I thought they'd have returned by now.'

So had Hannah. She fought back a sudden swamp of cold dread for Gracie. And for Molly. And for Jude. Where were they?

Chapter Thirty-five

Jude

Bloody hell, thought Jude, as he and the fellas from Luna Downs surveyed the body of water between them and the house he was aiming for. Two women waved from the verandah of the dwelling in the flooded paddock. Out front was a submerged car with water to the doorhandle. Nobody would be driving that anywhere. 'Let's get this boat off the roof.'

Jude began untying rope and once it was free, at Jude's word, his men all took a corner, lifted and flipped the boat into the water.

'Someone grab that rope and pull it towards me, backwards.' Jude pointed as he opened the swinging rear door of the vehicle and lifted out the outboard engine. As the flat side of the boat faced him, he bolted the outboard to the panel and threw in the oars in case needed.

Water poured off the road and down through the driveway of the rural store in a raceway. It was at least waist height and getting higher as it met the creek water in the paddock behind. He could see someone moving around in there and suspected it was the Jed he'd seen briefly this morning, the Jed that everyone seemed to talk about.

'Pop and Ben, head down and see if that bloke needs help and check with him that he's turned off the power.'

The two men nodded.

'Tesla and I will grab the two women and run them up to the doc's. Tell the bloke in the shed that, too, and ask who we should take the boat to next. Otherwise, we'll just work along the street.'

'Right,' said Ben, his red beard beaded with rain. 'On it.' The men waded off.

Jude climbed in and the boat seemed to tip precariously before it righted itself, but he didn't worry. He'd been mucking about in boats since he was a kid. 'Hold it until I get the motor going, Tesla, then wind in the rope.'

Jude pulled the cord of the engine, again and again, until finally it started with a puff of blue smoke and a few coughs, then settled into a whining hum. Tesla slid in over the side and wound the rope, and they headed across the water, small waves bumping like drum beats against the hull as they steered through the gate and up the submerged drive.

They pulled up to the verandah and the women leaned over. The redhead said, 'I'm Gracie. Thank you, Jude.'

He lifted two fingers in acknowledgement as they bumped against the rapidly submerging pylons. She knew his name even though she'd never met him. He guessed that wasn't odd given she was Hannah's best friend . . . or maybe it was just small towns where everyone knew everyone else's business.

He'd never wanted to be a part of this town, but it looked like fate had decided otherwise. He wasn't going anywhere. And frankly, maybe he'd needed a kick in this direction. 'Let's get you up to the rectory. To Hannah.'

The one Jude recognised as Molly from this morning gestured to a pile at their feet and made a circle with her hand. 'We have bags.'

Of course they did, and he had the feeling that was all they'd save from this place. 'Sure, the most important ones first until it gets dangerous and then you stop.'

Thankfully, the verandah still rose a little above the water. The whole village probably needed to get supplies from the only shop before all the power went off. Which led to a thought. One he should have had earlier.

'Have you turned off the power? If the level reaches the power points, then electricity can run through water.'

The women looked at each other. 'I'll go do that,' Gracie said.

She glanced back when Jude said, 'Flip each breaker off first, then turn off the main breaker.'

Gracie waved a hand in acknowledgement and spun away. Molly began handing down shopping bags with clothes and food until the boat looked like a rubbish barge on Sydney Harbour.

'Stop,' Jude said. 'Leave room for you and Gracie.'

Gracie had returned. 'Can you come back and get more later?'

'Put them up high on the verandah. When I know all the people are safe, I'll try to pick them up. If they're still here.' He tried not to see the flash of pain in her eyes.

By the time Jude had left the women with Hannah, the fellas were waiting for him at the bottom of the hill just out of the water on Hannah's drive. The driver from this morning, Jed, stood next to them.

'Thanks for taking my wife and Molly up the hill.'

'No problem. You're welcome. You finished in your store?'

'I've done what I can. We'll lose a lot. Mostly, I tried to save the supplies people will need when this is over.'

'Molly suggested we take extra folk to the church. Next door. You agree with that?'

Jed rubbed the back of his head. 'It's high and dry. And has power for the moment and a thrift store of clothes at the back for those who bring nothing. Plus, there's a water tank on the side of the building, so they've got water and toilets. Can't ask for more. I'm the local SES and it's evacuation orders for the low side of the street. They'll have to go to the church until we can find other accommodation.'

'You'll need someone sensible staying there in charge.' Jude had seen this scenario in Brisbane during the big flood. 'You won't want to waste the water or have problems. I don't know how long it'll take for more emergency services to come in. Other places are flooding too. The road is washed away to the west and the east has the landslide.'

Jed nodded. 'It'll take days, I reckon. As for someone being in charge at the church, Liam would be the best bet. He doesn't take crap and knows how to organise. We can do alternate days when he needs a break.'

The men piled in, and they turned right at the bottom of Hannah's driveway, towards all the houses on the same side as Jed's half-submerged store. Most had water up to their steps at the front porch, and low houses had water in through the front door. The deserted houses were silent and still, and the ones with families had scrambling people piling possessions high on tables on the front verandahs.

It wasn't too deep to drive out yet, but there was nowhere to go except up to the church. The level had risen even in the short time since they'd started down the street.

Jude's boat zipped over to each habited house and suggested the church. 'Evacuation order. If you get your car out now you should be able to park it in the churchyard. At the back as high as you can. Take bedding and food as the most important, but move now. It will be too late in half an hour.'

People blinked at him in shock. And gradually, their eyes cleared. Strange how things like unexpected emergencies could sometimes freeze your brain until you just ran around like a chook in a cage looking for something to peck. Or pack. The clarity of an evacuation order cleared some of that. 'Load the back of your car with essentials, people in the front. Best get going.'

When they got to single occupancies, one of Jude's men got out and helped the owners pack their cars. Jude would pick up his men from the church as needed, later. He and Jed pulled up at a derelict shanty set back from the road and surrounded by brown water. A grizzled old-timer glared out at them when Jude gave the order to move.

'Who are you, telling me what to do?' The old guy squinted at Jude.

'He's the bloke with the boat, helping you,' Jed said. 'The one who saved my wife.'

'Harrumph,' the old bloke said but appeared mollified. 'Probably won't get any higher, now's as high as it's ever been.'

Jed grimaced at the wasted time. 'My house is going under and they said it never has before. You'd be better to move instead of griping, Ned, or all the good places to sleep in the church will be gone.'

He glanced at the rusty Holden at the side of the shack. 'And your car won't start again if it doesn't move now.'

They turned the boat away and steered to the next house. Jude said quietly, 'What about Mavis? Her place is on the same side of the road as Audrey's. And yours. Think she's up high enough?'

'Liam's calling in on his way back with his tinny. They've got a hill and a caravan they're filling up with supplies. They'll be right on the hill. Archie will take care of his gran.'

Leo's friend Archie. 'He seems like a great kid. My son likes him a lot.'

'He's an absolute winner,' said Jed. 'He and Mavis are a team. You shoulda seen them in the fires.'

And there it was again. A mention of a past trauma that he'd heard about so often. It didn't go away, the PTSD of a natural disaster. Any disaster, really, but a natural one affected whole families, whole towns, whole countries. He was a part of it.

They steered over a fence towards a house set well back from the road.

Right now, they were living another one and no doubt it would become folklore in its own time.

Chapter Thirty-six

Hannah

Gracie and Molly had deposited the goods they'd saved and headed to the bathroom to take turns to shower. Now re-dressed, and sipping steaming cocoa, they gathered in the kitchen with everyone else. Oliver clung to his mother's leg, and Audrey had been cushioned in the corner of the kitchen on an armchair with her baby in her arms and a pink-spotted travel mug in her other hand.

The twins frowned over a jigsaw with the occasional cheating help from Molly as she pushed a relevant piece towards one of them. Every few minutes, Audrey's eyes would settle on her small sons and stay. Then she'd blink back tears and shake her head. Hannah couldn't imagine the emotional exhaustion Audrey suffered. Lost boys. A birth. A flood.

In fact, there were so many affected people in this room. Nell with her house inundated. The stress of almost being washed away in a truck with Liam. Reliving the loss of her possessions.

Gracie's house, the home she'd created with such love, currently being washed through with debris and moving water, with her and Jed's livelihood at the shop also washed through. Everything

181

left behind would be ruined. And somewhere out there, Gracie's husband could still be in danger.

Molly's brother and Nell's man hadn't come back, though Molly said he'd be fine, and their house, the one Hannah knew she shared with Liam though he mostly lived at Nell's, would be fine, too. But there was distress in her eyes that she tried to hide.

Yet Hannah was normal. Her house was safe. Sure, it was crowded with people, but that was no hardship. Although, even with what the others had brought, she didn't know how long she could feed them all. She shook her head. They would make it work. They'd pool their resources.

Then she thought about something other than food. Loo paper. Like in the pandemic. She had enough for one but not for ten. And other basics, like milk for the children. A task for her.

'I might see what's left at the shop before they close. We need milk, loo paper and candles,' Hannah said into the pensive silence. 'I want to do something useful before it's too late to get anything.'

'You are doing something,' Gracie said. 'You're housing all of us.'

Nell looked across at her, understanding in her eyes. 'Need to get out?'

Nell didn't miss much. She'd come to know Hannah quite well as they worked together, Hannah thought, and would know that sitting around was not her jam; she needed to be doing.

'One of us should go for extra supplies, before the shop is shut or empty.'

'Want me to go?' Nell asked, but her voice hinted that she wasn't keen.

'If you don't mind, I'd prefer to. I'll just grab some staples. It's not far.' Hannah tried to smile. 'Feels like I haven't been out for days.'

'Suits me.' Nell closed her eyes and her shoulders relaxed. 'I've already been out and used my Lady Luck supply.'

Hannah touched her arm briefly and squeezed. 'Hold the fort for me,' she said softly. 'Or hold the rectory, really.'

Gracie chimed in, 'You could drive to the bottom of your driveway. That would save you lugging the groceries up the hill. Especially if you're getting something heavy like milk.'

Gracie was right. The steepness of her drive was sure to make her slip in the wet with bags of groceries. Twisting an ankle wouldn't help anyone. 'Good idea. It's only a hundred metres to the shop through the churchyard once I get to the bottom of the hill. I can dump anything I buy in the boot and come back up the hill with them. That makes sense with the rain, too.'

All the women agreed.

Hannah donned a raincoat because she'd be walking through the rain if it started again. She collected a bunch of reusable shopping bags and took her keys down from the hook in the kitchen.

'It's slippery,' warned Gracie. 'Maybe reverse down? The water's flowing through the centre digging a trench.' She blew out a pained sigh. 'I've stuffed my car. It had water up to the windows by the time we left. Jed's not gonna be happy.'

Nell huffed. 'As long as you and Oliver are safe, Jed's happy.' Her pretended weariness at Gracie's theatrics was so heavy even Gracie smiled.

Hannah added, 'I'll do what you suggest. Might as well use the combined wisdom of women.'

'Brains trust, that's us,' Molly repeated sagely, and they all laughed.

But it was good advice to reverse so she didn't have to turn at the bottom. She didn't need to lose her car, too, like the others had.

Nell agreed. 'Are you getting much? Do you want me to come and help carry?'

Hannah shook her head. 'I won't ask for a lot. There'll be enough people looking for supplies. I just want to make sure we've got milk and other essentials. I've got a bread maker in a cupboard somewhere . . .'

'I know where that is.' Gracie's hand went up, one finger pointed to the sky.

'That's right. You and Oliver unpacked the kitchen.' Hannah smiled at the little boy who had left his mother's leg and wandered over to the twins to look at the jigsaw. 'I'll see if they've got a big bag of flour and yeast.'

Gracie nodded. 'Sounds good.'

Hannah patted her raincoat and slipped out the back door, where she stood unrestricted by the walls of the house. As she breathed in the rain-sodden air, she felt strangely, or maybe not so strangely, freed. Everything around her lay saturated, but at this moment it wasn't raining, and she sucked in another lungful of damp and her shoulders eased as she blew out a gust of liberation.

Breathe. She had so many people in her house. Lovely, lovely women, but she wasn't used to that. And it was such a huge day. And Jude . . . Where was Jude? Out there, saving people, too? She hoped Leo was okay if his dad was tied up here in town.

Jude must be somewhere in his boat. Selfless. Helping others. Surely, that meant he was nothing like Porter. She almost believed it now, without even seeing the good Jude would be doing. But trust was a hard thing. Hard to find and even harder to keep.

Something moved in the periphery of her vision, something unexpected, and she jumped until she realised it was Nell's dog, Grin. Another shuffle of movement from the other corner and she remembered the little calf. Poor little thing. She gave a moo, which sounded more like the bleat of a sheep than a calf, filled with misery. 'You need your mummy, baby. Powdered calf milk isn't as good. Keep everyone safe, Grin,' she said to the dog and Grin showed his white teeth and wagged his tail.

Hannah backed the car out, avoiding the temporary inhabitants of the carport by using the reversing cameras. Greatest invention ever, reversing cameras.

She retreated across the yard and eased slowly down her driveway, and the tyres bumped over the small culvert where the water had gouged out the gravel. Her house sat two-thirds of the way up the big hill, so the water rushed past her unpleasantly. She wished she'd driven frontwards and been able to see better, even if it meant a ten-point turn at the bottom. But if somebody wanted to drive up, she didn't want to block the way.

The car slipped and skidded and Hannah put her foot gently on the brake. Oddly, the horizon seemed to shift in front of her. The car dipped and slid, and she didn't know whether to accelerate to get a better grip or put on the handbrake.

Or was it too late to do anything?

At first, she didn't know what caused the wheel to jerk from under her fingers. The ground behind her sheared away. The car pulled sideways and plummeted faster. Despite jamming her foot on the brake, the pull of gravity jerked as her body tipped at an angle and she realised a part of the hill had given way.

Landslide.

And she was picking up speed – sideways.

Until abruptly, she hit something bone-jarringly solid, a crash that flung her against her seatbelt as her vehicle shuddered. And stopped.

There was an odd whining noise and then a clang as something fell and bounced on the roof of her car. A spark. What the . . .? A horrifying thought slid in through the shock. Electric and terrifying.

She turned her head slowly, looking out the rear window, which seemed almost level again. Half of it taken up by a splintered post of wood. A telegraph pole. Still standing. It hadn't come down. It would have crushed her if it had. But worse. In front of her, resting on the bonnet, a live power line skittered and sparked.

Chapter Thirty-seven

Jude

Jude skimmed around the slight corner in the main street and saw the low-lying house ahead. It had two storeys and the second floor sat perched well out of the water. Still, he didn't think it would take long for it to catch up with its neighbours and be inundated.

As they drew closer, they could see the woman leaning on the top balcony. Jed called out, 'Evacuation order. You need to come with us to the church, Mrs Bayley.'

She answered something, but they couldn't hear over the engine. Jude shut it off and hoped it would start again.

'You go save others. I'm fine here,' the white-haired woman, thin body hunched in a raincoat, called, waving them away.

Jude said, 'We might not get back to you in time.'

'We've all got time. And I've got a ladder to the roof. Won't need it, though.'

He reined in his frustration. 'Have you turned off the power?'

'I've got no power.'

'Have you got water?' Jed yelled.

'Got a tank, can't you see it?'

'The pump won't work without power.'

'I've got a tap on the tank.'

'Not upstairs you wouldn't,' Jed muttered. 'She'd have to come down and walk through the water at the side of the house to get to the tank.'

As if she'd heard him she said, 'I filled up the jugs with water. Go save someone who needs saving.'

'You should come now when we're sure we can help,' Jude said with authority.

'Not leaving,' she said and waved them away a second time.

The sound of a crash followed by a scream carried over the water behind them, and Jude shut off the voice of the recalcitrant woman. Then someone called his name.

'Juuuuude!'

He pulled the starter cord of the motor and steered the boat away from the double-storey house and back out onto the road through the submerged gates.

Over the sound of the motor, he just heard his name again. Terror on steroids and his gut twisted into a knot of dread. He knew that voice. Squeezing the steering arm of the motor more tightly, he willed it to go faster, but it couldn't.

'Don't like the sound of that,' said Jed, his face grim. Jude glanced at him – didn't he realise who it was? They rounded the corner.

And there was Jude's worst nightmare.

Hannah. Trapped. Terrified. Under threat.

Calling his name.

A power pole leaned precariously over the top of her car with one wire dangling over the roof and onto the bonnet. A landslip of dirt and mud and rubble had pushed her into the pole, but where she'd stopped was almost level.

'Hell,' Jed cursed. 'Where was she going? She's a doctor, not a fool.' And then, as if clocking the uselessness of that statement, he said grimly, 'Water and electricity don't mix.'

'She'd have a good reason. Shut up and let me think,' said Jude.

Jed shook his head. 'That's live. There's nothing we can do until the experts get here. Anyone goes near that, they die.'

The experts would be too late, Jude thought bleakly. The eddies of water thirty metres away were lapping closer, and for Hannah and the rescuers the options would narrow dramatically when the two met. It was bad enough with the wet ground.

He'd been here before. A clarity of purpose steered his mind. 'Had a bit to do with electrical rescues. Get on to the utilities and see about the power.' He glanced up at a pole to the left of Hannah. 'They should have already turned off the power to the whole town. Make sure they do that, now.'

Jed frowned but retrieved his phone to do as instructed. As they drew closer, but far enough away not to encourage a bow wave towards Hannah, Jude pulled to the side of the road. Jed said, 'Power number's engaged.'

'It would be. Get someone else to find a way around the blockage of calls. Tell them to ring you back when it's done.'

Jed nodded, pressed a number on his phone and spoke quietly.

The small tinny bumped aground, probably fifty metres from Hannah's car, which thankfully was out of the water. But only thirty metres or so away, the flood tide slid closer. She didn't have long.

The proper course of action was to sit it out and wait for a helicopter to drop in a linesman. Except it was Jude, looking at another woman he cared about asking him to save her. He hadn't been able to save the last one, and his heart lurched with desperate fear. No time for that. He climbed out and crossed the dry ground, not too close, but until he could hear her properly.

Hannah's arms waved. 'Thank God. Jude!' She brushed her hand across her mouth as if to wipe away the horror, her voice dropping in volume until he could barely hear her. 'Can you help me? Please.'

Jude held up his hand in the universal stop sign – both hands raised and palms out. 'Hannah. You have to stay where you are for the moment. We have to do this slowly and in the right sequence. Do you understand?'

She nodded. Grimly. 'Just get me out.'

'It's slow but you can do this safely.'

'Yes.' However, her face said she was taking a leap of faith in his words.

'You will get out of this.' Jude's voice stayed calm but firm. 'Do everything I say. I will see you safe, but I can't come and get you.'

Hannah gulped and nodded once more.

'I've worked in rescue. I've seen this before. While you're not touching the ground, you're okay.'

He watched her mouth working from where he stood as she struggled to control the panic. 'How did that end?'

Terribly, but he wasn't telling her that. 'Fine. I'll explain, but don't do anything until I say go.'

He waited until she blinked her agreement.

'Okay. Take a couple of deep breaths to clear your head so you can listen.'

He waited again, watching her shoulders rise and fall with the depth of each inhalation and exhalation. He needed a couple of discreet breaths himself. 'Are you ready to listen? Just listen. You with me?'

She gave him a thumbs up.

'What you have to do is leave the vehicle without touching it again. I'll explain how.'

He saw her head go back and the panic flared again in her eyes. 'It's okay,' he stressed. 'Not yet. Listen.'

He waited another few seconds until she'd gathered herself and was back under control. 'When I say, you have to jump, as far as you can. Feet together. Make sure you don't touch any part of the car when your feet hit the ground. No flapping part of the jacket touching. No raincoat trailing. No edge of your shirt. Nothing touching the car when you hit the ground.'

'I'm not your nimble kind of girl. Never could do high jumps.' The attempt at a joke felt heartbreaking. Jude swallowed to clear his suddenly tight throat.

Anxiety grabbed at his chest and he pushed it down. There she was. His bright and brave Hannah trying for comedy, even though it was the dark kind of humour. She could do this.

Her eyes were on his and he could see from here the fear she tried to hide. 'You'll be fine. As long as you keep your feet on the ground once you land. That's why I can't come get you. Why we can't reach you with wood. Can't pull you with rope. You have to jump clear. You can't just step away.'

He hoped that she wasn't only listening as instructed, but was taking it in.

Hannah nodded.

Jude said, 'What did I say?'

'Make sure no clothes are flapping. I have to jump clear, without touching the car as I leave. But can I touch the door to open it?'

'Yes. As long as you don't touch the ground. Just open the door without stepping out. But not yet. Not until I say go.' She had to stay calm, focused, unpanicked to have a chance.

He watched her mouth work. Then she said, as if to herself, 'Jump as far away as I can. Don't touch the car.'

'Good. But that's not all.' Her eyes were fixed on his again, all her faith resting on him. 'Once you land, stop. Keep both feet on the ground close together at all times.'

He watched her process that, emotions crossing her face as she imagined doing it.

'Do not lift your feet off the ground as you normally would when you walk. You have to shuffle.'

'Keep both feet stuck to the ground, you mean?'

He felt the first trickle of hope that they would get through this. He considered telling her she could hop like a kangaroo, keeping both feet together at all times, but decided she might fall and touch the ground with her hands. It was too risky and confusing. He had to keep it simple.

'Is that it?'

He must have paused too long while he thought it through. 'Not yet.' He paused for emphasis. 'Do not . . .' He paused again. 'Do not put your hands on the ground when you jump.'

She stared at him and he saw the panic rise. He had to cut it off. 'What did I say?'

She blinked. 'Keep feet together. Don't fall or put hands on the ground. Shuffle. Don't lift my feet. Shuffle.'

'Good. You'll probably get tingling in your feet or legs. You have to ignore that and just keep shuffling away with your feet close together and not lifting. Don't rush. You have to go slow until the sensation stops. You'll be at least halfway to us before that happens. Maybe more.'

'That's all?'

'Nobody can hand you anything or come and get you. It's up to you.'

He glanced again at the water creeping closer to the car, and wanted to say, *Stay. It's too dangerous. Wait for the power people.* But the water was coming, and she needed to get out before it reached the car.

'Just open the door,' Hannah recited quietly as if to herself. 'Wait. Make sure nothing's touching the car when you jump. Prepare and jump. Don't put your hands out to touch the ground. Keep your feet together. Shuffle.'

Jude could feel his heart pounding in his chest.

Jed whispered beside him, 'Jesus. You sure?'

'That's what the expert said last time. It's the only way to do it without the power being turned off.'

'I've got grey hair,' said Jed.

'I want to vomit,' said Jude.

Chapter Thirty-eight

Hannah

Hannah's heart pounded. It pounded so much that her ears blocked out Jude's voice. All she could hear was the *thump, thump, thump* vibrating in her chest, as though her heart wanted to jump out of the car with her.

Did he even know what he was talking about?

No, don't think that, she admonished. She had to have faith. She had to trust. Trust this man. Trust him with her life. He said he'd worked with rescue. He said he'd done it before.

Could she trust?

Yes, she realised, she could. Not simply because she was grateful that somebody knew what they were doing and was giving her instructions in this terrible moment in her life. It was that this somebody was Jude – that's what was providing the extra bit of faith she needed.

Okay, she decided. *I can do this. Like the first incision I ever made on a live patient. Follow his instructions, trust the process.*

Very, very gingerly, Hannah reached for the doorhandle. But then she remembered about the clothes. Was she wearing anything that could touch or drag, or be a draw to the electricity that pulsed around her car?

Her raincoat. She needed to get rid of the raincoat. It didn't budge when she pulled at it. Heck, she hadn't unclipped her seatbelt.

Would taking off her seatbelt cause a shock? She nearly asked Jude before her brain clicked back into gear. If she could touch the door, she could touch the seatbelt. As long as she didn't touch the ground until she jumped.

She unclipped the belt, then wriggled and squirmed to get her arms out of the raincoat, leaving the bulk of the waterproof material beneath her and tucking the sleeves under her bottom. She was wearing a fitted T-shirt and straight jeans. Nothing flapping there. And her hair was tied back with a band.

Okay. Very gingerly again, she reached out with her hand. 'I'm coming out now,' she called and pushed open the door.

Jude called back, 'That's fine. Don't step out. Just open the door and perch there.'

She did. She hung on with one hand on the steering wheel and one on the door, holding it open. When she pushed the door harder, it bounced wide, swung back and then settled fully open.

As she edged her bottom across the seat, the raincoat wanted to come with her. A sleeve fell out of the door and she grabbed at it.

A swear word from Jed.

She caught the sleeve before it touched the ground and dragged it back in. Her heart felt like it was cutting off the breath in her throat. Sweat broke out on her forehead as a sick feeling threatened to overwhelm her. She decided to drag the whole raincoat out sideways from under her towards the passenger's side in case it happened again.

'Breathe,' said Jude and she glanced across at him through the open door to see his eyes on hers. Drilling into her. Willing her to do all the right things. And something in that determined gaze settled her.

Breathe. Okay. She could do that.

Taking half-a-dozen long breaths, she looked up again. Right. She was ready . . . maybe.

Jed was chewing his knuckles and pacing. She sought Jude's face and thankfully his had remained calm. Determined. As if he believed in her. Instilling her with trust.

She looked to the seemingly innocuous ground that she was not to touch until she jumped. That was when she saw the water. It was much, much closer than she had realised. She was running out of time.

Hannah paused on the edge of the seat, running through the instructions one more time.

Jump.

Don't touch the ground with hands.

Shuffle.

She could do this. She would not fall. She would jump, keep her feet together and shuffle.

'Now?' she asked Jude.

'Go when you're ready,' said Jude, and his eyes held hers like he was holding her hand. But no one could touch her. This was just her. Which was really the story of her life. Being on her own, with no support, no people holding her.

Except Jude was holding her. From afar.

Hannah edged as far as she could while still on the seat and prepared herself. She worked out how she'd launch so she wouldn't touch the door, and where she'd land. Sucking in her breath, she looked once more at Jude.

He nodded.

Hannah jumped.

Chapter Thirty-nine

Jude

Jude blocked out Jed's litany of curses behind him. He kept his mouth shut, his whole being focused on only one person – Hannah.

He saw when she launched herself from the car, keeping her knees and feet together. He watched her knees bend with the impact and her arms and hands go out.

Holding his breath, his mind screamed, *Don't touch the ground. Don't touch the ground!*

Her hands came up fast, like she'd touched a hot plate. Which she nearly had – technically. She did well for a not-very-athletic woman. She'd done really well.

'Okay, shuffle,' Jude encouraged, in case she'd frozen with the fear of it all. His voice was level, his tone just a little bit demanding.

Her eyes flew to his and she sucked in her breath. 'I can feel the buzzing. You said I'd feel this, but it's . . . unexpected.'

'I'm waiting for you to shuffle,' he replied.

And all of a sudden she was moving, and he thought he was going to faint with the relief of it all. Feet jammed on the ground, she took tiny, sliding steps, keeping her knees together. Her terrified eyes were constantly flying to his, but she kept moving forward, shuffling as he'd instructed. Although she had a fair way to go before the water got to her, he wouldn't change what he'd told her to do. She'd needed the time to do it right.

'Come on, Hannah,' Jude muttered under his breath.

Jed was still swearing behind him, quite inventively, in short, staccato bursts.

Closer. She came closer. There were only six metres between them. Then he saw her eyes dart to the water that was closing in, and her body stiffened. They weren't out of the woods yet.

'Come on, honey, you've got this. Don't panic now. Stay calm.' His voice was slow but compelling. Her eyes flicked back to him and she nodded slightly.

'Nearly there.'

Shuffle, shuffle, shuffle, shuffle, shuffle. And then she was in his arms, sobbing, and he was crushing her into him, his own eyes damp, kissing the top of her head, her cheek, her mouth. And she was kissing him back.

'Excuse me, you guys,' Jed's voice interrupted. 'The water's coming and I'm not sticking around here with that power line.'

They broke apart just as Jed's phone rang. He answered and listened and then let out a short, sharp laugh. 'Apparently, the power is now off.'

'They could have done it five minutes ago,' Jude said as he put an arm around Hannah and hustled her back to the boat.

'Bloody oath,' said Jed.

*

A crowd of onlookers had gathered despite the floodwaters. Of course. They stood along the fence of the churchyard, and Jude steered the tinny straight for them. Mainly because that's where his boys were and he had nowhere else to beach the boat.

Nobody would be driving up Hannah's driveway anytime soon. He supposed they should all be thankful it wasn't the house that had slid down the hill, but he'd be ensuring that wasn't a risk as soon as he could get a professional to check it out.

Hannah had her head down, twisting her hands in her lap. Jed was next to her, his face curious, his hip almost touching her. Jude wanted to tell him to move, but he kept his mouth shut.

'Where were you going in the car?' Jed asked, and there was just a touch of disbelief that she could possibly have a good reason. It niggled at Jude that Jed's tone was judgy – it wasn't up to him to criticise – but Hannah just answered in her quiet voice.

'Milk for the kids while we could. I planned to walk along to the shop through the churchyard before the power went off.' She shivered and Jude wanted her back in his arms. To protect. Comfort. Hold. All needs he fought down.

She went on, as if talking helped settle her jangled nerves. 'I was just going to put the groceries in the back of the car and drive up to the house. There are ten people living there. I needed stuff . . . a lot of stuff.'

'Told you she'd have a good reason,' Jude said with deceptive mildness. But the undertone was *leave her alone*.

Jed shut up and even shifted slightly away from Hannah. The edge he'd picked up in the last year must be showing, Jude thought. He needed to pull that back, but the protectiveness he couldn't help around this woman was undermining his control.

Hannah's gaze shifted to him and she raised her brows. Her face softening, she brushed back her hair distractedly and closed her eyes as if in thanks. Then she mouthed, 'Later. We'll talk. Things I need to say.'

Then, suddenly, for Jude, the overcast day looked brighter.

Chapter Forty

Mavis

Mavis peered out the window. After the excitement of the morning and the boys finding the missing twins, she'd felt edgy.

After Archie's friend, Leo, had gone home with his dad and they'd had lunch, she took Archie aside. 'Boy. We should move that caravan they gave us last year out of the shed. Maybe to that higher rocky patch.'

'Okay, Gran. You want me to tow it with the tractor?'

Well, Mavis didn't want to do it. 'You reckon you'll be right with that?'

'Sure, no problem.'

Just like that. He was getting older, and she was getting too old. Turning into a wimp, in fact, but she hated reversing trailers.

'Do you think the flood's gonna get as high as the shed?' Archie asked.

She looked out the window. 'The ground's taken as much rain as it can. It won't if it stops now, but any big rain further up the valley will make it rush through this gully in a torrent. And that shed's lower than the house.'

'Crikey.'

'Ah well. If it does, it wouldn't be for long.'

He frowned in thought. The boy looked like a pug when he did that, she thought with a smile.

He said, 'It'd be a shame if we lost stuff again.'

'Hmm. I reckon there'll be some in town that'll get a shock,' she said. 'We might need to put up other people for a change, instead of them putting us up. Or maybe we can pass the van to someone else who needs it, now that we don't.'

Archie scratched his nose. 'We've still got the porta loo. You want me to take that up, too?'

'Only if you're willing to empty it when they leave.'

His horrified gaze met hers. 'I'd rather not.'

'You poor thing. Your great-grandfather used to dig a hole and empty the dunny can once a week. It didn't kill him.'

'Bet it killed everything else,' Archie muttered to himself.

'Leave it, then. If we have visitors, they can come down to the house when needed. Or you could just bring the van up here and park it next to the house. Then they can use the bathroom inside.'

He blew out a sigh. 'No porta loo needed, then,' he agreed, and she didn't miss his relief. The kid's face was a window into his thoughts, and they were a constant delight.

The rumbling sound of a truck coming down the drive slipped in through an open window. Mavis wandered through the house checking out windows as she went, the lack of curtains making it easy to see outside as she passed rooms to the front door. Down by the creek, something white in one of the trees caught her eye. But the truck grew closer.

It was a big truck, a blue one. One of Jed's. But it looked like Liam in the front driving. He had an aluminium boat on the back. *Hmm*, Mavis thought. *That much water in town, then.*

The brakes squealed and he stopped at the door. 'Hey, Mavis. How're you and Archie going?'

'All good. Just talking about moving the van up the hill in case we have visitors.'

'Not a bad thought.' Liam nodded at Archie as the boy followed her out. 'Archie.'

'Liam.' Men greetings.

Liam gestured to her house. 'Have you got enough supplies? It looks like Featherwood will be shut down for a while. Best not to drive anywhere unless you have to.'

She'd been living by that rule for months. 'We won't. And the boy got me to order home delivery last week. He loves it.'

'You like it too, Gran.' There was definitely a smile in the boy's voice, poking fun at her. Brat.

'True story,' she admitted. 'Anyway. It came three days ago with a month's supplies. We'll be fine.'

Liam glanced down to where the creek roared like a locomotive. 'Do you think your house is well out of the way?'

'The house should be, but the shed might go. We'll see. I reckon there'll be others with a lot worse problems than me.'

Liam winced, looking pensive. 'Already,' he said quietly. 'Nell's new house has been flooded.'

'Sorry to hear that. Glad she's okay, then?' Poor Nell. 'She's the nicest kid. It's good she has you.'

He smiled at that. A shy smile she rarely saw. 'I picked her up, but she's back to owning one bag of belongings.'

'Rotten luck.' Mavis had felt that last year, when her house went up like a torch. She and the boy were homeless until those strangers gave her a van, somewhere to live, while the new house was built.

Liam went on. 'She lost that big-horned cow she dotes on. It got swept away.'

'I'll keep an eye out. Where's she staying? With you?'

'In with the new doc, for the moment. A few in there with her. The rest at the church.'

'Crikey. If one of them needs a place to stay the van's here. And there's an extra room in the house if they need it. The boy can sleep on the lounge.'

'That's good to know. But the van might be good for a family, later.'

'We can connect it to the house for power and they can just come in here for showers and stuff. Or even take it away, if that suits.'

'We'll keep it in mind.'

'You do that.'

'If there's nothing I can do for you, I'll head back.'

'Be safe.' Mavis stood at the door and waved as he drove away, then she closed it and wandered down the hallway again. She glanced back to where she saw that white thing in the tree and turned to the boy.

'What's that down there? It wasn't there before, was it?'

Archie peered through the rain-streaked window. 'I'll just grab the binoculars, Gran.'

When he came back, he handed them to Mavis and she looked at him. 'Thanks, but you look. You've got younger eyes.'

The kid grinned, took the binoculars and adjusted them for his eyes. 'It's a cow. A white one. Could be Nell's, do you reckon?'

'What did she call it?' Mavis knuckled her chin. 'Remember, when it stayed at Gracie's?'

'Moo?'

'That's right. She called it Moo. I think I've got Liam's number here somewhere. Let's see if I can get him to come back.' Mavis went off in search of the number, but when she found it the house's landline was dead.

'Boy, you got your mobile phone there? Give Liam a ring, will you?'

Ten minutes later, Liam did return and they all pulled on gumboots and trudged down the paddock. Mavis grabbed a halter from the carport on the way.

Liam swung a chainsaw from one hand.

'Blimey,' said Mavis, once they all stood and stared at Moo. She had four hooves on the ground, but her head was stretched at an angle and her horns were caught between a fork in the tree. 'The water's gone down a bit and she's jammed herself.'

'She looks exhausted,' said Archie. 'But lucky to be alive.'

'I reckon that cow's not happy.' Mavis stated the obvious.

'I wouldn't be,' said Archie. 'She might want to trample us when she's free.'

'Hmm,' said Liam as he circled the tree. Moo's glassy black eyes swivelled as she watched him without moving her head. 'I'm thinking we just cut the branch that's holding her back.'

'She'll be terrified of the chainsaw noise.' Mavis stated the obvious again.

'She's terrified already,' Liam said. 'Just don't let her gore you when she's free. Those horns are impressive.'

'How about I put the halter on her now?' Mavis suggested. 'Tie it to another part of the tree so she can't pull away.'

'That'll work.'

'Want me to do it, Gran? I'm taller.'

'I'll do it,' Liam said. He made short work of the task. Once secured, he pulled the starter cord on the chainsaw and it roared into life. The sound bounced and echoed off the hills around them, and Moo's eyes rolled in panic.

'The wood splinters will hit her face.' Archie's features were creased with worry, and he pulled off his raincoat. 'I'll tie this over her head to protect her eyes. It might be better anyway if she can't see the saw coming closer.'

Mavis patted his shoulder. 'Good thinking, young brains.'

Together they wrapped the big head and horns, while poor Moo couldn't move anything except her eyes, though her hooves struggled uselessly in the mud as she tried to back away.

When it was done, Liam stepped in and carefully sawed through the thigh-thick branch of the tree that was holding Moo's weight. He stopped just before sawing all the way through and put the chainsaw aside, far enough from where the cow could reach when she was free.

'Okay. Take the raincoat off her face and step back. I figure the branch will break away when she moves.'

With a loud crack, Moo's body weight snapped the last restraint of wood and the big Brahman slid and landed head down, on the ground. She backed away, but secured by the halter rope as she was, she couldn't go far. Her muscled sides heaved and her eyes shone wild as she pulled, but it was a half-hearted effort. With a drooping head, she stood still, her last energy spent.

'Good girl,' Liam said softly. 'It's all right, Moo. You did well.'

Chapter Forty-one

Hannah

Hannah felt like a fragile glass test tube, ready to break. Because she was probably in that word she didn't want to use ever again – shock.

Adrenaline leaked from her bloodstream, leaving exhausted nerves and making her look like she'd joined the PTSD crowd. She'd lost her car. Her driveway . . . *It could have been worse,* her inner voice interjected. That was true, she had to admit. She could be dead. Fried like a prawn chip in a vat of hot oil. Except Jude had been there.

She shivered. And realised the boat had grounded outside the small store and post office, and she needed to get moving.

Jed stepped out and extended his hand to her. She took it. Something made her look at Jude when she did, though. His eyes had narrowed, blue sparks aiming at Jed, who dropped her hand as soon as she stood and backed away as fast and far as he could.

She knew what it looked like. She did not have the headspace for this, but inside, somewhere, a warm spot glowed from Jude's care. Like the tip of a pilot light in a stove – it was probably that tiny – but it still glowed warm.

Onlookers fell back as she walked past. There weren't many faces there she recognised. People from town who hadn't been to the doctor yet. She figured the town would be abuzz with gossip about the new doc's misadventures. This might actually bring in new patients, even if only to check her out.

She kept her eyes on the front door of the shop and forced a smile. Then stopped.

She turned, intending to walk back past the church, when she walked into Jude. He put his hands out to steady her arms before they collided.

'You okay?' He rubbed her goose-bumped arms and she realised she was cold. So cold. Deathly cold.

Jude's big hands felt warm and comforting. 'I just realised I can't shop. No money. My handbag's in the car.' She jerked her head but couldn't look in that direction. 'It was one of those things that might've flapped around and hampered my escape. I abandoned my raincoat, too. Anyway, I'm not going in there.'

Turning her, he gently faced her back towards the shop and reached into his pocket and pulled out his wallet. 'Take two hundred.' He peeled off four fifty-dollar notes from a wad.

Her stomach sank as a flashback slammed into her. Porter used to do that. He always had a wad of cash in his wallet. Why did Jude have so much cash on him? People – normal, everyday, law-abiding people – didn't do cash any more. They did cards or tapped their phones. They didn't have wads of cash.

Cold, criminal concerns crept insidiously closer and chilled her. They crushed out the warm spark inside her until it was bent and broken like a cigarette butt in an ashtray.

She stepped back and he had to sense her withdrawal. Although his black brows drew together, he said quietly, 'I withdrew money from the ATM this morning.' He shrugged. 'In case the EFTPOS machines went down.'

Oh. Right. Of course.

He jerked his head back in the direction of the power pole she knew was leaning over her car. 'Which they will do now, with the power turned off.'

He touched the small of her back, his hand warm, his voice calm, ignoring the revulsion she'd just sent him. *Not fair, Hannah. He saved your life.*

The spark spluttered and very faintly glowed again.

'You have a full house,' he said quietly. 'Buy what you need before everything goes. I'll get one of the fellas to help you carry the bags up the hill. I need to go back in the boat with Jed.'

He was leaving her? No. She didn't want him to go.

God. Her emotions were all over the place. It was one thing to be suspicious of him, but quite another to have him walk away before she could explain or apologise or thank him yet again.

'Hey, Ben.' Jude's voice carried. A man looked up and started towards them. Before he reached them, Jude said quietly, 'He's my most trusted bloke.'

The man was about thirty, with a short beard and green eyes, wearing a blue western shirt that looked worn but clean and was incongruously paired with footy shorts. Boots without socks and an easy smile completed the ensemble.

'G'day,' he said. 'Glad you got out of that car in one piece. Very brave.'

His words were unanticipated and frank, and Hannah felt her cheeks heat. Some of her embarrassment was caused by the thought of her notoriety, for being stupid enough to be avalanched into a telegraph pole. 'Thank you.' She looked at Jude. 'I had good instructions.'

He gave her a pleased look before turning. 'Can you help the doctor carry supplies up to the rectory, Ben? I'll pick you up on one of the runs when you're done.'

'Sure,' Ben said easily. 'Lead on, Doc.'

Which was how Hannah made her way back to the rectory with four bags of her own and Ben carrying eight.

She was exhausted by the time she pushed open the door, and he didn't even look winded. Whatever they did on that farm of Jude's sure kept them fit.

Nell met her with concern and a quick grab of the bags from her. Then she was bowled over by Gracie, who, as a small woman, packed quite a punch when she ran into you.

Gracie squeezed her middle, then squeezed again. 'My God, Hannah. You're all right? Jed told me what happened. You win in the danger stakes. That must have been terrifying.'

'It's not something I want to do again.' Even she could hear the shake in her voice. 'No one ever told me that going to the shops was dangerous.' Suddenly, she felt overwhelmed. 'Can you put these groceries away, please? I need to go to my room for a minute and . . . get changed.'

'Sure, of course. I'll make you a hot drink for when you come out. You can have a shot of whisky in it.'

Not in the daylight hours. 'Doctors don't drink in case emergencies arrive.'

'One drink won't kill you.'

'It can,' said the man at the door. 'All right if I put these on the kitchen table?'

Hannah's face flamed. 'Oh, I'm so sorry, Ben. Thank you. Yes, please.'

'I'll take them. I'm Molly. Thanks so much for helping Hannah. I haven't seen you around?'

'Pleased to meet you, Molly. I'm Ben. I do the cooking up at Luna Downs with Jude.'

'Well, you take these scones, they're just out of the oven, and they might warm you men up a little.' She handed him one to eat straightaway. 'It's my own recipe. I can share it, if you like. We sure do appreciate your help.'

'It's all good,' he said, chewing, then swallowed and dusted his hands. Now that the bags were deposited, he tipped an imaginary hat. 'You make great scones, Molly.'

There was something like admiration in his eyes, if Hannah wasn't mistaken, but she wasn't sure if it was about cooking prowess or he fancied older women. Molly had to be ten years his senior, but still a fine-looking woman with a beautiful smile. And she did make great scones.

'I'll just get on my way, Miss Molly.'

Molly laughed. When Hannah cast a look her way, she saw the other woman smiling as she lifted her hand to the window in a wave. It was as if her friend was saying, *I'm not dead yet*.

Now, that was interesting.

Twenty minutes later, Hannah returned to the kitchen wearing warmer clothes – she'd felt chilled and edgy, and not quite ready to be congratulated on her ability to survive. She might have surprised herself with that skilful leap from the car, but she'd not yet shed the belief that she'd been inept in putting herself in that position.

'Jed said Jude was amazing.' Gracie's voice was soft. 'And just a little bit scary. It seems our mysterious Mr Waugh has a bit of a crush on you.'

'I don't know about that, but I do know he's a good man to have around in an emergency.'

'Liam's heading back into town.' Molly rejoined the group after putting away all the supplies. 'He's checked on Mavis and Archie and they're fine.'

It's a tough gig caring about people, Hannah thought, and everybody in this room was doing it tough.

Nell said, 'Mavis found Moo, and Liam said he'll get the calf to her as soon as he can.'

Hannah smiled, noting the relief on her friend's face. Then she looked over at Audrey. 'Did you manage to contact your husband?'

'Yes.' Audrey stroked the baby's back. 'He's on his way home. It'll take him a couple of days. Hopefully, the roads will be open by the time he gets here.'

'That must be a relief. So pleased. Great news.' Hannah took the big mug of coffee Gracie handed her. Her nerves were beginning to settle, the twitches calming and her breathing easier.

'Sit back. Relax. What else do you have to do?'

'Nothing, I hope.' And that was the truth. Except she did want to talk to Jude. Once he'd finished saving the townspeople.

Remarkable how much she needed to talk to Jude.

The rain started up like bullets on the roof again – H_2O machine-gun fire – and Hannah realised it had grown dim, though it was still only afternoon, and there was no power for lights. She shivered at the thought of the people out in the rain. People who Jed had told her had chosen to stay in their houses rather than evacuate. She wondered if some regretted that decision now.

She imagined what could have happened if it had rained like this when she hit the pole . . . *No.* She needed to think of something else. Perhaps about tonight, when it would become really dark. 'There were no house candles left at the shop,' she said. 'I do have a heap in the bathroom around the bath.'

'Got them,' Nell said. 'I've put them in the rooms and Molly found a packet of matches.'

'Out of reach of the twins,' Audrey murmured, slanting a glance at the small, still absorbed boys. Molly had them colouring in.

Molly said, 'It's so good you have gas bottles for cooking, Hannah. I've started a soup. I brought bacon bones.'

'Soup is a great idea.' And the bread maker. They did have everything they needed to be warm and safe, and companionship for when it grew dark.

Molly nodded. 'We can easily jug water from outside at the tank tap. That makes us better off than someone in a city would be.'

Even if she didn't have a driveway any more. How were her patients going to get up to the clinic? And how were they going to get back down the hill? But she couldn't worry about that now. She simply didn't have the energy or the care factor.

Nell patted her shoulder as she went past, circling the room to prepare more candles for later. As if she read Hannah's mind, she said, 'The churchyard has a driveway. We'll take out the fence and go that way above the land slip. They were raising money for it to be rejuvenated anyway. I'm pretty sure Liam will help out there.'

And there they were again. Everyone pulling together, and suddenly, with the candles lit, even though it wasn't quite dark outside, the smell of simmering soup, the warmth from the stove and caring women around her, Hannah began to relax.

A firm, staccato knock had her gaze flick to the door. She knew that knock and she felt her senses come alive. She really was very, very conscious of Jude Waugh. And she had wronged him, even if only in her mind, and not to his face.

Molly opened the door and there stood Jude under the protection of the verandah awning. 'Come in.' Molly swept her arm towards the kitchen. 'Do you take sugar in your coffee or just milk?'

He looked across to Hannah and she stood up with her mug. 'Jude. Come through to my office.' It was the only private place in the rectory, and Hannah desperately craved privacy, now that Jude was here.

Jude smiled at Molly. 'Black and strong. And thanks for the scones. They went down well.' He slipped off his Driza-Bone jacket and hung it on the hook beside all the other rain gear. He'd left his boots outside.

Molly pressed a hastily made mug of coffee into his hands. 'Take this with you. I'll make more scones for you to take when you go.'

Which was how Hannah ended up in her office with the door shut and Jude standing with his back to it. Should she run at him and hug him, sit down and stare at him, or back up against the window to stop herself from doing either of those things?

He looked too good. Wet and wild, his black hair glistening with water droplets and his face rough with stubble. He wasn't helping the decision process, because all he did was lean back, broad shoulders outlined against the wood, and study her. With such intensity. Intensity that brought the heat to her cheeks and fired a glow within her belly.

'You look good,' he said.

'Better than I would have looked fried.' *What a stupid thing to say. Stupid. Stupid.*

He flinched and raised his hand. 'Don't even talk about it. I'll have nightmares as it is.'

'Sorry.' She was nervous, which was also silly. 'I didn't get to say thank you, Jude.' She blew out a breath and forced herself to relax. To enjoy the fact that he was here and she was alive. 'You were a rock out there.'

'You were . . . what's that word you like?' He smiled. 'A champion. So brave. Unbelievable.'

'Don't say that. I was scared. Absolutely scared witless.'

'You'd be mad if you weren't. But you still did everything you had to. And that's my definition of bravery.'

'Okay.' This was a lot, and hard to hear. She sat down suddenly. 'Take a seat, Jude. What did you want to talk about?'

That small half-smile lit his face. 'And I thought it was you who said we needed to talk.'

Yes, they did. She needed to get some misconceptions off her chest. 'I need to say things, clear the air. Apologise, maybe.'

He said nothing, but he did sit, so she stumbled on. 'I moved here running away from a relationship with a man. A man who turned out to be nothing like I imagined he was.'

Jude leaned back, his expression unreadable, giving no hints to his thoughts. At least he wasn't looking at the door like he wanted to escape.

She brushed her fringe out of her eyes. She'd started this and she wasn't even sure why. 'Porter turned out to be a swindler, a thief. A drug dealer with anger issues. I nearly lost my career over him when he was caught. I didn't know any of his backstory.' She rolled her eyes. 'Who am I kidding, I didn't even know his fore story.'

Still he didn't speak, but she didn't mind. Hannah needed to keep talking, to get this all out.

'Of course, he's currently in jail. I don't know when he's coming out . . . Frankly, I don't want to know. But I've moved away and hopefully he won't find me again.'

There was a flicker then. That flash of danger in his eyes, the one she'd seen directed at Jed. She should have been frightened, but oddly, she felt safer.

Jude leaned forward. 'How long were you with him?'

'Eight months.'

He sat back, looking slightly more relaxed. 'Not long.'

'Long enough.' It hadn't taken Porter long to take control from her. 'In just eight months, I found myself separated from my friends. Living on eggshells with his moods. And yet, strangely, I was still drawn to him. I don't understand any of it.' She shook her head, still baffled at the spell that had been cast over her. 'I'm just glad I'm free.'

Jude watched her face. 'Why are you telling me this now?'

Ah, the penny dropped for her. She hadn't been sure before, but she understood now. 'When I first met you, I wondered if you were that kind of man. A man with secrets and a past to hide. A criminal.'

'Did you?' His smile mocked her, yet he didn't deny it. 'Why would you think that?' Before giving her a chance to answer he said, 'Unless you were attracted to me?'

She glared at him. Earlier she'd kissed the man when he'd saved her, in front of others. 'That isn't the issue. Of course I'm attracted to you.'

'Oh, it goes both ways, Hannah Rogan.' This time when he smiled, it was long and slow. And then the smile disappeared. 'As to am I that sort of man, I guess it all depends on your definition.'

'Definition?' she asked with a frown.

'I came out of custody just over a year ago.'

Hannah's heart stopped. She knew it was impossible – she was a doctor, she knew her anatomy and hearts didn't stop unless there was a medical emergency – but it felt like it had. It felt like everything had stopped. Her breath, her heart, the blood in her veins.

He'd been in prison? A criminal, like Porter?

'You look shocked.' Jude's voice was so dry the air shrivelled.

'I am shocked. You're kidding, surely. I don't want that to be true.'

'That's the worst of it. There is a better side.' He watched her closely. Could he see the disbelief on her face?

'What's the better side?' She'd really like to hear an answer, because from her perspective, she couldn't imagine what that might be.

His shoulders lifted. 'I didn't do what they put me in there for.'

'And what was that?' This felt like a nightmare. She didn't deserve two nightmares in one day.

'They said I killed my wife.' It was such a matter-of-fact statement and all the more shocking because of that.

Hannah's heart did that stutter thing again. And then she frowned and thought back, replaying what she knew. 'Your wife died of cancer.'

'Yes. For the record, that's all she died from.'

'Then why . . .?'

'In the last two months of her life, she begged me to help her overdose. And I wouldn't . . . I couldn't. But she told her parents that I'd agreed to assist. She said goodbye to them.' He closed his eyes as if not wanting to see that memory. 'When she died earlier than expected, in their grief they pressed charges.'

'That's ridiculous.' Hannah worked through the probable scenario. 'They could have just checked her morphine levels. Or the amount of medication left.'

'Nobody checked anything.' He watched her, his inscrutable face on. 'There was a cremation and it was all too late. Then they brought up their word against mine.'

'How could they not think of Leo?' Her head shook from side to side, in a slow, horrified denial. 'How could they take both parents from their grandson? Create that greater damage?'

Still seeming matter-of-fact, though she could not imagine how he could be so, Jude replied, 'They wanted him all along and they got their way. Leo went to his grandparents. But when I was released, he chose, without hesitation, to come home with me.'

'So you both went back to Luna Downs?'

'Yeah. And in the beginning, it didn't work. I had too much anger. Too much bitterness. I just wanted to ride off into the distance on a bike and maybe power off a cliff.'

She winced this time.

'But there was Leo. My son. Our son. So we bumbled along for a while, me feeling sorry for myself and Leo not getting the attention he needed. He was isolated and with my moods getting blacker, he was struggling in a world that was bleak and miserable.'

'Sounds fun.' It sounded like the worst world imaginable after losing your loved one.

'Fun for a masochist, I guess. Then one day in Dorrigo, we stumbled across Ben. Hair everywhere, stinking like a dog. Drunk. I gave him five bucks. And he said, "You can't buy a drink for that." I thought about him on the way home. How cold it was up at Dorrigo. How pinched and miserable he looked. Lost, with not a single hope in the world. Ready to freeze to death for the sake of another drink.'

Jude was staring through her now, back into the past. This quiet conversation was so unexpected and traumatic, she wondered how he could be as stable as he was.

'Leo saw him, too. And we talked about the man, alcoholism, drugs. How that bloke was even more miserable than I was. Than we were. I wondered if maybe the way back to a worthwhile life was through helping others.'

'Not the easiest way,' she murmured.

'Maybe I didn't want easy. I told Leo it would be tough, but if he was okay with it I'd like to try. We both agreed and turned around, went back and got Ben.'

'You must be proud of Leo,' she said softly. 'Proud of his strength. His love.'

He looked up and met her eyes. 'Too right. I'm grateful for him every single day. And for Ben, now.'

This whole story fascinated Hannah. It made Jude a real person, with mistakes and wrong turns and leaps of faith, and not some hero riding into town to save the day. He had morals. She had needed desperately to hear that.

'So how did that go with Ben?'

'It was really tough. But in the end, Ben saved us all. After two months, he was dry and managing it well. No smokes. No alcohol on the place. And he was working, hard. Suddenly, I had another man's help. I wondered, maybe we could do it again for someone else?'

He lifted his big shoulders and that simmering coal flared to life again. Unfair, that's what those shoulders were. Then her thoughts were dragged back to his words.

'We went down to Coffs Harbour, found another young bloke around Ben's age and brought him back to Luna Downs. Poppy. Then Bill. Then Xavier. Last month, we brought back Tesla.'

'Interesting name.' But she was blown away by the philanthropy of it. The kindness, the strength of character.

He snorted a laugh. 'We call him Tesla because he's always sparking off about something that upset him. He's the hardest one of the lot. Spoiled as a kid, I reckon. He side-tracked me, so I missed it when Leo wasn't well. Which was why I nearly lost it to find my son so sick. Iris would never have missed that.' There was self-loathing in the words.

Iris. His dead wife's name. Not for thinking about now.

Hannah repeated what she'd told him at the time. 'Diabetes can be an insidious disease. Many don't see it coming until it's well established, like with Leo, or they're even in a diabetic coma.'

'Well, you saved him.'

'*We* saved him,' she corrected. 'Nell and I, and you bringing him in.' She paused and met his eyes. 'And now you've saved me. So we're even.'

He smiled and stood up. 'I'd better go. I need to get back home and check on my son. The men are happy to stay in Featherwood and help. I asked Jed to make sure no one offers them a beer.'

'More pressure for Jed.' Like Gracie's husband wasn't busy enough. But she smiled.

Jude shrugged. 'He wanted helpers. By the way, we'll divert your driveway next door when the rain stops. Geophysical engineers are coming in to ensure the whole hill isn't coming down, but nobody thinks it will.'

Another burden sorted. 'That will be amazing. I was concerned.'

'Don't worry until they tell you to. It's all cordoned off, but I brought back your handbag.' He reached into his small waterproof pack, pulled out the pink-starred clutch and handed it to her.

'Which reminds me,' she said. 'I need to pay you back the two hundred dollars.'

'Yeah, that's what I'm really here for,' he said. And he gave that crooked smile that made him so handsome she felt dazzled by him.

'There's a lot to think about in this conversation,' she told him.

'Then while we're here,' Jude said. 'I didn't like the way you looked at me when I pulled out the cash.' He watched her face. 'Guessing your ex did that, did he?'

'I'm that transparent?'

'Of course. You always are. Your face is a window into your soul, Hannah. I like that. You need to know I'm a moody mongrel, but I'm honest.'

She smiled. 'When all this is over, Jude, come have dinner at my house and I'll repay the cash.'

He laughed, letting his gaze linger over her face and down her body. 'When all this is over, Hannah Rogan . . .' And the way he said her name made the hairs rise on her arms. 'We'll go out somewhere wonderful. But right now . . .' He stepped closer and she stood up as well. 'I need to show you how grateful I am that you didn't die.'

Her eyes filled with tears. The sincerity in his words, the thought of how close it had been . . . Suddenly, she needed his arms around her.

He took another step towards her and she moved out from behind the desk and met him halfway. His eyes darkening, he crossed the last tiny distance and slid his arms around her.

'I'd really like to kiss you,' he said. 'I may be rusty. I haven't kissed anyone for twelve months. And I'm not even sure I should kiss you now. But I want to.'

She let the warmth from his hand seep into her shoulder and slide down around her waist. The weight of him against her felt too delicious. 'Do you think you can control yourself?' she teased.

His eyes darkened even more. 'Are you afraid?'

She was a little – of her own response. 'Not of you.'

'If you're afraid of you, then I'm interested in finding out why.' His big hand drew a hot trail up to her neck. The other was around her waist, drawing her closer until their faces were almost touching. 'But there will be control – until I don't have to.'

Their breath mingled. They were so close, with so much heat between them. Until their lips did touch and the need inside her roared into life.

Hannah closed her eyes. The feel of him – strong, potent yet tender. His mouth tasted like coffee. Hers tasted a little like coffee, too, she guessed. All heat and promise with undertones of wild.

Oh my. Oh my. Ohhh my.

That sparkler down in her belly flared instantly to life, a nimbus of light that grew into a cupful of belly heat.

He drew back. 'Mmm,' he said like he'd just tasted the best chocolate in the world. 'I knew it would be like that.' His eyes

224

were dark, bedroom dark, as they roamed her face. Hungry. A little bit possessive. Promising a time to come.

His fingers touched her cheek, the roughness of a worker's skin sliding down, grazing her bottom lip with tantalising torment.

'You're a stunning, gifted woman, Hannah Rogan. I'm a stonemason with a son. But if we had a chance, I think we'd be great together.'

'There is something hot about a man who works with his hands.'

'There is. I'll show you. One day soon.' Letting her go, he strode out and Hannah stared after him, on suddenly weak legs.

What the hell had just happened?

Chapter Forty-two

Jude

Jude thought he made the correct goodbye motions to the other women, but he didn't really see them as he passed. Blindly, he took the bag of scones held out to him, thanked Molly and walked towards the door on a mission. And once outside . . . he bolted. Strode away like a pack of feral dogs were on his tail.

He might have left his brain behind, though. It certainly felt like it had short-circuited. By the sweetness, generosity and that hint of playful teasing of Hannah Rogan, whom he wanted to carry off to a cave somewhere to keep safe. With just him. There was an intriguing innocence to her that even the scumbag she'd been tied to for eight months hadn't destroyed.

She was amazing. Enchanting like a fairytale, a princess he couldn't even aspire to match. Except when she was in his arms and he began dreaming. That had felt a fantasy, but he had plenty of future intent.

Imagine if she'd died today. His whole body shuddered at the thought. He couldn't lose someone else he loved.

He wasn't as brave as she was. So brave. So out of his reach.

He needed to get home. To think. To allow the terrifying afternoon here to fade back into the nightmare that it was.

He needed to make sure Leo was okay. That need grounded him, as it had done so often in the past months, years, ever since he'd first held the perfect, tiny infant in his too-big hands.

He'd phoned before visiting Hannah, and Leo had been fine then. Still, obstacles could happen to keep Jude from home. The world was crazy at the moment, and in hindsight, he should have brought Leo along, even if he'd dropped him with Mavis closer to town.

He'd left Xavier, the new guy before Tesla, with Leo. At the time, he'd not intended being away long – an hour at most. They'd gone to pull Liam from the washaway, but everything else had grown from there, and now he'd been away too long.

If he went home, it would mean he couldn't do anything else stupid, like kissing Hannah, promising a date and a possible future when he had nothing worthy to offer her.

By the time Jude skidded down the slippery path of Hannah's driveway, everything had gone to hell in a crazy waterworld of new flood heights and late-afternoon dimness. Though some parts were passable – just – he detoured via the churchyard until he could see the bottom.

He needed to get home before he couldn't.

Jed pulled Jude's tinny to the bank below the little shop and post office, with Bill and two passengers on board. Tesla and Poppy were helping two women out of the craft with steady hands and then pointing to the church.

He could see his vehicle just out of the water on the lower side of Hannah's disaster, where he'd unloaded the boat, but it wouldn't be going anywhere with the road so far underwater now. It would be deeper out of town.

He strode up to Jed. 'I need the boat. I'll have to go home and get Leo in case his diabetes plays up. The road will be deeper out of town and that's the only way I'll get to him.'

A mix of emotions crossed Jed's face, and Jude could tell he didn't want to give up the boat. After a pause he said, 'We've got a chopper coming in with supplies and some experts. Did you want to go that way? Maybe they'd drop in and pick him up on the way. Is there a clear space for it to land?'

There was a cement slab ready for the new shed just up from the house that would make a perfect landing area. 'That's not a bad idea.' But then he'd be well and truly stuck in town with nowhere to go. In his dreams, he could've asked to stay at Hannah's, but she was booked out. Maybe that was lucky.

Jed must have been thinking the same thing. 'You could stay at the church. We usually have the progress hall, but it's an island down on the showground.'

At least they had a high side of the street because the valley ahead of them was a sea of swirling brown water with Jed's shop and Gracie's house half-submerged. Along with every other house on that side of the street. It had to hurt watching them go under. He couldn't think of anything helpful to say about the devastation, so he settled for, 'It's good your town has a higher side of the street.'

'I wish I'd bought on it,' said Jed. They both turned at the sound of a truck engine, not something heard recently, and a big, blue truck lumbered into view, pushing a ponderous brown bow wave.

Jed said, 'Liam's back from Mavis's. We'll know about the road between here and there, and maybe you and your boy can stay with Mavis. That would give us backup on that end of town, so we can be there if she gets into trouble.'

'Assuming the chopper will bring him in.' Jude should have stayed home. But no. The boat had been needed and Hannah . . . Hannah had certainly needed him. No way could he wish he hadn't come in.

'I'm lead on the local emergency services.' Jed waved at Liam and indicated he park on the church driveway. 'I'll tell them Hannah said it was safer for Leo, which she would.'

'Yep, do it.' Just thinking about it made him want Leo here beside him now. 'As soon as you get the go-ahead, I'll tell him to light a signal fire so they can find him more easily.' He explained about the new cement slab for the helicopter.

'Got it,' Jed said. 'I'll give him a call now,' and he stepped away towards Liam.

Jude signalled to his men. They'd been helping the women carry groceries and belongings up to the church, but they were free now. They jogged over and he told them about the chopper. 'It looks like we're staying in town until the road opens again.'

Ben said, 'I reckon we can do a bit to help here, anyway, Boss.'

Jude nodded. 'It might keep us busy for a few weeks.'

'Or a few months,' Tesla said with a grimace at the devastation. 'The power won't be going on anytime soon.'

'Maybe a couple of years,' added Poppy, 'if this rain doesn't stop.'

The men seemed in good spirits. That helped. Thinking of bad spirits, he added, 'Are you blokes right not to take any drinks offered?'

Tesla looked away, but Bill and Poppy nodded. 'We've got this,' said Bill.

Good men, he thought, but inclined his head as if he expected nothing less. He'd have to take Tesla with him if he went to Mavis's. That wasn't a cheerful thought. But he'd taken on the burden of keeping him dry and he needed to see it through. Mavis would have to find the bloke something to keep him busy.

He pulled out his phone to prepare Leo. 'Bring all your meds, your sleeping bag, wear your gumboots and bring our thick work gloves. Bathroom bag and battery packs for my phone.'

'Got it.'

'That's my boy.' Pride swelled. So much had happened, but Leo had managed.

Leo arrived just before five in the afternoon in a swirl of water-splattered wind and noise. The helicopter landed with the geophysical consultants who'd come in to assess the landslide on Hannah's driveway and ensure the rest of the buildings on the hill were safe.

Leo stepped out of the aircraft with a huge grin on his face, and Jude smiled because he knew for a fact that Leo would have loved the ride. His son had been saying he was going to be a pilot when he grew up. A pilot. Jude didn't know how that would work with the diabetes, but he suspected it wouldn't be a goer, commercially.

That was stuff to worry about later, and for now, his son would be happy to bunk with Archie. The upside being Mavis had electricity and maybe even wi-fi.

Jed had moved his generator stock, and the shop was running the fridges and freezers with Jed's borrowed generators. The little petrol ones were doing the job, and the fuel supply was above ground in a standing tank. There wasn't enough portable power for the lights because they kept tripping the generators, but people were happy to look in the gloom for supplies.

Jed's diesel truck had been topped up before the drama started and would run for a week or more on the short trips out of town, a bonus Jed publicly thanked Gracie's nagging for. Apparently, his wife always did look ahead.

In the report of his latest excursion, Liam described the deepest part of the road being where Jude had pulled him and Nell from. The same place where Mavis had been washed away. That was between him and Luna Downs, so he could only drive the truck between town and Mavis's. Since there was nowhere else to drive with all the roads flooded, Jed offered total use of the high-wheeled vehicle in a swap for Jude's boat. At least until the water went down.

When the water went down. Who knew when that would be? A couple of days? The BOM was saying another week of rain, but if they didn't get any heavy falls upstream or over Featherwood, the creek would rush away as fast as it had rushed in. Then the long, painful recovery could start.

Liam turned to Jed. 'Hey, we found Nell's cow. Stuck in the fork of a tree, but alive and washed all the way down to Mavis's. I've freed her, but we need to get the calf back to its mother ASAP.'

Jude's attention caught. 'Was it a white one?' He shook his head in disbelief. Hannah would be happy. 'We thought we saw a cow go past. It's nice to have a good news story. If you phone Nell to get her ready, we can take the calf when we go to Mavis's.'

Liam grinned and pulled his phone from his pocket.

Jude turned to Tesla. 'I need you to go up to the house at the top of the driveway and someone will show you where to find this calf. Find a rope and bring it down. We'll use the rope to tie it up in the back of the truck, to stop it from jumping out.'

Tesla jerked his head once and strode off to the path through the churchyard across to Hannah's driveway.

Jude wondered if he needed anything else from the shop for Mavis. She had said no, just come, but maybe he'd pick up some eggs and long-life milk, if there was any left. He gestured to his son.

'Did you bring all your diabetes stuff?'

'Everything's in a bag.'

'Good. Can you think of anything extra we should take to Mavis that they might have in the shop?'

'What's for dinner?'

Jude handed Leo two fifty-dollar notes. 'Grab dinner for five adults, make it something you can eat, and then we'll head off.'

Chapter Forty-three

Hannah

There was nothing anybody could do until the water receded. A town of one hundred and seventy people – a hundred and seventy-one, Hannah thought smiling, including her as a permanent resident – with everyone accounted for and only minor injuries. That was the main thing.

Those who resided on the church side of the road stayed lucky, except for one gully-lying house. Those on the lower side lost everything that had been left behind. In nature's irony, during the fires the year before, the most burnt dwellings had been on the high side of the road.

Mother Nature, the great leveller.

Where possible, residents on the high side of the road in their new houses took in their neighbours from across the street. Like Gracie and Jed to Hannah's. The rest went to the church, though not many ended up needing to bunk on the ecclesial floor.

That night, the churchyard glowed as a fairyland of torch- and candlelight and small fires, with the smell of barbecues and the low chatter of voices filling the atmosphere. People told stories of other floods and little miracles like Nell's cow, and for a first night, it wasn't too bad. Except everyone knew the hard part was to come. Tonight was for celebrating no loss of life. Tomorrow they could think about the loss of everything else.

Most of Jed's hardware supplies in the rural store had been trucked up the hill to Hannah's shed at the back of the rectory as the water climbed the walls in the store and shed. He'd figure out later how he was going to get them down again.

During the two days while they waited for the creeks to fall, those staying in the rectory helped sort supplies in Hannah's shed in preparation for the big clean-up. Four dozen buckets, each with cleaning gear and heavy gloves, were assembled.

Jed had a couple of dozen pairs of gumboots, though thankfully, most people in town had left home with their own on their feet.

Because Nell was minding Oliver and Audrey's boys with Molly, Hannah and Gracie handed out flyers on the high side of the street. One was medical from Hannah, about the dangers of contaminated water and the need to wear thick rubber boots and gloves, long sleeves and trousers when working with contaminated flood water. It also included information about treating any scratches for infections, being wary of conjunctivitis with unprotected eye splashes and throat infections without masks. The sheet listed her emergency phone number for questions.

Another flyer was about entering damaged houses; taking a torch and watching for missing floorboards, and being aware of falling plaster and ceilings. Those with gas bottles needed to beware of leakage and breaks. The flyer also urged people to comply with stay-away orders until the local SES declared they could go back into their homes.

Nobody was happy. Waiting for a city-centred decision on their own property was not the Australian way, but Jed had found with the presence of Liam – and his personal desire to check out his own ruined house and store, which he was resisting – that people did listen.

'Just wait,' he said. 'As soon as it's safe, we'll all get in and take photos. Nobody moves anything until we take photos.'

'Who wants photos?'

'For insurance.'

'And what if you haven't got insurance?'

'Take photos in case someone offers to replace what you've lost.'

On the morning of the third day, the clouds skittered, the sun shone weakly and overnight the last foot of water disappeared off the road. Still lying in the paddocks, brown sludge centimetres deep squelched around Gracie's and others' houses, littered with bizarre articles shifted by the flood waters. There was even a quad bike on a low-lying roof bowing the tin. The town's power remained off, and people were allowed back into their homes to take stock of the damage.

Hannah and Nell went with Gracie for that first look at her house. Hannah knew it had to be heartbreaking. The road had washed away between Mavis and Nell's place, so Nell couldn't get to her own house until the road was repaired to a drivable condition. Liam and Jude were going to try to make a causeway later in the day for temporary access, just until the council could get in and do the heavy-duty work. If they were successful, Jude could get home to Luna Downs, as well.

They trudged down Hannah's driveway in their boots until the roped-off area of the landslide appeared. Everyone stopped. And gaped.

Hannah couldn't look at the spot, so instead she looked at her car, off to the side, and the end of the pole lying on the ground. Someone – Jude? – must have moved it.

'Oh, Hannah,' said Gracie.

'I don't want to think about it.' Hannah started moving again, and thankfully, they crossed into the churchyard and left the scene of Hannah's nightmare behind them. Now she could push it to the back of her mind, to the place where monsters and horror stories were relegated.

'Molly must have wanted to come with us,' she said, to change the subject.

Gracie glanced sideways, agreeing with her eyebrows. 'Mol will be here as soon as Audrey's husband arrives. She said she'd bring Oliver later. I don't know what we'd do without her. She's such a champion with the kids.'

Like her friends, Hannah had dressed in gumboots and long sleeves and trousers. Thick leather gloves sat in their pockets, and each carried a cheap plastic bucket of cleaning rags and disinfectants and brushes.

Jed had lined up the pre-packed buckets outside the general store to give away this morning. Buckets they'd all prepared yesterday as they waited for the water to go down.

A surprise benefactor had been Hannah's father. He'd rung and offered financial assistance, which Hannah had declined. But when he'd pressed, she'd accepted it for the town. 'You can pay for the cleaning buckets and what's inside them.' Jed had been going to give them away, and Hannah knew Gracie was having a fit because each one cost forty dollars to replace.

'That doesn't sound enough,' her dad had said.

'There are four dozen of them. And the gumboots – you can pay for the gumboots, too. There are two dozen of them and they're heavy-duty ones, so they're not cheap. How does that sound?'

'Good. It sounds good for now. It's still not enough, but when I come to visit, I'll think of something big. Let me know if there's more before then,' he said and deposited the amount into the Farmer's Friend bank account as soon as she finished the call. Gracie heaved a sigh of relief and Hannah smiled.

That had been yesterday, and here they were with buckets paid for by her dad, walking down to the road towards heartbreak and hard work.

Gracie stopped and stared and then lifted her chin.

Hannah wanted to hug her friend. 'Should Jed be with you instead of us?'

Gracie's smile turned a little fixed, but she shook her head. 'Jed's needed at his store. He'll have his work cut out for him there. The sooner he has it up and running, the sooner he can offer supplies to those who need them. Many will have to work on their own houses and fences. Liam's with him and Jude's coming . . .'

Hannah faded out for a bit there. Jude was coming? Helping the townsfolk? Getting involved again, despite himself? Well, she guessed he couldn't get home yet, but still . . .

Gracie was saying, 'With the extra men to dry it out and clean, they can start bringing the stuff back down from your shed. The shop is mostly wood and corrugated iron and will hose down. Jed has a truck with a tank and hose he keeps for summer fire protection. They'll use that to clean.'

'Don't you want him to hose your place out first?'

They'd reached the road – a silted line of brown mud with ankle-deep tyre tracks and footprints crossing back and forth.

Gracie looked across the paddock to her house forlornly sitting in a puddle. 'It needs emptying first. Plus, my house has always been a woman's world and it's fitting that I have my friends with me when I see it for the first time.'

Hannah squeezed her friend's shoulder.

'And tomorrow we'll all go to Nell's house,' Gracie continued, all stiff-backed and stoic.

Nell jammed her lips together and lifted her chin. 'We will. But not tomorrow. Once we've finished here.'

Hannah listened in admiration to these two amazing women and their determination to meet the challenge head-on. They all knew it wouldn't be a quick fix. But they were in it for the long haul. They were the brave ones.

Gracie's house was old and big, and despite it being six steps off the ground, the water had come halfway up the windows.

Liam had said the wood could dry out better than a newer house, but they'd have to throw out the carpets, and strip off any wallpaper. Apparently, houses with gyprock – the newer houses with the internal wall linings – would have to be stripped down to the joists because they'd grow mould and rot. Gracie had wood plank walls. Nell's had gyprock.

Bizarrely, Hannah had learned, old houses made with intact asbestos would dry out well. Asbestos could handle water. The danger with it was related to owners pulling it down when they didn't need to and ending up with a pile of dangerous asbestos they had to dispose of.

The women sloshed down the road in their boots past the Farmer's Friend, a scene of masculine activity and muddy forklifts reversing that they decided to avoid, to the gate of Gracie's driveway. They stopped for a moment. Gracie considered the house in the paddock and lifted her chin. And a small battalion of brave women with buckets set off for the task.

Hannah's eyes widened at the detritus beside the driveway and in the paddock. They passed three children's schoolbags, and when Gracie opened them to find a name, inside she found lunches lovingly made and untouched. In the end, the flood had come so fast. Plastic bags of sandwiches and apples and drink bottles, all coated in brown, waited but would never be eaten.

There were two lawn chairs, tumbled and broken, a bedraggled mop, a tricycle with a red plastic seat and tangled vines in the spokes of the wheels. A pram and a lawnmower were entwined in an odd embrace. A three-burner barbecue upside down was entangled with a pair of flippers. How strong the current must have grown to be able to drag all these things along.

After sloshing through the paddock and the soggy driveway to the house, Gracie, who was in the lead, stopped.

'Can you wait a sec?' She didn't turn, only the question floated back to them as they all stood at the bottom of the stairs.

'Of course,' said Nell and Hannah together.

Gracie put her hand on the rail then lifted it quickly. She wiped her fingers, leaving a dark-brown streak down her trouser leg. She wiped them again and then pulled out her gloves, placing them slowly over her hands, each finger lodged in properly, taking her time. She wasn't looking at the house, just looking at her hands.

When she was ready, she straightened and put her hand back on the rail and climbed the rest of the stairs. 'It's slippery,' she warned.

'Okay,' Hannah responded, while she and Nell waited to be invited in.

Gracie pushed open the slimy door and it jammed on the swollen carpet runner. She pushed harder and a stream of dirty water gushed out. 'Right, then,' she said quietly and shoved it wider until she could see into the hall.

A cloud of the dank, contaminated wetness of sedimented flood pong, a stink that must have hit Gracie first, rolled past and down to Hannah and Nell waiting at the bottom of the steps. Hannah blew out through her lips and tried not to breathe. Pulling a mask out of her pocket, she put it on. Nell glanced at her.

'I'm not keen on getting any of that water into my mouth.'

Nell pulled hers out, too. 'Good thought. Hey, Gracie.'

Gracie turned and Nell said, 'How about a mask so you don't get splashed in your mouth?'

Gracie nodded and followed their lead. 'And you'll need your gloves on. Welcome to my nightmare, ladies. Please come inside.'

Everything is brown, Hannah thought. Even colours that weren't brown were brown. Soaked and silted and slimed. And brown. Hannah could feel the slime beneath her fingers whenever she touched anything or rested her hand on a surface. Even through the gloves, and through the masks, it stank. Featherwood had septic tanks and they'd all been submerged and mixed into the flood waters.

'Photos first,' said Nell.

Hannah hadn't remembered. She'd had the sudden urge to try to fix this for Gracie as fast as she could. But there was no quick fix. There were days and weeks of work, possibly months. And replacement of everything left behind.

Gracie said, 'That's right, photos. I reckon if we all take them and a couple of videos each, you could AirDrop them to me and I'll put them in a folder. That way, we should get most things recorded.'

She looked across at Nell, who was staring down at the wet carpet. 'We'll do the same at your house, Nell.'

Nell nodded, chin up, eyes narrowed. 'Yes.'

While she'd been taking photos of the bathroom, Hannah accidentally snapped a photo of the raw grief on Gracie's face as she stood in the doorway to Oliver's room. Leaning her shoulder against a clean part of the frame above the waterline, Gracie's face had drawn tight and then crumpled.

Hannah put down the phone and stepped closer.

Gracie said, 'I was given so much before Oliver was born. Things people made. And after. It's all ruined now. And all the things Jed restored for me. The furniture I sanded and painted. All Oliver's lovely clothes. And books. And toys.'

She blinked away tears. 'I can't believe a month ago we had a party here. The house looked so beautiful. Gifts people brought for his birthday that day. All gone, too.'

Nell came up to stand beside her, and said softly, 'They're just things, Gracie.' She hugged her gently. 'I learned from last year that only people are important. And memories, they're important. Your lovely party, and what it meant to have such a gathering for Oliver. That sisterhood is still there. That's what matters, Gracie. All the people are safe.'

Gracie straightened off the door, sighed and nodded. 'You're right. But it's sad.'

'It's not sad,' said Hannah. 'It's heartbreaking. But we'll get it right. In time.'

Gracie said softly, 'And, in time, if we get it right . . . What if we fix everything, restore what we can, buy new what we can't, and then a flood comes through again?'

Nobody had an answer to that.

'It's the home of my heart,' Gracie said.

'So let's put it back together,' Hannah said gently. 'And worry about the future later.'

Once the photos were done, the clearing began. They decided to leave the carpet for the men because it was just too heavy. Unless they could cut it up into little pieces, maybe, and take it out a piece at a time? Perhaps they'd try later.

They concentrated first on the kitchen. Opening all the windows – only one had been broken – and stripping it out. They could draw water from the tap outside on the tank and they started on the bench, strewn with flotsam from all over the house that had ended up there.

The fridge had to be thrown out. In fact, all the electrical appliances needed to go. Gracie cautiously hoped she could save the fuel stove. Strange she used to dislike it, she said, with it being so hot in the summer, but now it was more an old friend that she hoped she could restore.

Under the kitchen sink, the plastics cupboard looked so revoltingly dirty Gracie was keen to put all the containers in a big, black plastic bag for the tip.

Hannah wrinkled her brow. 'Put them in the bag, sure, but I'll take them home. We have a big bottle of Milton in the surgery for sterilising baby bottles. I'll make it up in the bath and start soaking things that can go into bleach. I'll stack them and put them in my shed in a new plastic bag until you're ready.'

Nell tilted her head and smiled at her. 'That's a good idea. And they're not heavy to carry.'

Gracie blew out a breath. 'Thanks, Hannah. I guess this is what they mean when people say don't be silly by throwing everything out.'

'Many things have to go,' said Nell.

'But not everything,' said Hannah. 'And we'll think twice with articles you care about.'

With the three of them working, it still took until lunchtime to clear out the kitchen. They left the fridge where it was but pulled it away from the wall. The pile of slimy brown rubbish grew beside Gracie's ruined car and accumulated outside on the flattened, sludgy grass. They hadn't even used their buckets to clean with yet, but soon they would start.

The kitchen floor, like the rest of the house apart from the destroyed rugs, was wood. By the time they'd finished stripping out the last removable item, they were ready for Jed to come in and spray at least the kitchen walls, floors and cupboards with clean water. Then they could start scrubbing.

Chapter Forty-four

Jude

Jude knew he should get home to make sure Xavier had control of everything at Luna Downs. Plus, he needed to stop being a burden on Mavis. Though Mavis had surprised him with a burden of her own. But he couldn't leave these people he'd just met in Featherwood because they didn't deserve this disaster. Nobody did.

Many hands didn't make it lighter, they just made it that little bit faster. In truth, he couldn't quite get over Jed's good humour and philosophical nature. The man was an optimist of the die-hard kind. It was a wonder his wife hadn't pressed a pillow over his head while he slept at night.

Jed kept saying, 'It could have been so much worse.'

This from a man standing in a pool of mire and maelstrom of wreckage in his store. All the windows had blown out with the force of the water, the tin walls had buckled and the doors wouldn't shut. The man was mad.

He caught Liam's slight smile as he shrugged. 'Have you been over to see your house yet?' Jude asked.

'Nah, Gracie will say if they need a hand.'

Was he kidding? Surely, his wife needed him. *More facial Tontine therapy needed right there*, thought Jude.

'I'm going over in half an hour,' said Liam. 'You wanna come, Jude?'

Jude shovelled another pile of wreckage and juggled the spadeful outside. 'Why would I if Jed isn't?'

'Because Hannah's over there,' said Liam with a sly grin.

Stirrer. Normally, nobody would dare to pull Jude's tail. At least, nobody had ever done it and lived, anyway. Liam liked to live dangerously. Jude stared stonily at him. Liam's smile widened and there was just a hint of the tiger beneath.

Jude kept his face straight. 'Mongrel,' he said mildly. Then added, 'Sure, I'll come.'

Liam laughed and Jed looked between them with a 'what did I miss?' question on his face.

They went across at twelve, squelching through the paddock in their gumboots. 'How long do you reckon this will take to dry out?' Jude asked.

Liam shrugged. 'It depends on the rain, doesn't it? A couple of weeks. We'll see it all grow back soon. We have a fair bit of fencing to do, though.'

Jude glanced sideways at Liam. 'So do you work for Jed? Or are you just like his fairy godmother?'

Liam looked at him – straight-faced, irritated – and Jude smiled. *Gotcha*, he thought. *Here's back at you for that Hannah comment.*

'Mongrel,' said Liam, and Jude's mouth twitched.

'Jed's my mate,' Liam supplied finally. 'Let's say I'm independently wealthy and don't need to work. He needs help and he makes me laugh.' He glanced briefly back to the shed, where Jed had the battery radio blaring, and they could hear his surprisingly deep and rich baritone singing along. 'When I came back from the army, I didn't find much amusing. Didn't talk much, either. I reckon if it hadn't been for Jed, I wouldn't have been ready for a relationship, ready for Nell when she came along, and that would have been a damn shame.'

Jude thought about that. About getting over trauma and hard knocks, and the loss of a loved one – like him losing Iris, or in Liam's case, probably the loss of mates in a war. So Jed was a friend who made Liam laugh. A friend who needed help. Who gave Liam purpose until he found his feet.

Jude could see how that worked. Jed wasn't a fool, but he was naive in what he believed as the inherent good of people. He believed in someone's word because Jed's word was his life and how could other people not be the same?

Jude was too cynical for that. And he suspected Liam was as well. So Liam and Jed were an odd pairing, but they also made some sense. Hadn't Jude done something similar with Ben and the guys?

Right on cue Liam asked, 'What's the story with your fellas? They your fairy godmothers, or is it the other way round?'

Jude's mouth twitched again. He couldn't remember the last time he'd smiled twice in an hour. Except when thinking about Hannah. 'Hardly. I keep them dry, fed and clothed, and they work for me. They're not my mates. They're more like down-on-their-luck cousins. They can leave anytime they want.'

'But they haven't?'

'Not yet.'

They made it to the steps just as Nell came out with a black plastic bag that rattled and bulged with whatever it held.

'Need some brawn, sweetheart?' Liam asked, and his lady blushed. Jude looked away and up at the kitchen windows, where he saw Hannah's face, and it felt as if the sun had come out. His mouth curved and he lifted two fingers in salute.

Nell was saying, 'We need the fridge outside. That would be really great. It's the last thing and strong as we women are, we can't move it.'

Liam jerked his head towards Jude. 'Good news I brought the ring-in, then.'

Jude raised his brows. 'I'm a ring-in, am I?'

'You're a bit of a princess, but I reckon you can carry your weight.'

'You're spoiling for a fight.' He saw Nell's face and lifted his hand in an 'ignore us' gesture. 'I'm joking. We've been sledging all morning.'

Hannah came out, and again the day grew brighter, and he forgot all about Liam and Nell and taking the mickey.

He scaled the steps like he'd been pulled on a string. 'How's it going?' he asked, his voice low and his head tilted down to her.

She smiled like she was glad to see him. 'Did I hear there were strong men out here?'

'Ha,' Liam said, 'they only say that when they want us to lift something.'

Jude shrugged and smiled at Hannah. 'I'll take it. Nell mentioned a fridge. Is that all that needs lifting?'

*

It wasn't just the fridge. It was the carpet. And the lounge. And the dining-room table, although it went out onto the verandah because they were going to clean and restore it to its former beauty. Along with the matching wooden chairs. All the cushions were for the tip, though.

They moved the mattresses – there were four of them, and they were heavy blighters – and more rugs and a couple of armchairs. 'You've got a teepee of ruined furniture and furnishings, Gracie.' Jude stared at the mound. 'Or a large bonfire ready to light at the front of the house.'

'It has to go to the tip,' said Liam. 'There are too many plastics. Public works will come get it when the roads open.'

The remaining furniture, wood or steel, had all been shifted out to dry on the verandah. It would take days of work, but it could be restored if someone wanted to do the man or woman hours.

Hannah had a decent-sized pile of plastic bags stuffed with things she was taking back to her place to clean. It looked like a lot of work to Jude, and that was just getting it over there. He turned his mind to working out how he could make it easier for her. 'How about I bring my vehicle over from where I unloaded the boat? We can pile it in there and at least we can drive it as far as the path at the church.'

'Yes, please. That would be great.' And the smile she turned on him made the whole afternoon worthwhile.

'I'll get the boys to help shift it up to your house.'

'Then I'll have to figure out where to put it all.'

He thought about that. 'Start in the carport. Now that the calf's gone, we'll sweep it out and you can bring each bag in one at a time to clean.'

They worked it out and Jude brought his car across and didn't get bogged, despite Liam's scepticism. And Hannah smiled at him with gratitude. They made his day, those smiles.

He glanced back at Gracie's house. Regardless of the hours of work, they hadn't done much at all towards making it liveable. And they were nowhere near getting the power back on. That would take weeks and new electrics. He couldn't see Gracie and Jed moving back into the house anytime soon. Months probably.

He said as much to Hannah as they loaded his car.

'I think you'll be surprised,' she said. 'Gracie's keen to go back to basics. Using oil lamps and the fuel stove, if Liam can get it going again. Apparently, it fuels the hot water system, as well.'

'What about a fridge and phone charging?'

'She said Jed's got a generator that will do the job, and with a new water pump she'll have the kitchen running again soon.'

He hadn't thought about doing the whole thing without power rather than waiting for it all to come back. Man, they were resilient, these people. And he didn't like to have to admit they were more resilient than he'd been after Iris. He'd shut down for a while and he'd had a fully functioning house.

'So you might not have lodgers for the next month, after all?'

'I guess that depends on Nell's house. Nell's is more modern and Gracie's is mostly wood. But I'm sure she and Liam will be resourceful.'

'No doubt.'

'Plus, she can always move into Liam and Molly's house, too.'

'So that leaves . . .?'

'Audrey's husband arrives today.'

He'd forgotten about Audrey, the baby and twins. 'How did her house fare?'

'Audrey's had enough bad luck, so I'm happy to say she got off lightly, flood-wise. The water didn't come up her paddock all the way like at Nell's. She's on more of a hill than I thought she was. A bit like Mavis.'

She grinned at him. 'How'd you go staying out with Mavis?'

'She is one tough nut. Real farming stock. And Archie knows his way around the farm work, too. I think Leo's found a second home.'

'I suspect there are worse places to feel welcome than at Mavis's.' Hannah's eyes sparkled and he enjoyed her delight. There wasn't a lot to be delighted about in his world except for Leo. Yes, thank the stars for Leo, too.

Hannah went on. 'She's funny. Though I haven't known her long.'

'She's been very good to us. And Tesla. I had to take him with me in case he went on a bender.'

They heard Liam's phone ring and everyone stopped to listen. There was no privacy here. 'Yes, Jed?' A pause. 'Have you?' Another pause. 'Did he? And after that, then? When?' After a short pause, he said, 'We'll be there.'

Jude looked at him with the question and Liam said, 'Jed's found a bloke with a backhoe.' Then he said to Hannah, 'He's willing to work on a small bypass for your driveway now, if you're happy with that?'

'Absolutely.' The idea that people would be able to drive up and down her driveway was a step in the right direction. It would make life easier for Jed with all the transfer of shop supplies, which was probably why it was prioritised.

'Jed said he'd make a small detour around the slip that's enough to drive up if they have to. He'll dump some gravel on it.'

Hannah nodded vigorously.

'Then the bloke is going to help us with that washaway between Mavis and Nell this afternoon,' he told Jude. 'Five o'clock. I said we'd meet him there.'

'A backhoe.' Jude rubbed his chin. 'Maybe we can knock it over in a couple of hours, at least enough to be able to drive over it.'

'Yep,' said Liam. 'I'd like to get out to Nell's place, and I'm guessing you'd like to get home.'

'Yeah, I'd like to go home, check it out, make sure everything's fine, but I'll be back. And once the roads open, there's nothing to stop that.'

Liam flat-stared him. 'You decided to be part of the community, did you?'

Jude flat-stared him back. 'Most of you, anyway, are not bad people.'

It took until late afternoon, but Liam and Jude and Bob the backhoe man created a drive-through causeway where there had been a crevice and wall of broken road. That was good enough for off-road vehicles, anyway. If they had another gully rusher, it'd probably all wash away again.

'It should do until the council can come and do something. They'll make it more substantial and permanent,' Bob said, and they waved him off as he bounced away on his backhoe down the road.

Both men drove separately back to town, with Jude peeling off to Mavis's to pick up Leo and Tesla. From there, they'd head to Luna Downs.

Liam was picking up Nell, then heading to her house to see how it had survived.

Chapter Forty-five

Nell

Nell sat beside Liam, bouncing on the truck seat through the ruts and potholes and finally over the new culvert he and Jude had built today with the backhoe man.

It was nearly dark, but she'd wanted to come today. The thought of lying in her bed at Hannah's for another night imagining the worst made her skin itch. And Liam had understood. He always did.

They were getting close now.

She'd been there for Gracie's first sight of her house and now it was her turn. Her belly roiled, and she immediately thought of last year and the ashes and ruin. That visceral pang of loss and disbelief.

Having seen Gracie's poor house, at least she knew what to expect. The brown sludge. The stink. Hopefully, they'd find the actual dwelling still standing.

Inside, she expected hers to be as bad as Gracie's. But when they bounced up the rutted drive and over the hill, she could see the water had receded all the way back to the creek. Yes, the flats were trodden brown grass and her gardens had been buried and driven through when Liam had come to get her, but the house was still there.

She stared disbelievingly. The flood mark on the wall at the front was so much lower than she'd expected. True, the water had gone through, but it hadn't risen much higher than when she'd left – maybe knee height, at worst.

Her heart began thumping because there was a possibility that the possessions and pieces she'd put on the bed and on the table could be safe. And in the cupboards? Maybe halfway up the cupboards would be okay, too? Maybe not everything had been ruined. Maybe not even her mattress . . .

Inside, where she rushed as soon as Liam had stopped the truck, the top shelf of the cupboards was fine. It was a little damp with moisture, but not wet. The bottom shelves, well, yes, they were ruined, and the contents were thrown around with the water and coloured brown, but unlike Gracie, Nell didn't have cupboard doors. So really, they could just pull everything out from knee height down, discard them and then clean the shelves.

She turned to Liam. 'It's not so bad.'

He pulled her back against him and studied the room more pragmatically. The rugs were sludgy and the couch was ruined, as were the bottoms of the curtains. 'It's a lot.'

'No, not compared to Gracie's loss.' And those spoken words were accompanied by a funny sickness in her gut. 'Oh,' she said quietly, and pulled away, walking quickly through to the bedroom.

Her eyes widened as there, on the bed, untouched by the flood, sat the small table and chair that Liam had made for her. She bit her lip hard, struggling to comprehend the obvious. Her most treasured possessions were safe. She tried as her throat closed to hold back the tears. She hadn't lost what she thought she had. And she didn't know how she felt about that.

Liam came to stand beside her and smiled. 'You lifted them up.'

'I did,' she said, but her voice choked out the words on a sob.

He squeezed her gently. 'What's wrong, love?'

She felt like an idiot. She didn't lose control. Ever. 'I should be happy. Should be over the moon. There's really not that much damage.'

'I think you're a little bit early with your optimism,' he said. 'It's not great. Have you been taking lessons from Jed?'

She laughed at that. 'No, but compared to Gracie's house . . .' She sobbed once.

'Ah,' he said, and pulled her close against him. 'You don't have to compare to Gracie's. You lost everything last year. None of this feeling guilty, because Gracie's house is more badly affected than yours.'

Is that what this was? Survivor's guilt? She looked at him. How had he known that? God, she felt so stupid.

She took a deep breath and leaned up and kissed him. She was still weepy but better, and feeling grateful for the man holding her. So grateful. 'I think you're right. I am feeling guilty.'

He pulled his arm tighter around her and nudged her into his chest, leaning down to kiss her gently on her lips. Tenderly. And then a little bit insistently, until he groaned. 'I've wanted to do that for days.'

Her mouth curved under his. 'Me too.'

He hugged her closer before he let her go. 'So how about you move in with me and Molly instead of staying at Hannah's? We'll get this done from there, and then you can come home.'

'Do you think it needs much structurally?'

He narrowed his eyes at the wall boards that were already swelling. 'The lower gyprock needs cutting out, and any of the particle board in the kitchen, but it's not major, just fiddly. And the water didn't go as high as the power points. It depends on how long it takes to source a sparky to come out and check that it's safe. Then there's the painting.'

She teased, 'I could do what Gracie's suggested. Get one of Jed's generators and just live with lamps.'

He smiled. 'And a barbecue because you don't have a fuel stove. Or a hot water heater that's connected to the fuel stove. But you could live without hot water.'

'Hmm. Maybe I'll live with you and Mol. Until I can get the power on.'

'I have a really nice bed,' he offered solemnly.

'I know,' she said just as solemnly. 'I've actually spent a few nights there.'

He tugged her hand and pulled her away. 'It's getting dark. We'll come back tomorrow. Let me show you my really nice bed.'

She laughed. 'As long as you show me your really nice shower first.'

He stopped and pulled her even closer, looking down into her eyes, his face serious and full of admiration and something that made her heart rate bound as if she was running uphill.

Two spots of colour grew high in his cheeks and she understood suddenly that he was embarrassed. 'And when your house is done, how about we have a party here, just a few friends, and maybe your mother and mine.'

A party? To celebrate the house again? And then she knew. Her dear, sweet, inarticulate man.

'What are you saying, Liam?' She furrowed her brows, pretending to be confused, but inside her heart thumped and her breath hitched. 'You want to party with me?'

His mouth curved into that smile that could melt her bones. He saw her understanding. And her happiness. 'Party. In so many ways. Yeah.'

His finger lifted and stroked her cheek with all the tenderness he always showed to her. 'Will you marry me, Nell? Here in this home that you love. Please. I'd get down on one knee, but . . .' They both wrinkled their noses at the muddy floor. 'And we'll party right after we get married.'

She leaned up and before she kissed him said, 'I can't think of anything I want to do more, Liam.'

Chapter Forty-six

Hannah

Suddenly Hannah's house echoed with silence again. There were no childish shouts, toddler squeals, baby cries and women talking. Even the dog and the calf were gone. Jed and Gracie, plus little Oliver, would be a part of the household for a while yet, but they were all down at Gracie's and wouldn't be back for half an hour.

She had time for a hot shower, thanks to the gas gods who allowed cooking and hot water, and then to sit in silence before they came home.

Molly had departed, but in typical Molly fashion, she'd changed all the sheets in the now empty rooms – and taken them with her to wash – and cleaned the bathroom before she left. Apparently, Liam had rung and shared the news that Nell would be moving temporarily to their place, and Molly had left to make a feast for tea, taking Grin, Nell's dog, with her.

Hannah, Molly and Gracie would go with Nell tomorrow, because Gracie said her house would take weeks and maybe they could sort Nell's much faster.

Audrey's husband had arrived and taken his family home to the fabulous news that their dwelling had remained untouched in all the disaster. Hannah admitted to a silent relief for herself, because living with a brand-new baby and two four-year-old twins had certainly been a little too interesting. She was happy to have them, but now that they were gone, she wished the growing family well.

The hot stream of shower water pummelled the tension from her shoulders, and the slight ache in her back from all the lifting today eased as well. Soft light from the candles increased the calm seeping into her, and she leaned her head back to put her face under the spray. Darn if she couldn't manage fine without electricity. For a little while.

Although, Jed had installed one of those small generators outside the kitchen to run the tank pump and the fridge, and an extension cord ran through to her office to a four-switch power board, ready for use if they had a medical emergency that needed power. That also meant she could charge her phone when needed. And she had wi-fi from her phone.

Hers was a whole different world to that of the families along the street below. She was so lucky at the top of the hill. Lucky also that her hill hadn't avalanched down and taken the house with it when it took her car.

Unfortunately, someone in town with a phone had sent a dramatic video of the vehicle and the telegraph pole – thankfully, after she'd jumped out and Jude had taken her away. Thank the small mercies for that, but it had still made the six o'clock news. Which was why her father had contacted her and offered help. He'd recognised her vehicle.

She turned off the shower and stepped out. Then she dried quickly and dressed, rubbing inexplicable goosebumps, because suddenly she felt oddly nervous. A shiver ran through her, and as if in answer to her edginess, her phone rang. It was Jude. Who had she expected? But instantly she felt safer.

'Hey.' His deep, intimate drawl caused that *Jude spark*, which was what she was calling it now: the warmth that seemed to flare in her belly when she heard his voice, or when he was standing close. Or when she thought about that kiss. 'How are you?'

She knew now that she could lean on him and he on her, so why didn't she just tell him how she really felt? 'Honestly?'

'Always,' he said, and she liked the sound of that, them being honest with each other all the time.

'Okay, then. I feel better just hearing your voice. I was sitting here thinking about the fact that everyone had seen my car on the six o'clock news, and whether Porter would see it in jail.'

'You can't worry about stuff like that.' His voice was gruff. 'And I'm only a phone call away. Don't ever think I won't come.'

'I do feel better knowing that.' And that was just about enough honesty for now, she decided.

'How's your house?' he asked.

'Surprisingly empty. I think it echoes.' She glanced at the clock on the wall. 'Another ten minutes and Gracie, Jed and Oliver will be back. But for the moment, it's very peaceful on my own. How's it going for you at Luna Downs?'

'Better than town. We had no water problems and we've still got power coming in from Armidale.'

'What about the man you left in town?'

'Tesla is doing a great job. I'm proud of him.'

'Are you coming back in to Featherwood tomorrow?'

'Yep, we'll all come in. The fellas and I will go to the Farmer's Friend. The most sensible thing is to get the store up and running so people can buy what they need to do their own repairs.'

'Jed will be pleased for the help. What about Leo? Are his sugars keeping stable?'

'Pretty much. He's good with what he eats. He said Archie promised to let him know if he was acting strange, so I'm happier for him to help if he's got Archie with him.'

Clever boy. 'Kids are so adaptable.'

'More than me, I reckon.' She smiled at that. 'Thought I'd send them over to help Gracie, so that I'm not far away in case anything happens. I worry he'll do too much, have a high or low. Or that he'll sit down somewhere and no one will notice he's unconscious.'

And there it was. The ever-present worry and responsibility he still had to get used to. 'That's unlikely, Jude.'

'But possible,' he said.

'Yes, it is possible, but everyone's going to Nell's tomorrow, even Gracie. We're going to try to knock it over in a day before we all go back to Gracie's. The boys could come with me.'

'I'm fine with that. He'll be with a doctor and a nurse.'

'And Archie.'

'That's true. Young Archie has brains, too,' he said, and she could hear the smile in his voice. 'I'll check with Mavis if she's okay with that.'

'Liam's right. You have become a part of the community.'

'Liam talks too much,' he pretended to growl, and she smiled and heard a truck pull up outside. She knew the sound because Jed had driven up and down since the driveway had been fixed picking up supplies from the shed. 'Jed and Gracie are here.'

'I'll let you go,' he said, but it didn't sound like he wanted to, and the thought made that *Jude spark* spread wider. 'It's great talking to you.'

'You too.' Wonderful, really. 'Thank you.'

'Bye,' he said, and before she could reply the line went dead. It had been good talking to him. She had the feeling that there'd be more of those conversations. She hoped so.

Feeling still a little dreamy, she filled the kettle with water and put it on the stove to heat. Her guests would want a cup of tea, right after they had a shower.

Molly had left a big bowl of aromatic bolognaise in a pot on the stove. All Hannah had to do was boil pasta. Easy-peasy, and the amount might even fill Jed.

Chapter Forty-seven

Mavis

It was two days after her dunking, the day after the little twins were found, that Mavis began to have pains in her chest. At first, she thought she might have inhaled some water and was brewing a chest infection, but she didn't have a cough. Or, more likely, it was delayed muscle strain from when she'd been hanging onto that steering wheel so tight – like the Grim Reaper hangs on to his scythe. And it had gone away for a couple of days.

It had been a big week and she'd never really been right since that scare in the river. She didn't think she could ever drive a car again, even though she'd managed to take Jed's small truck to the doctor's that day. She'd been shaking by the time she got home and had decided it was the last truck she'd drive.

What sort of life was it if she was too old to drive a car? Her eyesight was going and she was losing her nerve. She never wanted to be old. But the kid had staved it off for a few years, anyway. If she lived through this, Archie could drive from now on. They'd only be going to Featherwood, after all.

But today, she couldn't ignore the dull ache crushing the centre of her chest and along her jaw. It was definitely getting worse, and now she felt sick and faint. She'd been trying to hide it from Archie while she made breakfast, but he watched her closely, frowning, his gaze narrowed, his mouth tight.

'You okay, Gran?'

'Fine. Indigestion. Toast's stuck.' She pulled her hand away from her sternum and smiled. It was probably a rictus of a smile 'cause the kid didn't look reassured. 'Hurry up. They'll be here soon. I'm so glad you have a good friend in Leo. I like his dad, too.'

Then the big off-roader pulled up, and Archie kissed her when he left. He didn't always do that, and she savoured it. His young cheek against hers. The smell of him. Sunlight soap and sweaty hair.

'Love you, Gran.'

'Love you, too, kid. Very much.' He'd changed her life. 'And I'm proud of you for helping people today.'

'I could stay home if you're not well?'

'Off you go.' *Breathe.* 'Take your lunch.' *Breathe.* 'Hurry up.' She had to keep her sentences short because the breathlessness was getting worse. If she didn't shut up he'd stay, and the last thing she needed was the kid to be here if she died.

He hung back, not sure what was wrong but not feeling it was right. Observant little blighter. And he had good instincts. Too good. 'See you when I get home.'

'And I'll want'—pause for breath—'to hear all about it.' She was having trouble getting the words out, but the car was here and they were waiting.

She gestured to the door. 'Go.' She put a bit of mean into it, to make him leave.

Finally, after one more worried backward glance, Archie ran down the steps and climbed in. Mavis watched, fist pressed hard into her sternum, until the truck disappeared from view.

Chapter Forty-eight

Hannah

Just after eight-thirty, Jude dropped the boys off at Hannah's house, and she decided she liked starting her day like that. Seeing Jude. He wore well-fitting jeans and an open-necked, long-sleeved shirt, the blue of which brought a sapphire tinge to his grey eyes.

'I thought you might like some fruit.' He brought her Granny Smith apples in a box with lemons and limes from his orchard, and she got to watch as he carried them into her kitchen, all broad back and strong arms.

As he leaned to put the box on the table, she teased, 'An apple a day keeps the doctor away.'

His eyes narrowed as he pretended to take the box back. 'You won't get them if that's true.'

And now she was blushing like a schoolgirl. This man made her silly. 'They look wonderful. Thank you.'

'Leo has his bag and Mavis packed Archie a lunch, so the boys are right for food. Just ring if you want me to come get them, otherwise you can drop them at the Farmer's Friend on your way back.'

'Got it.' They shared a smile and then he was gone.

*

Five minutes later, Hannah climbed into her slightly worse-for-wear car. 'Okay, boys, let's go. Early start. It's going to be a big day.'

The boys climbed in after they'd exclaimed long and loud over the telegraph-pole-shaped ding in her boot. She'd have to get that fixed when the roads reopened, because right now she couldn't use her boot. Everything they carried for the day had been tossed onto the back seat to jostle for space with the boys.

Once they were all sitting in the car, she heard Leo say to Archie, 'Well, go on, ask.'

Archie cleared his throat. 'Um, Dr Rogan . . .'

She smiled into the rear-view mirror. 'Call me Hannah, both of you.'

Archie said, 'Hannah,' in a small voice. 'I'm a bit worried about my gran. I don't think she looked well this morning.'

Hannah frowned and clicked the handbrake back on again.

'I wondered if we could just drop in quickly.' Archie's sentences gathered speed. 'And check on her. Check she's all right.'

Their eyes met in the rear-view mirror, and Archie's were filled with concern.

Hannah's heart went out to the kid. She'd seen it before, the almost grown-up protectiveness of the woman who was his world. 'Of course. What do you think is wrong with her, Archie?'

'She was rubbing her chest.'

Hannah blinked and said, 'Hang on a sec. I'll grab my medical bag, just in case.' She opened her door and hopped out, strode fast into the house and picked up the black zippered case. On a considered thought, she took the AED off the wall of the surgery, where it hung for emergencies. She didn't want to need an automatic defibrillator, but chest pain was a good reason to take it.

She dropped all the equipment onto the passenger's seat, and she climbed back into the car. Once buckled in, she connected her phone to the Bluetooth and punched in Nell's number, then began driving down the driveway.

It took several rings before Nell answered. 'Morning, Boss. What do you need?'

'Have you left Liam's place yet?'

'We're just about to. Liam's coming with me today, seeing as Jude's helping Jed.'

'How about you meet me at Mavis's? Archie said she had chest pain this morning, and I'm concerned.' She glanced in the mirror when she said that. *Damn*, she'd forgotten the boys were there. Archie's eyes had widened.

Nell said, 'Will do. Be there in ten.'

'Okay. We'll be there about the same time. We'll check Mavis – just a quick visit, I'm sure she's fine – and then head out to your place.'

'Sounds good.'

'I've got the boys in the car.'

There was a pause before Nell said, 'Got it.'

Chapter Forty-nine

Mavis

Mavis watched the big four-wheel drive vehicle rumble out of the driveway carrying Archie with the Waughs, thinking, *Goodbye, my darling boy.* She was no fool.

She dug into the drawer under the telephone and pulled out the letter she'd written to Archie three days ago, after her conversation with Jude. Grasping it in her fingers, she sank into the soft lounge chair she liked to watch television in. The one the kid used to fight her over when it first arrived, purchased with the insurance money from the fire. Now he didn't even try to beat her to it. They'd had a good thing going.

She'd had a word to Jude – she'd caught a lucky break having him stay with them in the flood – and she'd liked everything about the man. So she'd asked if anything happened to her, could he take Archie like he took those alcoholic fellows. Keep him until he could inherit the farm she'd willed to him. She'd explained that Archie's mother couldn't take the farm, that it was in trust with a trustee, but she could take her boy back to hell. Mavis had left her money, but she would lose it if she took Archie away from Featherwood.

Jude had said, 'Is there something you're not telling me, Mavis?'

'Well?' she'd pushed. 'Will you, or won't you?'

'If the worst happens, then yes, I will,' he'd replied, gaze narrowed but unflinching. And she knew he wouldn't go back on his word. They'd phoned the solicitor and talked it all through. Tied Jude in with Gracie and Jed and Archie's wishes like Jude suggested.

Jed had been the first she'd thought of for Archie after that doctor's appointment in Armidale but Jude was a solid bloke who had Leo. She liked a lot about Leo, and Archie would need a close friend when she was gone. The specialist told her she was a time bomb and needed to have a big operation to try to fix the blood supply to her heart. In Sydney. But it didn't look good.

No way, Mavis had scoffed. Her heart was wearing out because she was old. Old didn't need fixing. It needed rest. Looks like she was going to get rest.

She'd continued to Jude, 'I've got money. Gracie's the executor of my will, and a bloke in Armidale is the trustee, so they'll make sure the kid pays his way.'

'He won't need money to stay with us. But you made Gracie executor, not Jed?' He'd looked surprised and she'd laughed and shaken her head.

'Gracie has the money head on her shoulders and Jed's brain's up there in the clouds with all his newfangled ideas.'

The pain swamped her and the dizziness grew. Mavis let it have its way. *At least I managed to avoid the flu needle*, she thought with a weak smile. And Archie had got his tetanus jab. Score one to the old bird.

She and Archie had been through some tough times, she knew, but he'd be a strong, kind man when he grew up because of it. She smiled sadly. It was a terrible shame that she wouldn't be here to know the man he'd be.

Odd thing, this, to know she was dying. One saving grace that she was here on her own farm, not dependent on strangers in her last moments.

Light spiralled down as the pain opened like a flower in her chest, until, in a flash, it was gone.

Suddenly she was young again, side by side with her lovely William, their beautiful daughter, the farmhouse newly built. Mavis smiled.

Chapter Fifty

Hannah

Nell and Hannah arrived at Mavis's at the same time.

Hannah got out with her bag and the AED and leaned in the window to the boys. 'How about you let us go in and have a word with your gran, Archie?'

In her head she was thinking, *Great-grandmother, not gran.* Mavis was no spring chicken, but she was fit. Look how she'd bounced back from that dunking the other day.

The boys nodded and stayed put, and she and Nell walked together to the front door. Nell took the AED from Hannah. Liam came over to stand beside the boy's window.

As he leaned on the car, Hannah heard Liam say, 'You did a good job telling the doctor.'

'She said I had to listen to my instincts,' Archie responded.

And then they were up the stairs and knocking on the door. They knocked twice with no answer, so Hannah turned the door-handle and stepped inside, with Nell on her heels. Down the hallway and into the kitchen, then through to the little living room.

They could see the back of Mavis's head. She was facing the television. 'Mavis?'

When they moved forward, they found her smiling, but when Hannah touched the pale, wrinkled skin of Mavis's hand, it had already chilled. Mavis was long gone. A white envelope fluttered to the floor.

Archie sat on the floor beside his grandmother with his head on her cold thigh, the open note in his lap. Nodding. Holding back the sobs, saying, 'She died at home. She wanted to die at home.' Over and over.

Dear Archie, my mate, best great-grandson ever.

Sorry I have to leave, but I've had a good life. The doc in Armidale said I was a time bomb – it's much less time than I expected, though.

I'm pleased I got to spend my last time here with you and not in some Sydney hospital. You remember that.

Of course, you do what you think is best, but I did ask Leo's dad if he'd take you if anything happened, seeing as how he takes vagrants. I reckon you'd be fine.

Nah, you're a good kid. The best. I've loved every minute of having you. I reckon I lived this extra two years because of you. And anyway, I probably would've got booked if I got you to drive for the next five years without a licence.

I left you the farm. It would've been better if you were eighteen, but rent the place out until then (Gracie will help

*you), and you can teach Leo about cows and move back in
when you finish school.*

Love ya. See you in the next life.

Your gran

Chapter Fifty-one

Jude

Mavis had the biggest darn turnout for a funeral that Jude had seen for a long while, and the people who couldn't fit inside the church spilled out the doors and filled the whole churchyard.

The bells rang in farewell to one of the building's most consistent Catholic churchgoers, and the arched windows were open so the mass carried to the outside through the frames. Several strategically placed microphones and speakers Liam had helped arrange meant they could all hear.

Jude couldn't forget the day Mavis died. Hannah had been amazing, so gentle, sitting beside the boy as he said goodbye, saying, 'Take your time, Archie. She loved you so much. She'll always be with you.'

Now, today, Archie held it together like the champion he was during the long Catholic mass Mavis would have savoured. They'd suggested a shorter one, but Archie had shaken his head and said, 'Gran liked the long ones.'

Archie's mother, Mavis's granddaughter, had been as burnt out and lost as Jude had suspected she would be, and during the interview with the solicitor afterwards, she'd suggested she (and her sleazy boyfriend) could sell the farm and take Archie back to Sydney.

Archie had turned panicked eyes to Jude, and he'd shaken his head and mouthed, *No way*.

When the solicitor explained that Mavis had left Archie the farm and her granddaughter a lump sum of equal value which would be redirected to a charity if she took Archie away from Featherwood, Archie's mother had left in a huff with the cash.

Archie went home with Jude and Leo but asked if Jed and Gracie could move into his gran's house while theirs was out of action, so it wouldn't be empty. He took his gran's favourite chair with him to Jude's, and Jude's team whipped up another room at the end of the woolshed so Archie had his own space.

As Jude had hoped, after a few, tiny, teenage skirmishes, Archie and Leo became inseparable. It was Leo who told Archie that his mother's ashes were scattered on the hill overlooking their house at Luna Downs, and plans were made for Mavis.

Two months later, on the day Mavis would have turned eighty-two, Jude watched Archie carry the urn up the hill on Mavis's farm in front of them all. The afternoon was still and beautiful, blue skies and the occasional butterfly and soaring birds amidst the sound of cicadas in the grass and trees. They were having a picnic beside the water tank on the hill, and Jude carried the folded table to set up on.

They didn't need chairs because Archie and Leo had been tractoring stones from Luna Downs, and with Jude's help had fit them together to create a circle of benches with stone ends, where a dozen people could sit in a semicircle and look out over the house below and towards the creek.

A person could see nearly all of the farm below, and Archie had wanted to bring his great-grandmother's ashes up here on an auspicious day. His shoulders were straight and his head held high, even if his lips were jammed together. The kid had an inner strength that made Jude want to lay his hand on his shoulder. But this strength was Archie's gift to his gran and all Jude could do was marvel.

Leo and Jude stood behind him on one side, and Gracie and Jed on the other. Jed had an esky with cold drinks. Nell, Liam, Hannah and Molly carried baskets of food and flowers, and once they reached the top, they set about creating a joyful space to celebrate her life over the checked tablecloths that were Mavis's favourites.

Once it was done, Archie stepped forward from where he'd been staring at the house. He said simply, 'Thank you for doing this and sharing it with me.'

He turned the urn slowly in his hands, shook his head and looked at the sky. 'That's where she is. Up there. And everywhere. Not in here.' His chin went up. 'Gran, thank you for being there when I needed you. I know you'll always be here for me.'

He unscrewed the top of the urn and began to sprinkle the cremation ash into the wind that carried drifts out over the edge to the paddocks below. The granules disappeared into the grass to become part of the hill.

Chin up, Archie turned back to Jude, who nodded approval, and the kid forced a smile. 'Let's eat.'

*

In the weeks and months during the flood recovery, Jude's Crew – the name coined by Jed – had become a thriving business known for good work at reasonable prices. For those families affected by flood damage, it had proved incredibly difficult to source tradesmen from the big towns with the whole state suffering under widespread devastation and need.

For Jude to be paid, he needed an ABN, especially for insurance work, so that had been the path he was pushed down. A path that took him and his band of not-so-merry men out of Luna Downs and into Featherwood as required.

And they were required a lot.

Jude's Crew worked their way down the lower side of the main street of Featherwood, stripping out walls and electrics, and then, when the house bones were dry, restoring and rewiring.

Tesla, jolted by desperate people needing help, had admitted that prior to his wife and children leaving him, he'd been an electrician with a gambling and drinking habit. Hence the sudden and debilitating descent into vagrancy and loss of self.

Once his credentials had been confirmed, it seemed Featherwood could heal faster than likewise affected towns because of this core of determined workers and Jed's seemingly unending supply of building materials.

Every flooded house needed all the power points and switches removed, and sometimes even light fittings, if the building had been immersed past its ceiling. Jed began to build two flood mounds, like islands in the middle of his paddock, one for Gracie's house and one for the store, to future-flood-proof the buildings. It would take a while.

Until everything was completed, they'd be staying at Archie's rental property. When they could, they'd restore their own house, but for the moment they showered Mavis's little home with love and concentrated on the store.

Jude watched Hannah settle into the life of the only GP in Featherwood, but something had happened between them. There was no doubt she'd pulled back from him. Despite the phone calls, and the drop-ins when he took Leo to see her, he'd noticed her growing reserve, and he had no idea why. In the early days, he'd dared to hope they were moving forward, but lately, he'd begun to think she'd changed her mind about their connection.

Did the fact that he had five men, plus two teenage boys, as his responsibility act as a deterrent, or had she just gone cold on him?

Or was it something else? A worry? Something she wasn't telling him?

Either way, he wanted more and didn't know how to shift on. He felt like an idiot but he cared too much to blow his last chance. He needed advice. Eventually, he manned up and asked for it from Liam, knowing he would hate every second of the experience.

He found Liam unloading a truck of feed bags at Jed's store. 'Mate. Reckon I've done something to annoy Hannah?'

Liam paused, furrowing his forehead. 'Why ask me?' He went back to unloading, leaving Jude nonplussed.

Jeez. Not a helpful response. 'I wondered if Nell had said anything.'

'Nope,' Liam said, stone-faced, still moving bags from the forklift.

Jude raked his hair. Maybe this hadn't been a good idea. 'What do you mean, nope?'

Liam shrugged. Scratched his ear. 'No, Nell hasn't said anything.'

'Well, do you think you could ask her?' He'd known this would be hard, but not this hard.

Now there was twinkle in the mongrel's eye. A shake of the head. 'Nope.'

Jude resisted the urge to shake the man. Liam would just shake him back and then where would they be. Pushing like schoolboys. He nearly smiled at the thought. 'You're not very helpful.'

'Cry me a river,' Liam quipped, and then he smiled. 'You want me to be helpful?'

Finally. As he suspected. He'd been having him on. 'Yes.'

Liam shrugged. 'Take her a bunch of flowers and ask her out. Finalise the time.'

The obvious – it couldn't be that easy. 'That's it? The big advice?' Great. 'Do you reckon it will work?'

Liam shrugged. 'Dunno. Good luck. I'm not a fortune-teller.'

What a waste of time. And embarrassing. Jude turned to leave, depressed.

Liam said quietly, 'It's good to see you squirm. It took me a year to ask Nell to marry me. I thought I was the only useless one at making a move on a woman.'

The next time Jude drove into Dorrigo for supplies, he bought a big pot of sunflowers. There wasn't much choice and he'd never been a carnation fan. He'd always bought irises for Iris. That had made sense, and it only happened once a year when they were out in flower for a month.

But Hannah was Hannah, and for some reason sunflowers made him think of her. He saw them at a farm gate on the way into town, and they'd stayed in his mind during other options. Hannah was bright and vibrant, and she suited sunflowers. But the pot was huge.

His life was never easy.

He turned up to Hannah's back door, not the surgery entrance, after five-thirty, thinking that the consulting rooms closed at five and everybody should be out by half past. Except that he walked straight into Nell with his gargantuan pot and the flowers waving like a choir ready to launch into song.

'Ohhhh, nice flowers,' said Nell. She smirked. Smirked!

'Yeah.' Of all the luck. He bet she'd tell Liam and he'd be in for a ribbing. 'You should get Liam to buy you some.'

Nell showed her teeth and there was a little bit of wicked in it. 'He told me he suggested flowers to you.'

'Did he.' After saying he wouldn't ask Nell for help – the traitor. Jude couldn't think of anything else to say, so he settled for, 'Is Hannah in here?'

Still grinning, Nell nodded. 'Indeed she is.' And on her way down the path to her car she hummed that song about pina coladas. Bloody stirrers. Both of them.

He waited until she'd gone. No way was he doing this with her watching. Nell drove out and he moved to the back door, put the flowers to the side out of sight and knocked.

There was no answer.

Maybe she was in the shower or changing into her flannel bee pyjamas. He smiled as he wiped his pot-stained palms on his legs. Or she could be slipping into something slinky? *A man could dream.*

The door opened, and Hannah stood there wrapped in a white towel, all rosy-skinned legs and long neck and damp décolleté. Better even. It seemed entirely possible he'd died and gone to heaven.

'Oops.' She shook her head at him. 'I thought it was Nell coming back. Come in, Jude. I'll just get dressed.'

Such a crying shame, his libido yodelled. 'You don't have to on account of me.'

'I definitely do, especially on account of you.' He heard the smile in her voice as she disappeared out of sight. 'Put the jug on.'

He could still come in. The door hadn't shut in his face – he'd take that.

He cast around in the kitchen and saw the long-spouted kettle on the stove. Carried it to the sink and filled it from the tap – the electricity was back on in Featherwood, so the tap worked and he didn't have to go outside to get water from the tank.

The power had taken six weeks.

Six weeks of expensive petrol generators for those lucky enough to have them.

Six weeks of candles and people cooking on their barbecues, rain, hail or shine, with so much bottled gas required that Jed had bought a franchise in refillable gas cylinders.

Six weeks of filling jugs with water from a tank outside, grateful that they had a tank. At least the rain had made sure all the reservoirs were full.

Once public works had been through and the trucks came to clear all the rubbish that was sitting in the streets, and the council came and resurfaced the roads, they'd been able to see what needed doing.

Jude's Crew became the sought-after team, something he hadn't expected. And the genuine appreciation of service was doing the fellas more good than all the months of work on the farm had achieved. There was work enough here for another year.

He'd even accepted the truth that he had real friends in Liam and Jed. For a man who had held himself apart for so long, he was now on a first-name basis with the whole town.

He enjoyed his verbal sniping with Liam – the bloke was a stirrer – and they both enjoyed the mutual sledging they indulged in, though it annoyed the women. He liked Jed, too, though he still shook his head at the man's optimism, or maybe that was envy – with his beautiful, loving wife and son, and Gracie knowing her man wasn't perfect but adoring him, anyway.

Nobody cared about him that way. He couldn't even pin down Hannah to one night out, let alone a discussion of the future. He'd known from the moment he met her that she was the one, his light in the darkness he'd climbed out of, but he still felt she was out of his league. A doctor. Gorgeous. Yet that didn't stop him wanting to get to know her, to pursue this attraction and hope. To let her warmth and humour and kindness wash through him. So here he was, in one last-ditch effort, despite the cooling off he'd been subjected to over the last weeks.

Hannah came back, bringing with her the scent of citrus and flowers. And wearing a pair of white linen pants and a soft blue top the same colour as her eyes. He liked the snug V-neck.

'So, Jude Waugh. Welcome. To what do I owe the pleasure of this visit?'

Suddenly, it was easy to tell the truth. He didn't need a prompt or a suggestion for that one. 'I have a gift for you, and a lifetime ago, we talked about a night out. I want to set the date.'

He watched her face but couldn't read the expression. Her smile had disappeared as if she'd thought of something that troubled her. He didn't want to be that something that troubled her.

She said, 'I'd like that,' but there was caution in it, and she tilted her head at him. 'When?'

'Friday. Dinner,' he said, off the top of his head. What day was it today?

'Done. And the gift? Can't see it?' She looked amused now, because his relief must have shown.

'Ah.' With a smile, he turned back and opened the back door.

'Spare me, it's not an animal, is it?' There was definite concern in her voice – she still hadn't got over having the calf as a lodger – and he laughed.

'It's quieter than that.' He reached down and picked up the pot, then brought the profusion of sunflowers into the room like an armful of happy faces.

She laughed out loud, her delight obvious. Score. 'Oh, they are glorious. And just what I needed.'

He put them inside the door on the floor and they lit up the room. Perfect. Like she lit up any room she was in for him.

'Thank you,' she said shyly, 'I really do love them.'

'Friday,' he said. 'I'll pick you up at six and we'll go out to the place on the escarpment past Dorrigo. They have a restaurant there.'

She frowned in thought for a few seconds, then her face cleared. 'Lookout Mountain Retreat? I saw that when I went to Coffs Harbour one day. Have you been there?'

'No, but I know people who have. They said it was great.' He shifted uncomfortably. He was no good at this stuff.

'Sounds great. I'll look forward to it.'

Okay. Glad you like the flowers. I'll see you then.' And he was outside the door and back in his truck before he knew it. God, he was hopeless.

Maybe that's why it was taking so long to break down Hannah's walls. Was it his fault? He really did need to lift his game.

Jude drove away from Hannah's, thoughtful and more than a little frustrated. They could be good together. They should be great together, because she needed someone like him to remind her how amazing she was. It hadn't all been awkward.

He loved the way she'd allowed him into her home while she dressed. As if she trusted him. He'd watched her when she'd told him that people said they appreciated her, as if she wasn't used to compliments or admiration. Which was crazy. She was a star. The champion she called others.

His eyes searched the road ahead as he drove, watching for wildlife, thinking about Hannah and wishing he was still there with her in his arms. He should have kissed her after she kissed him that time. He wished she was in the seat beside him now, because there had been a bond between them.

He mulled over what he'd learned today. She wanted to see him. Wanted to go out with him. But something was holding her back. She had good friends here in Gracie and Nell, and now she had him. If she'd take what he offered, she could have more. He wanted more. He wanted everything. Forever.

Hopefully, even if it was to be gradually, she'd learn that they were all to be relied upon, and until then he could wait.

Chapter Fifty-two

Hannah

Friday arrived and ramped up Hannah's misgivings. Maybe she wasn't ready for a relationship, even if she'd been drawn to Jude the first time she'd seen him.

To be honest, she'd found she couldn't look at another man because they all paled beside him. So on the surface, she must have decided he was for her, but whenever he tried to draw closer, she felt herself push him away.

Hannah rose from behind her desk and stared out the window instead of calling in her next patient. What was wrong with her? She'd been in Featherwood for three months; three months of country medicine challenges. On top of that, she'd been caring for hurting patients damaged by the scenes they'd been caught up in and the losses they'd suffered during the floods.

Many still suffered as one by one the houses were stripped to bare bones and rebuilt, and it meant smiles were slow to come and the scale of the disaster kept spirits lowered. Every time it rained, people withdrew into themselves, as if preparing to suffer again.

The town, and she, needed a lift, and here was Jude offering her one tonight. He was offering himself, really, and she should be stepping forward into his open arms. Instead, she'd been building a wall against a relationship with him, and she didn't know why.

Jude arrived at six as he said he would. Of course.

She heard his rumbling vehicle come up the drive at one minute to the hour, and couldn't help that extra glance in the mirror.

Nell had suggested this dress, and Hannah tugged at the bodice. It wasn't low-cut, but the swell of her breasts was visible, especially when she moved. Still, it was the colour she'd been after, as if the brightness of the yellow would boost her spirits and make her brave. And it matched the sunflowers. She loved those flowers.

When she opened the door and found Jude standing there, she sucked in a breath. He wore dark trousers over muscled thighs, white shirt open at his strong throat, broad shoulders backlit by the afternoon light, and full lips curved as his gaze roamed over her. Why on earth was she resisting this man?

'You look beautiful,' he murmured, his eyes darkening in appreciation and intent, leaving her in no doubt that he liked what he saw.

'So do you.'

He quirked his lips. 'No, I look handsome.' He held out a small posy of exquisite wildflowers, and she took the rough bunch with a little spurt of wonder. They were different lengths, purple and yellow, and obviously hand-picked. 'I found these on the side of the road,' he said.

'You must have left early.' Feeling oddly shy, she waved her other hand. 'Come in. I'll put these in a vase and then we can go.'

Jude remained where he was, leaning one large shoulder on the doorframe, and she could feel his gaze on her as she moved towards the cupboard. When she found a vase of the right size, she turned back to face him. 'Not coming in?'

'I can watch you from here. I've been thinking about you all day.' He smiled, clearly not worried that he was giving himself away at all. 'Nice thoughts.'

Her own mouth twitched. She concentrated on adding water to the vase, but she felt his intensity, and the heat seeped through her skin and into her belly. He'd been on her mind, too. But she'd been thinking she shouldn't encourage him until she had something to offer. The truth was, she was afraid of how much she wanted him. And here she found herself again, grasping for why that was a problem, why unease hung there, without success.

As if he'd read her mind, he said, 'Stop overthinking it and just come out with me.'

Could she allow someone else to make the decision for her? It seemed so easy, and maybe that's what she needed.

She nodded, relieved, slid the posy into the water-filled vase, picked up her purse and went to where Jude waited. 'Thank you for the flowers.' She reached up and kissed his cheek, and then pulled the door shut behind them.

As she climbed into his big car, he held her door like she was important and precious, and then closed it quietly. Striding around the other side, he opened his door, and then he was inside with her, his presence filling the cabin. His scent, his mass, his obvious pleasure at having her there were a potent mix.

There, it was done. She was leaving with him, and there was no more indecision. She relaxed back in the seat and allowed the hedonism of Jude caring for her to settle around her like a warm cloak.

It felt wonderful. *He* was wonderful. What was wrong with her?

They drove into the twilight, with the green paddocks and gurgling streams in front and the setting sun behind them. They travelled up and over hills and then down into the old-fashioned but appealing township of Dorrigo, moving past gardens and older-style houses and shops, until finally they came to the top of Dorrigo mountain and the Lookout Motor Inn, where the restaurant was housed.

They entered through the big doors, with Jude's hand on the small of her back, and Hannah welcomed the fire crackling in the grate. It wasn't something she expected, but it added to the cosy, relaxing atmosphere. Their table held low candles and flowers, and she noted that the menu was extensive when it was handed to her. She needed this beauty, this affirmation that there was sweetness and little pleasures in the world.

Finally, her puzzling misgivings slid away and she could relax. 'I'm impressed,' she said. 'I had no idea this place was here or would be so wonderful. Thank you for bringing me, Jude.'

'My pleasure. And you deserve it. You've been a rock for the townspeople, did you know that? Featherwood appreciates you.'

Her eyes lifted to his in embarrassed confusion. 'You more than me. You, Liam and Jed's store, and Jude's Crew. Your men have already given some people back their lives as you restore their houses faster than anyone expected.'

He shook his head. 'That helps. But the town sings your praises, you know. You listen and smile and invite them back to offload when they need to. You care, and I'm seeing the improvement in morale after people see you.'

She squirmed, thinking she'd done nothing special, but she hoped the improvement was true. Not that Jude would have said if it wasn't. 'Well, thank you, but that's enough praise flinging. Let's talk about something else.'

He smiled, tilting his head at her as if she charmed him. 'Archie is settling in well at Luna Downs,' he said.

'Dear Mavis. I didn't know her long, but I feel there's still a gap where she used to be. I used to run into her all the time when I went down to Jed's store. She'd pick Archie up from there after school. Archie must miss her so badly.'

'I asked him again if he wanted to go to the agricultural boarding school. Mavis suggested it in our one conversation about it. Archie said only if Leo goes.'

Hannah laughed. 'Touché, Archie. What did you say?'

'I said that was up to Leo, although, I'd hate it and I'd stress about his diabetes.'

She watched his face. 'It's not so bad an idea. The school would have an experienced nurse on staff. The boys already travel forty minutes each way on a bus, and a boarding school would offer sports and social skills he won't get here. I went to boarding school and there are definite good points. They could come home for weekends and have the best of both worlds.'

'Except I'd miss Leo. And now Archie. I can teach them what they need to know. Archie can stay as long as he likes with us.' He waved that away as if it had become something he wasn't sure he wanted to talk about. 'So you went to boarding school. Tell me about your childhood.'

She shared a couple of amusing stories about school, sneaking out once and getting caught, and tricks they played on the teachers that backfired. She even touched on her father's preference that she call him by his first name. How she disliked being called Honey or Sweetie. And about her kind and stay-at-home mother dying when she was seven, and her dad always searching for another soulmate in the wrong place and attracting the wrong women who didn't last long.

She didn't mention the fact that she'd had to learn to be resilient and independent and not expect anyone to champion her beyond normal friendship. Although, she suspected that Jude read between the lines.

The food arrived, local produce and perfect, and the conversation even better, once she started Jude talking about the improvements they'd made at Luna Downs.

Afterwards, they were more at ease as they drove home. Jude played quiet music on the excellent speakers, and she leaned back against her seat and closed her eyes, savouring the serenity. Yes, of course she'd found quiet and relaxing times in her life, but this capsule of serenity with Jude was something she didn't think she'd ever felt. A horrid premonition brushed her neck. She hoped it lasted.

When he followed her to her door and kissed her sweetly, and then with more toe-curling intent, she wanted to ask him to stay, but something still held her back. Jude being Jude, he saw that. She almost wished for that decisive Jude to take the initiative. Instead, he stepped back, and with a wry smile wished her goodnight.

It wasn't Jude that was the problem. She could see a future with him. A glorious one, if the way he kissed continued down the path she hoped it would one day. She was the problem. She just couldn't put her finger on the foreboding that stopped her going further.

She needed to sort herself out, she decided, because Jude wouldn't wait forever.

The following Thursday, Hannah's phone rang with *No Caller ID*. It happened with her patients sometimes and she'd seen tomorrow's appointment book. It was full, and she hated saying no to worried clients before the weekend. 'This is Dr Rogan.'

'Have you missed me, my Hannah?'

The unexpected shock of Porter's deep, seductive tones dripped ice down her spine. Hannah's stomach lurched and she felt the nausea at the back of her throat. It was too visceral a reaction to a man she never wanted to see again.

'I changed my number.' It was a stupid thing to say, but her brain had frozen. She needed to do better.

'My Hannah. You haven't answered. Have you missed me?' His voice was slightly slurred, drugged or drunk, she guessed, and the tone held biting venom.

'Not your Hannah.' She struggled for a dry, dismissive pitch, determined to hide the shock that made her throat hurt. 'They let you out.'

He scoffed. 'Ah yes. Only got me on the lighter charge. I've paid that debt and here I am looking for my girl.'

Oh no. She swallowed back bile. 'I'm not yours.'

He ignored her, going on silkily, 'But my girl seems to have left town. Left the state, actually.' He paused. 'Went south.' Then, 'I think she's playing hide-and-seek.'

So he knew she'd moved. Maybe knew she'd moved here. 'How did you get this number?'

A quiet, chilling laugh rang down the phone, making Hannah recoil. 'Babe, it was too easy. Dr Google told me. Your number, address, even your visiting hours.' She couldn't miss the threat in the last sentence.

And damn it, she did have a webpage. 'What do you want, Porter?'

'You, of course. You should've stuck around. Where's the loyalty?'

Her heart thudded in her chest and her mouth dried in disgust. 'We're finished. I have a new life, Porter. Make yourself one.' Her finger aimed for the red 'end' button, but she didn't close off in time.

'I'm coming for what's mine.'

Hannah stabbed the button. The phone rang again almost immediately, and she didn't want to look at the number, but when she did, she paused. RR – her father. Although she still had to brace herself to answer, suddenly, ridiculously, she wanted her dad in a way she hadn't for twenty years.

'Hello, Richard.'

And then he ruined it. 'Hello, sweetie.'

She shut her eyes. 'My name is Hannah.'

'Oh, okay. You sound upset.'

Because she was. She hadn't even begun to think straight after the last call. 'I just had a phone call from Porter.' Normally she never would have shared that, especially with her father.

'I thought,' Richard's voice steeled, 'he was going away for years.'

So had she. 'He was acquitted of the main charges, apparently.'

A silence and then, 'How about I come visit? I've checked out the flights and they travel several times a day from Sydney.' He said it slowly, casually, as if ready for her to push him away. Which usually she would have – she had done since her mother died and the first new woman had moved in.

Such was her brain fog, so large her distress, so stupidly she clung to the idea of not being here alone if Porter showed up, she said, 'Yes. If you'd like.'

'I'll fly out to Coffs Harbour tomorrow, hire a car and arrive in the afternoon. Would that be okay?'

She realised now her father had been so surprised that she'd said yes, he was coming fast in case she changed her mind. She'd spent her whole teenage years declining his help, then put herself through med school with the money her mother had left in trust for her. Her father she'd barely seen.

'Look, really you don't have to come,' she said.

'It's the first time you've said yes,' he crowed. 'I'll be there with bells on, Hannah.'

Hannah sighed. He'd used her name. *That was way better than 'sweetie'.*

'Fine, Richard. See you tomorrow.' Hannah pressed the button to end the call, and said out loud, 'What on earth have I done?'

But just for a moment, she'd forgotten about Porter, so that at least was good. She couldn't imagine what Featherwood's reaction to her dear, theatrically larger-than-life, womanising dad would be. But it wouldn't be boring. She spread her hand over her face and closed her eyes.

Her phone rang again, causing her heart to jump. This time it was Jude. 'I wish you'd phoned five minutes ago,' she blurted, then squirmed at the neediness of that, thankful he couldn't see her face.

'Shame. I wish I had, then,' he said, and she could hear the smile in his voice.

As if she'd wiped a filthy window clean, she realised now why she'd been reluctant to drop the last barriers between her and Jude. Porter. She'd never felt it was over. Oh, she didn't care for him any more. God, she didn't want to see Porter ever again. Even his name made her ill. But what she didn't want more than that was to bring that kind of trouble down on Jude. Jude, who had suffered enough already. Jude, who would stand between them without hesitation and put himself at risk. She'd known all along that if Porter came, there would be trouble.

Jude had had so much trouble in the past and he did not need hers. He had Leo's diabetes to be vigilant over and Archie to care for, as well.

There was a leashed protectiveness in Jude that he extended out over people he cared about, and she knew that somehow she'd been drawn into his bubble of care. She had no doubt Porter could cause disaster, and Jude didn't deserve disaster.

'Is there a problem?' he asked.

Pulling herself back into the call, she began to respond but then hesitated. She'd already told her father, she reasoned, and Jude needed to know sometime. Still, she couldn't seem to get the words out.

'Hannah?'

'My father's coming to visit,' she finally said, 'tomorrow.'

'Is that a good thing?' The smile was back. They had discussed her hedonistic old man a few times now. And there'd been the donations to Featherwood in the flood.

'He's coming to stay for a few days.' And then before she chickened out she blurted, 'I had a phone call from my ex.'

'The bloke from Roma?' All humour had disappeared. The question asked quietly, intense, concerned.

'Yes. Beau Porter. I'd just hung up when Richard rang. When he offered to come, I said yes.' She was talking to herself more than him, really, explaining how it had happened. She sighed. 'My father will cause mayhem.'

'You'll have someone in the house with you. A man. That's a good thing.'

Maybe he was right . . .

'Do you think this Porter will try to contact you in person?'

Yes. This was her very real fear, now that she'd seen through to the conscienceless villain beneath the shine and remembered the threats. 'Yes.' The sound was smaller than she'd intended, so she cleared her throat and said more clearly, 'Yes. He said as much.'

'Then I'd better come tomorrow and put that bolt and chain on the door we spoke about way back. And we could lend you one of our dogs? We have enough to spare since Archie came.'

Hannah smiled. 'I don't need a dog.'

'Are you sure?' Jude was quiet, persuasive, leaning on her to consider. 'There's a lovely bitch here that Archie's been talking about finding a home for. You could keep her just until this is over.'

This. Her problem that he wanted to share as his. She smiled again at the phone, feeling better already. 'Now I really do wish you'd rung before RR. Such sensible suggestions.' Unless Porter wasn't playing with her from afar . . . What if he was already here? She swallowed. 'Thank you.'

But that too lacked substance. And Jude must have heard the anxiety in her voice, because he asked, 'Are you okay?'

No, I'm not, she wanted to say. And she was thinking that maybe she was getting worse as it all began to sink in, piece by fearful piece. 'I'm fine.'

Silence. Then, 'You're not. I can hear it in your voice. How about I come over now and put the bolts on your doors tonight. Then you can sleep better.'

'Tomorrow will be fine.' But the words lacked conviction, and Jude was no fool. *No, he certainly isn't.*

'It's not even five-thirty,' he said. 'Give me twenty minutes. I'll give Jed a ring and he can leave the bolts in his mailbox if his hardware is shut. The job will only take me a few minutes.'

She should say no. She should just suck it up and be tough. Instead, she heard herself say, 'I'd like that. Yes, please.'

Jude arrived in nineteen minutes, carrying a small paper bag from the Farmer's Friend store, a drill set and a small bag of tools.

Following him pranced a bouncing blue heeler that reminded Hannah very much of Nell's Grin, though quieter and with less apparent teeth.

Jude waved his hand. 'This is Mimi. She's housetrained, but she can stay outside if you wish. She doesn't bark unless there's a problem and she's very happy to come on a holiday. You don't have to worry about her with patients or children. Mimi has lovely manners, but if you'd prefer to keep her in the laundry, inside, she won't complain.'

'She sounds like a saint.'

'She is. Saint Mimi, yes.' He smiled. 'When I told the boys about a possible unwelcome visitor from your past, Archie wanted me to tell you to keep Mimi and listen to your instincts.'

Hannah had heard that before from Archie – it was Mavis's advice. The kid was still missing his gran. But it was good he was up to sharing her guidance with others. 'You tell Archie, I will. Thank you.'

But now with Jude here, dropping everything to fix a bolt to her doors, and her dad coming tomorrow, she began to feel a little embarrassed. She moistened her lips as she followed Jude, who carried his gear through the house to the front door. 'Maybe I over-reacted.'

Jude put down his tools and turned to face her. 'Every time you've mentioned this guy, there's something in your voice that says he worries you. I hear it. Your survival instinct kicking in. So go with Archie's advice and stay safe.' He pointed at the door. 'Let's get this done.'

Maybe he was right. 'Can I make you a cup of tea or something while you're doing it?'

'Sure.' He smiled over his shoulder at her. 'Black. No sugar.'

She knew that, but she just nodded and went back to the kitchen to put the jug on and dug the sausage rolls, which Molly had dropped off via Nell, out of the fridge. She needed to learn to make these. Molly had said she'd teach her.

Nobody could refuse a homemade sausage roll, and she'd learned the Featherwood knack of setting up impromptu picnics that the others seemed so adept at. Something about squirting the tomato sauce into a bowl made her think of that gathering of townspeople when she first arrived. Mavis came to mind again.

The cheeky dryness of her comments. Her love of all clothes maroon. All the women on Gracie's used-to-be-gorgeous back verandah that had been washed through with brown sludge. The way dear Mavis had cut up the sausage rolls and put the sauce in the dish was a bittersweet memory, and made Hannah look back and think about the months she'd been here, the people who'd touched her, and whose lives she'd touched as she cared for their health.

She'd let them near to her but not close – always drawing away from the commitment that she was staying. She'd put it on hold because in the back of her mind, her instincts had worried that Porter would turn up and bring it all down like a house of cards.

She went out to where Jude was fixing the bolt and the chain.

He looked up briefly, saying, 'Nearly done here.'

'Jude?'

His hand stilled mid-movement with a screwdriver, his arms taut and the muscles defined. Then he stepped back and smiled, as though he had all the time in the world for her. As though she was the most interesting person he could possibly talk to.

How on earth had she brushed all this aside because of Porter?

'When all this drama with the ex is over'—then she remembered RR's impending visit—'good grief, and my dad coming . . .' She shook her head, drifting slightly.

'Hannah?'

She blinked and found him watching her. 'Oh, sorry, just thinking about my dad . . .' She trailed off. 'What a fiasco.' Focusing, she lifted her chin. 'Anyway, after all that, I'd like to go out to your place and see Luna Downs. See what you've done out there. See Archie's room that he told me about the last time Leo came for an appointment. Just get to know a little more about you and what's important to you.'

His eyes warmed, then darkened. 'I'd like that, too. I haven't asked because I didn't want to push.' He shrugged. 'I got the back-off vibe,' he said.

That made her mouth twitch. 'I know. I've had an epiphany. That I didn't want to ask because of my worry that Porter would come and ruin everything.'

Putting his tools down, he straightened and closed the gap between them, his rough, workman's hand cupping her cheek. 'I wish I'd known that before.' He stroked with his calloused stone-mason's thumb across her mouth, sending shivers through her. 'You just say the word and I'll stop the world, including him, from bothering you.'

There it was – the protection mode that could destroy him. 'And that, my dear sir'—shaking her head at him, she stepped back—'is why I've been trying to keep you away from this disastrous man who could ruin your life again.'

'Let me worry about me.' He said it quietly, and then his tone changed. 'Was that rumour about the cup of tea true?'

It seemed they both wanted to change the subject. She lifted her chin and pretended hauteur. 'When you've done your job on both doors, I will provide a repast that involves more than tea.'

'Really.' His eyes darkened again as they met hers, and she blushed like a twit.

'Not that sort of repast.'

'Darn,' he sighed dramatically, then lifted his head and sniffed. 'Smells pretty good.'

'It is good. People who install deadlocks out of hours on fair maidens' doors deserve sausage rolls made by Molly.'

'Molly's homemade sausage rolls?' He might have moaned just a little, and even touched his chest. 'Be still, my beating heart.'

When it was done – when both doors were secured with a slip-in chain and his tools were back in his car – they sat side by side at the kitchen table, with Mimi next to Hannah's chair.

'How does she know I'm the person she's guarding?'

'Because I told her the one that smells good is her new boss.'

'Is that so?' Hannah slipped a piece of sausage roll out of the side of her hand and Mimi took the morsel delicately with her teeth and no exuberant slobber as Grin would have done. 'Very ladylike,' she murmured and could see how this new addition to her household could easily make her presence precious.

Then she leaned over to Jude and rubbed his cheek with her nose. 'You smell good.'

'You're playing with fire,' he said, and she sat back with a smile.

'I'm building up to it.'

'I'm patient,' he said, but she had the feeling that even his patience was straining. It was a stimulating idea and she felt her spirits lift.

Jude and Hannah took their time, laughing over the antics of the teens in Jude's house as it grew dark, and Hannah savouring the company of this man, who looked at her with appreciation and that hint of desire in his eyes that he couldn't quite hide.

Yes, she thought. When all this was over, she and Jude needed to have time together, though goodness knew how they could do so alone with his cast of thousands at Luna Downs. Her mood brightened. They'd just have to spend the time here.

'I'd better go,' he said, and she knew he didn't want that as much as she didn't want him to go.

'You'd better. I'll have to be organised tonight for Richard's arrival. I won't have time tomorrow.'

Jude smiled at her underlying impatience. 'I'll look forward to meeting him.'

She blew out a breath at the thought of her father meeting Jude, and possibly the stand-off to come. 'Yes, that will be interesting.'

He rose and slid his hand over Mimi's ears. 'You look after her, dog. Stay.'

Mimi settled back down on the wooden floor and Hannah appreciated his thoroughness. 'I remember your words, the first day we met,' she told him.

He raised his brows in question.

'You said I needed a chain on the door and a dog.'

He nodded. 'And a surveillance camera. I'll look into that tomorrow.'

He would too, and more, she was sure. 'Thank you, Jude.'

'You're very welcome.' She followed him out, as if she needed to be there with him just those few extra seconds.

He leaned over and kissed her lips. 'Sleep well, dear Hannah.' Their mouths drifted together one more time and he said against hers, 'We really need to move on from this.'

She smiled against his lips. 'I'm thinking soon.'

'Good.' Kissing her hard, he turned to go, and she knew he'd decided he either went then or never. There was something very flattering about a man who was tempted to stay but cared enough to go.

She leaned on the doorframe and watched him climb into his

big vehicle, the dog warm against her leg. The engine roared, the headlights came on, and Hannah blew out a breath.

From a bad afternoon, it had turned into a lovely evening. With lovely Jude, though she couldn't imagine he'd appreciate that nickname. She smiled and watched him drive away.

Almost immediately, her phone rang. *No Caller ID*. A shudder ran down her spine.

She didn't answer it. Instead she backed into the house with Mimi, pushed both locks into place and shot the bolt in the kitchen. Then she went through to the front door and checked the same was secure there. It was. She also checked the windows – all were secure. Perhaps the timing of the call was coincidental; it didn't mean he was out there.

A text came through. *How touching. That won't do. You're mine.*

Hannah shivered and called the police. Mimi pushed her shoulder into Hannah's leg and barked.

Chapter Fifty-three

Jude

As Jude drove away from Hannah, his neck prickled with disquiet. She'd looked calm, and the dog had certainly taken to her, making her feel a little more secure. Regardless, it hadn't done much to allay his concern.

His gut screamed that he should have suggested she come back to Luna Downs for the night. Even though the only place he could offer her to sleep was his bed, in a long house of men. Excellent thought though it was, he doubted she'd accept him moving into the lounge room. And he didn't want to rush the best part. They'd waited too long and he wanted to take a long time loving her.

His mind replayed the fact that she was worried enough about him to try to keep him safe. She had admitted that she wanted more but had pulled back to keep him from risk. He didn't think anybody had ever done that for him before. Even his first love, Iris, had done the opposite to keeping him safe by suggesting he help her overdose, even if it meant he could be imprisoned.

Well, he guessed he had survived, but there had been a cost. And here was Hannah. Sweet Hannah. Pushing him away from her because she didn't want him caught up in the mire of her ex-boyfriend's stalking.

To hell with that. He slowed the truck, picked up the phone and dialled Leo.

'Yes, Dad?' Leo sounded alert and happy, which was always a relief.

'How's everything at home?'

'Good, no problem.' Leo and Archie had slid into a seamless friendship of mutual respect. They watched out for each other.

'I'm having one of Archie's instincts at the moment. And even though I'm driving your way, I think I'll turn around and stay the night at Hannah's. I've got a bad feeling about it all.' It was funny how that had come out of his mouth all in one piece, as if he'd been thinking about it the whole time but just hadn't worked it out in his head.

'Okay. We've got dinner sorted here.'

'Good. I'll come home in the morning as soon as Nell comes into work. Ring me for anything straightaway.'

'Will do, Dad.'

'How's Archie?'

'He's fine.'

'Tell him Mimi was a big hit, and Hannah said thank you.'

'Will do.'

'Okay, mate. Ring me if you need me.' He hung up and then pressed Hannah's number. The last thing he wanted to do was frighten her by driving up the driveway unexpectedly.

'Jude?' Her voice was shaking. What the heck had happened? His heart rate spiked. 'Are you okay?'

'I got a text. He's watching from somewhere. I'm scared.'

Hell, he should not have left her. 'I'm on my way back,' he said.

'Good. I rang the police. They said they'd come, but it will be at least forty minutes.'

'Ten minutes and I'll be there. Keep everything locked.'

Her sharp laugh sounded too much like a sob. 'I can manage that.'

His hands tightened on the wheel until the leather creaked in protest. Just what had this guy done to her?

'How about I stay on the line until I get there? You don't have to talk.'

'What, just prop you on the kitchen counter while I think about what to have for dinner?' He could tell she was trying hard to act normal.

'Perfect. I can imagine you moving around. By the way, I'm staying tonight and won't leave tomorrow until Nell comes in.'

'Oh, that is good news. Thank you. And food. I'm not sure I can eat, but I can certainly feed you.'

He heard the crack of the fridge door opening, and the rattle of drawers. Too scared to eat? His lips compressed. What had he been thinking to leave? 'I'll see what I can do about your appetite when I get there.'

She laughed. It was shaky, but it was real. 'Well, we've eaten all the sausage rolls.'

'A very nice entrée it was, too.' He was keeping it light as he watched the lights ahead of him cutting through the night to her. 'I'll thank Molly next time I see her.'

'How about . . .' Her voice grew distant. 'Steak and some onion? I can take a couple of bread rolls out of the freezer, add lettuce and tomato and some of Molly's relish?'

'Sounds perfect.' He glanced at his watch. 'Five minutes and I'll be there.'

There was a pause, and he was pretty sure he heard her sigh. Then she said, 'I'll put the jug on while I'm waiting.'

Another kilometre eaten up. 'You do that. How's Mimi?'

'She's not barking or growling. Just the once when he rang. I think she felt my fright. She's the only thing that kept me sane and not ringing you straightaway.'

'We'll talk about that when I get there, too,' he said. 'You'll have to thank Archie for me coming back – I was listening to my instincts.'

She did that strange, half-strangled laugh that tore at his heart. Soon he would be there.

'I'm turning into your drive now,' he said, his eyes scanning the trees and the edge of the drive and across to the churchyard. As much as he could see through the light from his own headlights, there was no movement he could discern. No one.

He pulled up in his usual place across the yard. After turning off the engine, this time, when he got out, he locked the vehicle and took the keys with him. He'd stopped doing that recently. Since he'd learned to trust Featherwood. Trusting the people around him.

That wasn't a sensible option now.

The back light shone, but she hadn't opened the door. *Good girl.* 'It's me,' he said into the phone, the line still open. 'I'm coming to the back door now.'

He saw her white face at the window, then she opened the door, her eyes immediately scanning the yard behind him.

He stepped in and closed the door, then pulled her into his arms.

Chapter Fifty-four

Hannah

Jude's arms felt so solid. Warm. Safe. She hadn't thought she'd feel safe tonight.

'Thank you. I can't tell you how glad I am to see you.' She knew she shuddered against him as he held her, clamped to him, stroking her hair, but with the heat of him warming her, the panic was subsiding. Mimi pushed her nose between them then she circled their legs, her tail wagging, and the awful tension she'd held since the text and its underlying threat began to ease.

'It's okay, Hannah. You did well. Did anything else happen? Any more calls?'

'Some noises outside. I have no idea what they were, so they could be normal.' She shook her head. 'Nothing else.'

Cool, calm, professional Dr Hannah Rogan was not herself, she knew that. And she could see Jude thinking it.

'Do you need to talk about what happened in the past with this guy? Because he certainly has you worked up.'

It wasn't surprising that he'd asked. 'Maybe later, when I've calmed down a bit.'

'Of course. Later is fine. Can I do something to help in the kitchen?'

'Help me work out how much to feed the dog. Stupid I know, but . . . I've never had a dog.'

He looked at her. 'Really?'

She shrugged. 'I told you I spent most of my childhood at boarding school.'

'What about after school?'

'University. As a young intern, having an animal wasn't fair to the dog because I was never home. I needed sleep, not company. I don't even know what to buy for dog food.'

Something landed on the roof – with a crash.

Hannah jumped and grabbed Jude's arm. 'What was that?'

'It sounded like a branch dropping on the roof.' Jude's voice remained calm, quiet, matter-of-fact, and she willed her heart rate to slow down.

'You have that big tree that leans over one corner of the house.'

She did. And sometimes the branches dropped. 'I might get you to arrange someone to trim that back for me so it stops doing that. Especially at night.'

'Easy,' he said and rubbed her back until she felt herself begin to relax again. Relax as much as she could when her brain chanted, *Porter, in all his drug-crazed madness, could be out there.*

She strained, listening, but the sounds had stopped. Thank God Jude was here. 'Okay. I'll take one falling branch on the roof, but just one.'

He smiled. 'Did you want me to go outside and have a look?'

She shook her head vehemently. 'God no, I don't want you to go outside at all.'

They both listened. There were no further noises. 'Fine,' he said. 'As much as I'm enjoying this . . .' Kissing her again, he gently peeled her arms from around his neck. 'It's getting a bit hard to resist you when you're so close and smell so good.'

'Let's not resist, then.' Lying in Jude's arms forgetting the world, now that sounded really, really fine at this point.

His mouth came down to her ear and said very quietly and with intent, 'When we make love for the first time, it will be a much more romantic scenario than you scared out of your wits and seeking shelter.' The look he sent made her blush from top to toe. 'And wayyyy more fun.'

'Okay, then.'

He stepped back. 'So we were talking dog food.'

She laughed. This man. Her hero. She loved him.

She froze for a moment as the words ricocheted through her brain like spinning silver spheres in a pinball machine, the reverberation knocking walls down in her brain and spinning others. She loved Jude. No question mark. When had that happened?

Hannah blew out a stunned breath and shelved that enormous, complicated thought for later.

Jude was saying, 'You can't go wrong with raw food for your dog. If you don't fancy making it yourself, which you might not . . .' He smiled, and she suspected he couldn't see her chopping up roadkill or something similar. He was right.

'. . . you can order it from Jed's store. Mimi likes eating twice a day. As she's not a working dog, give her half a cup of kibble at night; I brought a bag with me. And half a cup of raw-meat mix in the day.'

'Got it. I thought dogs ate bones?'

'A raw bone once a week will keep her teeth in good health. Jed buys them for the customers.'

She was feeling better. Normal conversation and a fast learning curve on dog food. Normal was good.

Suddenly, Mimi barked loud and vicious right before something smashed into the kitchen window. A jagged crack appeared along the pane, then there was another crash as something long and black smashed against the window again. Her window. He was smashing her house. A sudden surge of protective anger flooded her mind. *How bloody dare he.*

Jude spun her back against the central wall of the house, then slipped away from her to the outside wall to peer cautiously through the cracked window. He swore softly.

In that moment, Hannah was more angry than afraid at the realisation that Porter wouldn't stop until he'd destroyed her things. Jude's car. Them. He was too off his face for any coherent thought, she'd bet. *Damn him*, she was over it.

This was her house. Her life. Her man. Damn Porter for trying to ruin it all.

'We have a problem.' Jude stating the obvious. 'He's tall, thin and dressed in camouflage.' He pulled out his phone and pressed a button. 'And he's laughing like an idiot, so totally high as a kite.'

Jude spoke into the phone. 'Leo?' A pause. 'Put Ben on, please, mate?'

After another pause he said, 'We've got trouble here and I need reinforcements. Hannah's called the police, but they'll take a while to get here. Bring everyone. Leave the boys locked up with the dogs. Can't fit them in or we'd take them to Gracie. I'll ring Liam.

Bring the men up to Hannah's and park beside my truck. Don't get out until I tell you.'

There was a bit of silence, then, 'I don't think he's got weapons . . .'

Hannah's heart felt like it stalled before it took off again at a gallop. Guns? Knives? Jude looked at her and she held up her hands. How could she know? How dare Porter bring this violence to her town.

'None used yet. Maybe bring a decent piece of wood each, for self-defence. Nothing illegal. We don't need you guys getting into trouble. You got it?'

Hannah looked in shock at this cold-faced stranger who had taken control. He cut that call and made another.

'Liam. Hannah's dickhead ex has turned up at her house. I'm with her inside. My men are coming, the boys will have to stay at Luna Downs. Can you ring Jed, tell him to come as reinforcement? Together. Not alone. Thanks.'

Another window crashed and an eerie, jeering laugh echoed from outside. Mimi's sudden ferocious barking made Hannah's heart double its pace. This was a nightmare. And wrong on so many levels.

Jude held up his hand to Mimi, saying firmly, 'Quiet.' She stopped instantly, and the sudden silence filled with another crash.

'I'm going outside.'

She launched herself at him. 'Don't! I saw him kick a man on the ground once. He didn't stop. That's when I knew I needed to run.'

Jude stared at her for a moment before nodding. He clearly wasn't happy and was staying inside for her, she knew, rather than himself, but he didn't know this crazed Porter. Finally, he said, 'I can wait for the men.'

Hannah's phone rang. *No Caller ID*. She held it out to Jude, but he shook his head. 'Answer. Put it on speaker.' He touched her arm. 'I've got you.'

Yes. She couldn't wait to talk to him, actually. She pressed the 'answer call' button.

'You've got a boyfriend inside with you, Hannahhhhh.' Porter's voice was manic, obviously slurring, and wild with glee. 'I've got a tin of petrol. Matches. How about I burn his car?'

'Pull back, Porter,' she snarled. 'This will not end well.' Although she knew they were wasted words – maniacs couldn't hear others – she felt better.

'You can stop it all by coming outside, sweetie.'

'You're sick.' She spoke slowly. 'And high. The police are coming.'

He laughed. 'Then I'd better get you out fast.' The line went dead.

Jude's car. He would burn it if he could. Hannah wanted to pull her hair. 'I'm so sorry I dragged you into this,' she told Jude.

Jude waved that away. 'It's not your fault. It's this guy's fault. Do you have an extinguisher?'

She rammed her hands through her hair. Extinguisher. A requirement. 'Yes, I remember Nell ordering it.'

He touched her shoulder again. Reassurance they had this. 'Pull it out and have it ready in case we need it.'

She walked unsteadily through to her medical observation room, almost shaking with rage. *Damn Porter*. She could kick him.

There, under the sink, she found it. The red fire extinguisher lifted out easily. She reread the instructions about pulling the pin and pointing away from people. Well, she wouldn't mind pointing it at Porter, that was for sure. Or hitting him over the head with it.

She returned to the main room. 'Here it is. It's new and full.'

'What type is it?' he asked.

She read it again. 'Dry chemical.' Might sting if she sprayed Porter.

He nodded and pulled his phone again. 'Tesla, tell Ben the guy is threatening to burn my car. Wait for Liam to get Jed, then all arrive together and make three points. See if we can box him in with me at the house and the other two cars at angles.' He paused. 'Okay. No heroics.' He hung up.

'They're just parking at Jed's,' he told her. 'We need to wait until Liam arrives.'

She thought of Nell's ex-special-ops man. 'Knowing Liam, he won't be long.'

Jude met her eyes and smiled grimly. 'My thoughts exactly.' Then crinkled his brows at her and smiled slightly as if puzzled. As if noticing the change. 'You look better.'

She narrowed her eyes at him. 'Yeah. I'm more ropeable than scared, now. He broke my window.' She lifted the long wooden rolling pin she'd liberated from the kitchen and slapped it into her palm. 'I want to do a bit of defending myself.'

His brows lifted but he smiled. 'No heroics from you, either.'

The sound of vehicles heading up the driveway roared in through the broken window.

'Show time,' Jude murmured. He moved to the back door and pulled it open on the chain, enough to see through. 'You're outnumbered, Porter,' he called out.

Hannah had a surreal moment, thinking how strange it was

that Jude remembered a name she'd only mentioned a few times. As if he'd marked it in his brain in case he needed it.

'Gonna have a little fire,' Porter mocked, coming into view as he left his cover. 'You can prevent it all if you come out, Hannahhhh.'

'Not happening,' Jude called back.

Porter hefted a red plastic jerry can and began to splash the petrol on Jude's car in messy arcs. The liquid glittered in the back porch light and the stink of petroleum floated on the breeze that had sprung up.

Jude unlocked the back door as Liam's ute crested the rise in an arc of headlights and noise, almost flying through the air as it hit the top bump. He pulled past the house and to the far right, then executed a perfect handbrake turn to stop facing the house. His headlights were shining directly on Jude's car and the man gesticulating beside it.

Jude's men roared in behind, a full load in the Luna Downs truck, and stopped just inside the entrance to the left. The headlight-targeted vehicle sat in the middle of the yard, with Porter dancing around it like a maniac waving his can.

Doors opened as men climbed out. Five from Luna Downs, and Jed and Liam, tall and muscular and towering over the rest at the other side.

The idiot splashed petrol everywhere, half of it going on himself. He spun to the newcomers. 'I'll burn you all,' he sneered, and ran towards them, arcing and splashing the petrol in their direction.

The last of the flammable liquid hit the dirt and dribbled, the container empty, and he flung it down and backed away. Pulling matches from his pocket, he waved them at the newcomers and laughed.

Jude called out, 'Don't. You'll go up yourself, you idiot.'

Porter spun their way. 'You're next, Hannah,' he crowed, struck a match and threw it towards Jude, but suddenly, in a searing shaft of flame, the petrol exploded backwards, turning Porter into a column of fire.

Porter screamed, an ear-shattering, drawn-out shriek, and ran towards the house, a human torch, trailing flames and aiming for them.

Ben, without warning, took off across the space and thwacked Porter in the knees with a long piece of wood, and the flaming man went down short of the house.

The other men closed in, one grabbing the garden hose, and Hannah pushed past Jude, lifted the extinguisher and sprayed Porter from head to toe. Too bad if the chemical was a problem; they could hose it off.

Liam and Jed were controlling the spread of fire that threatened to crawl to Jude's truck with their own extinguishers, and Jude took the extinguisher from her hand to give to Tesla.

Ben hosed the chemical off Porter and Hannah kneeled down beside him. When Ben dropped next to her, she sent him in for the medical bag in the hallway cupboard.

Porter was alive, in shock, and she suspected his knee was dislocated, but incredibly, he hadn't been aflame for more than a few seconds and most of his clothes were intact. She suspected he would have inhaled and damaged his lungs, though. He was luckier than he deserved, but still the relief was there that he probably wouldn't die. She was a doctor. She'd do what she could. She had an oath.

She leaned in and gently felt around the charred collar of his neck for a pulse. His eyes opened and he blinked lashless eyelids, his skin red and blistered, but only small patches were badly burned. 'Guess that was pretty stupid,' he croaked, sounding for that moment like the Beau Porter she'd once thought a nice guy.

In the distance, a police siren wailed.

Ben came back with her bag and she drew up an ampoule of morphine and put it aside. Assembling an IV line, she flushed it, gave the bag to Ben to hold up high, flushed it, connected it to the cannula and injected a quarter dose of the morphine into a side-line. At least she could take the edge off the pain until he could be transferred to hospital. She couldn't give him too much in case his breathing deteriorated. She'd check with the paramedics if they wanted her to give more when they arrived. It was all she could do.

It was a long night until the ambulance and police had gone. Hannah had given her statement and Liam handed over the memory card from his dash cam, which had caught all the action.

Hannah couldn't help wondering how it could have been more horrible until she remembered what could have happened if she didn't have these friends around her.

She looked for Jude, found him talking to Ben, and felt herself thaw a little from the cold of dreadfulness that had settled over her. If she hadn't left Roma, this could have been her trying to stay alive on her own.

Porter had been helicoptered away, suffering more as the shock wore off, but his drug-fogged brain had caused his own horror. Hopefully, he'd get help for his addictions, and prison time might help him turn the corner back to the man he used to be.

Tonight had given her the chance to stop blaming herself for being weak. For allowing him to affect her for so long. The rage she'd felt had burned away the victim she'd still felt she was. She wasn't a victim. Not any more.

'You okay?' Jude asked, his warmth coming closer, his hand easing around the small of her back to her hip, pulling her into him. It felt wonderful and right. And she leaned into him.

'I'm getting there,' she said, the words quiet, still too tentative. But the warmth of his body behind her felt so good, and unconsciously, thankfully, she tilted her head back and closed her eyes for a few seconds. Safe.

His other arm came around her waist. 'The boys are going home with Ben and the men. I'm staying. Is that fine with you?'

'Oh. Yes.' Hannah blew out a long, pained sigh. 'Very fine. I was dreading the night.'

Across the parking area, the other cars started their engines, headlights coming on. Liam and Jed waved as they drove away. The Luna Downs vehicle revved, warmed up, and that too followed down the rain-damaged driveway.

The night grew silent, and it was just them now. Them and the memories and the scars on her property.

'Come inside,' Jude urged quietly.

She did. Jude's arm propping her up, propelling her forward, and on her other side, Mimi brushed against her knee, sharing more warmth.

The tang of petrol still hung in the air, but that horrid, acrid stink of scorched flesh had blown away. How would she ever forget this night?

She struggled for something light to break her own tension.

'At least you got your car washed,' she said, and he shook his head at her weak attempt.

'Ben and Tesla did it. They said they didn't want someone to drop a match near me.'

'Ben was amazing,' she said, remembering. 'I'm so impressed with the way he knocked Porter down.'

'You did amazing first aid.'

She had done basics. 'We gave him a chance, but there was nothing we could do once he struck that match.'

'You can't help stupid.'

'I know. He burned up his brain months ago.' But she winced at the awfulness of the memory.

Jude must have noticed because he said, 'Did you hear what Ben said to me?'

She looked up at him beside her as they walked.

'He told me it felt good to save me for a change.' His beautiful mouth curved. 'I think he's taking lessons from Liam in stirring.'

She smiled. 'You really like Liam, don't you?'

'I appreciate him.' There was an amused glint in the Jude's eyes. She liked it.

'I appreciate you,' she said.

'I'm counting on that, and more.' He bumped her shoulder with his. 'I'm also counting on the fact that you promised me the use of your shower one day.'

She thought back to that day. The day he saved Mavis. The day she began to really value him. 'I did, didn't I?'

'Indeed, and I'm cashing in.'

'You can go first.' She should really feed the man. She'd promised him food hours ago. 'Are you hungry?'

'Not for food,' he said. 'But I was thinking we could share the shower.'

The water ran hot, filling the bathroom with steam. The lighting dim with the candles, even though they had electricity if they wanted it. Jude helped her remove her clothes, and she wasn't sure how it happened, but she'd discovered he had this strange knack of just rolling them off her like a magician. She slanted a look at him. At least the dimness helped the slight embarrassment of him seeing her for the first time. Her chin dipped.

His finger came out and he lifted her face. 'You are incredibly beautiful.'

She blinked. 'It's the candlelight. It's very flattering.'

He shook his head, smiling. 'No, it's the woman in front of me.'

The warmth in her belly turned into a blaze. 'You have far too many clothes on,' she whispered. And suddenly, he had none. Smart man. Just needed prompting.

'Speediest clothes shedder in the west?'

'Something like that.' Taking her hand, he led her, naked, into the spray. The water was stinging and stimulating, and so, so freeing of the stains from the night.

He picked up her soap, lifted it to his nose, watching her face as he inhaled the citrusy vanilla she loved. His face came close as he leaned down and gently brushed her lips with his, all the while rolling the cake between his big, rough hands until they were lathered in bubbles.

Soap slid over the top of her shoulders, one swirling, rough palm on each side, as he circled her shoulderblades. She couldn't help her tiny shuffle closer, her eyes drifting closed as she savoured the strong feel of his hands on her skin. His fingers slid down her spine, down over her hips, circling, stroking, kneading the ache in the small of her back above the crease of her buttocks. And then up and down in a convincing sweep of warm fingers until he kneaded the tension in her neck and shoulders.

She squashed against him, her breasts flattened into his chest, as his hardness pushed against her abdomen. He kissed her gently, tiny nibbles and caresses, and Hannah allowed the sensations to fill her mind behind her closed eyelids.

Her shoulders drooped, bringing her forward further until her forehead rested on his chest. It felt so, so good that she groaned in pleasure. The water tumbled over them both, and she imagined soap frothing at their feet as her tension washed into the drain with the suds.

Nothing, nowhere, no-one, had ever felt this good.

Gripping her elbows gently, he turned her and pulled her back firmly against his chest, until she could feel the hard length of him behind her. Swirling the soap again, Jude's sculptured arms slid around her as his oh-so-clever hands caressed her throat, her neck, above her breasts and under them. But he travelled down, not up, and she squirmed against him. 'You missed a bit.'

He laughed into her head. 'Impatient,' he whispered as he teased down the outside of her thighs, across her belly, and back to the underside of her breasts.

'Just so you know, we're not making love here, this is foreplay.'

'What is this thing you call foreplay?' she whispered, a teasing laugh in her voice at the wonderful sensations flooding her belly and core. Her hand slipped back to stroke him, delighting at his indrawn hiss of breath.

Rough voiced, he growled into her ear, 'This is worship I've wanted to give you for way too long.'

Anytime. All the time. Again. 'Can we do this over? Tomorrow? Because I could see myself becoming addicted.'

His laugh stroked her low and deep, rumbling in his chest against her face. 'We can do this every day if you'll have me.'

She tilted her head up and reached to kiss his throat. 'I think I can handle that.' And things moved on until finally he lifted her from the shower, wrapped her tenderly in a towel and carried her to the bed.

When Hannah woke up in the morning, Jude's long, powerful, naked body was curved around her like a heated silver spoon. His strong fingers were relaxed in sleep as they draped over the top of her waist, pulling her hip in towards him, his breathing deep and peaceful. He was fast asleep, and yet she knew if she moved, he would wake instantly to check that she was okay.

He was a wonder. A phenomenon she had no idea had existed. She'd had little time for boyfriends before Porter, and after the first night he had always been a first-to-sleep, last-to-wake kind of guy. She hadn't known she'd been missing the extras. Like the gifts that had kept coming last night and this morning. Because Jude . . . well, Jude was something else.

He'd taken her to places she had no idea existed. He'd taken her to pieces and put her back together better than before. And the reactions he'd drawn from her – she didn't even know she'd been capable of so much response. This world he held out to her felt fragile and very, very beautiful, as if she was a queen in his realm. Just thinking about it made her eyes sting.

There were so many ways he'd shown her he cared: he'd turned up when the twins were missing; he'd talked her out of the power-pole danger; the bolts on her door; bringing Mimi. Most tenderly, he laughed with her, and directed her thoughts so she could concentrate, and he'd been there last night, when she'd needed him most. In fact, he was still here, this morning, when she needed him again.

Last night his presence had kept her sane.

This sudden explosion of feelings and revelations seemed so much to take in. It was a lot to dream. That she and Jude could go on to grow even closer than now. That he could be a part of her life. And she could be a part of his. Always.

And then she remembered her father would be there today and she groaned.

Chapter Fifty-five

Jude

Jude was there when Richard Rogan descended on the rectory. Hannah had pleaded with him to come for the royal arrival, so he was here. As if Hannah needed him to greet her dad. He didn't understand, but for Hannah, he would always be there when she needed him.

Along with Nell, Molly and Gracie, who had been hovering around Hannah all day after her traumatic time the evening before.

Hannah's silver-haired parent pulled up in a BMW sports with the hood down, and climbed out of the low-slung car with the ease of a much younger man. He had to be sixty, but it was hard to tell. Jude suspected this man with his debonair scarf, linen shirt and Italian shoes would be outside the box in more ways than one.

He heard Hannah sigh in exasperation at the overt display of wealth, but her father's happiness at seeing Hannah could not be disputed as he swept up his daughter in a warm hug.

'Beautiful girl, look at you. It's been too long since I saw you.'

'Richard. You look well.' She hugged him back, and after a searching look into her face, he kissed her cheek.

'Too long,' he repeated, and there was undeniable honesty in those two words.

Jude wondered who'd been avoiding whom and suspected it had been Hannah doing the evading.

They both turned to Jude.

'And who is this?' her father asked the obvious question.

Hannah extended her hand to Jude and pulled him closer, not letting go once she had him against her side. 'Jude Waugh. Richard Rogan. Jude and I have become very good friends since I moved here.'

Jude offered his free hand to shake, luckily his right one, and wondered why Hannah was making such a statement. He was happy but interested in her reasoning, sensing her awkwardness.

'Jude? I thought that was a girl's name.' The man's smile hardened, watching Jude's face with narrowed eyes.

'It's not something I worry about,' Jude said lightly, pretending to flex and looking down at the older man with a twinkle he couldn't suppress. 'A man could be called anything and sound like a girl.'

The man looked slightly disappointed that Jude hadn't bitten. 'You and my baby are close, eh?'

'We are. Hannah's friendship means a lot to me. It's good to meet you, sir.'

Hannah looked at Jude with pleading that said clearly, *don't leave me*, so he guessed he was staying, despite feeling like a third wheel – or a six-wheeler with all the girls there, too.

As if satisfied he wouldn't run, Hannah let go of Jude's arm. 'These are my dear friends, Gracie, Nell and Molly.'

'Hello, lovely ladies. Such beauty in threes.' Richard twinkled and kissed each lady's hand, taking his time as he finished lingering over Molly. Molly blushed like a schoolgirl and Hannah shook her head.

'I warned you, Molly.'

Molly, still blushing, slanted an amused glance at Hannah's father. 'And he's just as much fun as I thought he would be.'

Hannah rolled her eyes. 'Come inside, RR, and see the rectory. Hopefully, you won't be smitten by God's wrath as you enter for your extravagant lifestyle.'

'Big words, child, and you wouldn't know anything about my lifestyle since you won't come and visit me.' But he stood back. 'Please, ladies first.'

The guy was smooth and over the top. And amusing. Trying not to laugh, Jude wondered if the man was checking out Molly's backside more than he was being the gentleman. *Dysfunctional families*, he thought, *gotta love 'em.*

Chapter Fifty-six

Molly

Molly *saw* Hannah's father. As if she recognised his cheeky essence. Watching him climb elegantly out of his flashy car, strong and lithe, wearing a scarf, she smiled. Of all things. A scarf. In Featherwood. Bless him.

But he looked fine. And even though she'd been warned he was a player, she couldn't help the catch of her breath. *Goodness.* A strong, muscled sixty. Broad chested, charismatic, too-white teeth. But there was goodness in him, as well. There was no bad boy there. Maybe a little boy trying to be bad.

But she *saw* him. She saw his overwhelming love for his daughter. His hesitation. The expectation of being rebuffed. Molly's soft heart ached for the father he'd tried to be but hadn't been able to achieve. She could help there.

She saw through the over-the-top bonhomie of a man pretending to be something he wasn't. *Oh, you gorgeous, silly man*, Molly thought. *You. Just. Come here to Mama.* Though she was twenty years younger, she suddenly felt like a wise woman on a mission.

Jude and Richard – he'd already become Richard and not

Hannah's dad in her mind, interesting – were busy eyeing each other. Old bull. Young bull. How droll. And how lucky, how fortunate was Hannah, to have these two beautiful men loving her.

But Richard needed loving, too. For the first time in many years, Molly felt the swell of hope, excitement and wonder that she might just have found the man for her. Finally. She didn't have time to muck around. She'd wasted too much of it already.

The family greetings were over and he was heading their way, his smile infectious, trying to be a little bit wicked. No, she decided, he certainly was no bad boy, just a man who had lost too much and had been looking in the wrong place for happiness.

She waited while he kissed the fingers of Gracie and Nell, cheeky devil, and then he was there, bending over her fingers, clasping her hand in his big, warm one. Meeting his eyes, she told him she saw him without words. As she smiled at the blue twinkle, and twinkled back, a flash of awareness flared between them. A crackle of understanding. A pull. He blinked, tightening his hand on hers. Then he kissed her knuckles with an extended flourish, lips lingering, staring into her eyes.

'Molly,' he said.

'I'm here,' she answered, but she couldn't help the heat that rose in her cheeks.

Hannah said, 'I warned you, Molly.'

Molly, still blushing, slanted an amused glance at her. 'And he's just as much fun as I thought he would be.'

Within a week, Richard had moved into Molly's farm and Liam had moved out. Within a month, Richard and Molly had eloped.

He called her his goddess and she honestly adored him as much as he adored her. And finally, she'd found someone she could cook for.

They'd both been delighted at Hannah's shocked face when he and Molly had impishly flashed wedding rings after their elopement. Hannah had been dumbfounded, and Jude had raised his brows in as much of a show of surprise as that inscrutable man allowed himself.

Molly's mother had laughed and said men could have children well into their sixties, which was a daunting and exciting thought, but Molly would just leave that up to God.

Her farm, their farm, in no way resembled the original building Richard had first moved into, and the grounds now contained a tennis court and swimming pool. Molly had laughed, shaken her head at his desire to spend, and taught him about bees.

There was such joy in her family accepting him, though her brother, Liam, still hadn't recovered his equilibrium at his sister's much older husband.

'I'm pleased for you, sis,' Liam had said. 'You look happy.' He'd shot a glance at her husband. 'Though I'm glad I don't have to live with him.' Her man was larger than life and as subtle as a bulldozer. She loved him so much.

Together, she and Richard weren't just happy, they were ecstatic. Richard had found his soulmate and he also had his daughter back in his life.

Chapter Fifty-seven

Hannah

On the first Saturday in November, nine months after the floods in Featherwood, Hannah Rogan sat on her front porch with her father and sipped delicious homemade lemonade. They watched the crazy traffic on the usually quiet road as people prepared for Featherwood Celebration Day.

'I never imagined you could settle here and still be busy and happy.'

'We travel.' Richard inclined his head. 'But coming home is good.'

'You've made your impact. I think you know more townsfolk by name than I do?'

'Darling, you are considered a saint by this town. And I haven't been this content for many, many years.'

Hannah suspected twenty-five, to be exact. 'Molly looks happy.'

Richard's smile beamed. 'We both are.'

'You were luckier than you deserved.'

He shook his silver head in mock sadness. 'Always so harsh to your poor old dad. Molly is a goddess who adores me as much as I adore her.'

And his new wife, Hannah thought, *has found someone to run a little wild with*. Their antics were a joy to watch. Embarrassing sometimes, but a joy.

Today, Richard and Molly would be standing beside Archie to cut the ribbon for the brand-new, architect-designed, Mavis Maloney Memorial Children's Playground – which Richard had been elated to be able to make a very substantial donation towards. With a covered waterpark feature for hot days, twin flying foxes over bouncy turf, a dinosaur slide with four different gradients, swings for all ages and plenty of covered picnic tables for families to enjoy, it was a place Mavis would have loved.

After the opening, the town planned to celebrate the resilience of Featherwood from the flood, along with a sombre glass raised at the two-year anniversary since the fires.

This small town had a big heart and impressive toughness, and Hannah felt honoured to be a part of the community. With Jude by her side, she finally had found peace, contentment and love.

It seemed her father felt much the same way, because Richard appeared to find it hard to prise himself away from the place for longer than a few weeks. Hannah suspected some of that was because he and Molly were both holding out for grandchildren. Although, Molly had whispered, Richard had agreed that if they were blessed with their own children that would be wonderful.

Now that was scary. Hannah could have a brother or sister the same age as her and Jude's baby if they both fell pregnant at the same time. Hannah had been struck silent, and Jude had raised his brows when she'd shared the thought with him. But his eyes had twinkled.

Hannah watched a car pull into the Farmer's Friend across the way, and Jed came out to chat to the driver. Gracie was there as well, big, pregnant belly out front. Hannah sighed and her father, noticing, patted her knee. 'It must be special, to watch the young families you care for grow larger.'

'It is.' She turned to face him, seeing the familiar blue eyes and the laughter lines that had grown dear again. She also saw the silver hair and ageing skin, and with a jolt she realised he wouldn't always be there. 'It's very nice to have you here, too.'

'You're glad? Finally,' he crowed. 'Molly said it would come out in words, eventually.'

Yes, she thought, she had so much to be glad about. She was here with her dad and Molly married in Featherwood living on Molly's farm, Jude was building a new house on Luna Downs for after they were married, and her work was an integral part of a community.

She glanced right to where her now two-lane entry had been resurfaced in a very stylish driveway all the way up the hill to the surgery. Richard had told her he liked the way the carpark had come up, too. The pressed and coloured concrete, almost thirty centimetres thick, stylishly opulent in a way Featherwood had never seen, could carry even Jed's blue truck and made the entry an all-weather proposition.

'The driveway looks good,' he said with satisfaction.

'It's too grand.' Hannah shook her head, wryly.

He'd used the same concreter who'd built his driveway at his estate in Sydney. 'It didn't stop Jude's Crew from learning the process to add to their repertoire.'

'Hmm,' Hannah said.

'I can't go having you wash down the hill again if we get more rain,' he said, and they both shivered at the thought.

'I agree,' Molly said, as she appeared in the doorway, her

beautiful eyes twinkling. 'Some people should learn to say thank you and accept the gift in the spirit it's been given.'

Hannah's face softened. She winked at Molly, then leaned in and kissed her dad. 'Thank you, Father.' She smiled at him. 'Imagine if you didn't have Molly to remind us how lucky we are to have each other.'

For a second there, she thought she saw tears in her dad's eyes as he caught her hand, lifted it to his lips and kissed her wrist. 'I haven't told you often enough. I'm so proud of you, Hannah.'

And this, here, was an unexpected joy she'd found in Featherwood, a closeness to her dad she'd been missing for so long, that she'd thought had died along with her mother. And it was growing stronger every day with Molly's nurturing.

Hannah's wedding would arrive in two weeks, and Richard and Molly had taken control of the planning because Hannah and Jude had wanted to elope. Why not? If they could, she could. Molly had shaken her head and said Featherwood needed a couple of good weddings to celebrate.

So she and Jude met the Anglican minister who shared the church with the Catholics, and found him delighted to perform the service. 'Anything that brings people inside the church makes me happy,' he'd said. 'Then there'll be children to christen.'

He had no idea. He could have more than he expected if Molly proved fertile. The thought made Hannah smile.

She'd been informed the reception would be held in the marquee constructed on the large, open area behind the rectory. Richard had wanted to fly in his favourite chef and team from Sydney, but Molly had won, with the dinner catered for by the local branch of the Country Women's Association.

Hannah had laughed and Jude had shrugged. Her Jude was happy with anything that made Hannah happy, saying if Richard wasn't thrilled, it wasn't his wedding.

Hannah loved Jude. Hannah loved her family. And Hannah loved her Featherwood life.

Acknowledgements

Floods have been a destructive part of so many Australian lives. That rush of powerful and deadly water, the devastation afterwards, and the heartbreak of loss and muddy filth has always carved deeply in memory and emotion and brought out the best, and sometimes the worst, of us. To those who woke to find water rising through their homes in the dead of night, I offer my heartfelt admiration for your resilience. I've tried to portray the devastation and hardship of floods, as well as the comfort and comradery of community in shared disasters. But only you know the reality of recovery.

When my husband and I first moved to the northern New South Wales town of Kempsey in the early 1980s, we were impressed with the sports fields and parks, but we also knew that houses had once stood on those low-lying open areas and that the floods had caused their demolition years ago. The locals still spoke about the 1949 flood that submerged most of the town. Six people died, 15,000 cattle were lost and 56 houses and homes were washed away.

In the time we've lived and worked there, we've seen the water-craft sloshing up and down Belgrave Street in flood – with my husband in his ambulance – waiting for boats to arrive over submerged bitumen with the injured or the ill to transfer them to the hospital on the hill. I've been on stand-by for helicopters bringing labouring women across swollen waters.

Lately, Australian towns have suffered deeply again. In early 2022 the northern rivers had the biggest flood in modern history and Lismore is still to recover. Devastation down southern and western New South Wales, Victoria, Brisbane, Western Australia . . . when you start looking, there are so many areas in Australia affected by flooding. Heroes and hardship everywhere. So I wanted to offer this book to give a glimpse into the suffering and heroics of a small town in flood, the people who push on and those who put themselves at risk to care for others.

As the River Rises is also a book about general practice medicine. I loved highlighting Hannah's new world as a doctor settling into a small community. These brilliant health professionals are such valuable resources, and their commitment is something we prize very highly. Hannah's horrid history with her ex is sadly very possible with the explosion of illegal drugs across the country, and my heartfelt appreciation goes to the brave police who put their lives at risk as they strive to eradicate the suppliers and criminals who ruin so many lives.

Jude is a favourite hero of mine, and his story of wrongful accusation came from a true story that sparked the idea for this book. Plus, he's such a great dad and friend, and I think a little hot – he makes me smile. While his dream of rehabilitation for those sleeping on the street is more wishful thinking than fact, dry communities are moving forward with great success. Huge kudos to the tireless workers who provide hope and support and succour for those in need of a blanket and a roof over their heads. Sometimes the light of hope is that catalyst for change. Good endings do happen.

As always, I would love to thank the team at Penguin Random House: my awesome publisher, Ali Watts, my wonderful editor Amanda Martin, designer Louisa Maggio and Katherine Furney in publicity, who works so hard to let readers know my book is out in the world and waiting to be found. Thanks also to Alexandra Nahlous and Sarah Fletcher for your insight and polish.

Special appreciation to my first reader and super-savvy writer friend Bronwyn Jameson for your amazing input with that first draft. I love your sense of humour in dealing with me. You are a great mate.

To all the amazing reviewers who do such an amazing job of sharing their thoughts on my fiction, I thank you. Writers know the best chance of their work being read is through word-of-mouth recommendations.

I also would like to thank my agent, Clare Forster, who is never too busy for me and is the person I turn to for career advice and as my sounding board. Thanks, Clare.

Thank you to my writing friends in RWAus and RWNZ, where I found our lovely Maytone group – special mention to Trish Morey, who always provides forward motion when I lose my way. To Jaye Ford/Janette Paul for being my writer buddy and sounding board when we're at retreat, and all the WWOW writers at lunches for motivation. And Annie Seaton, who always says, 'You can do it', when I'm running for a deadline.

Then there's my hero: my husband. No acknowledgement would be complete without the man who makes me laugh every day. Dearest Ian, my love, my best friend and my biggest fan – I am *your* biggest fan. Thank you.

ACKNOWLEDGEMENTS

As always, it takes a village to write a book. And that's what I love about writing – we give, we learn and we share so that we can create books that touch our readers, experience magic moments and inspire the joy and satisfaction that comes from creating a story we love. I hope, dear readers, that you'll love *As the River Rises*. Thank you for your wonderful support. xx Fi

FIONA McARTHUR

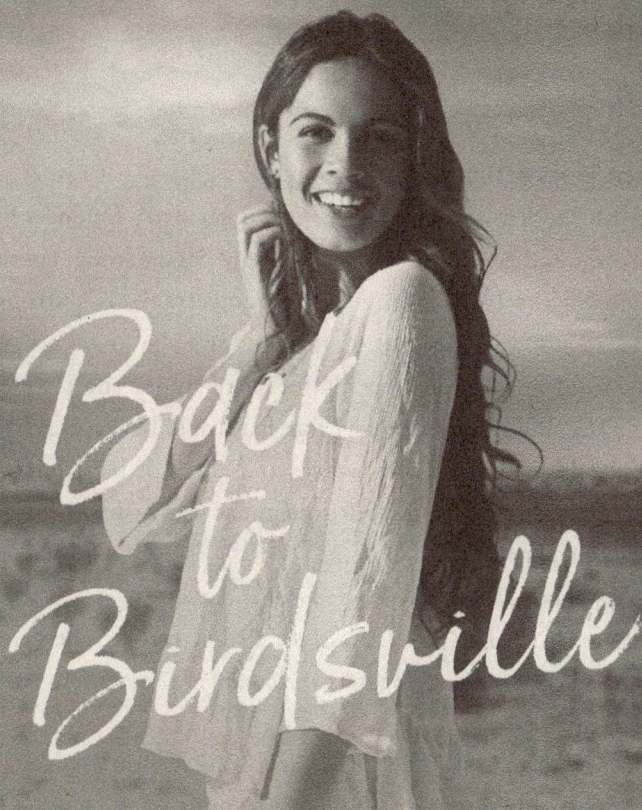

Back to Birdsville

READ ON FOR A SNEAK PEEK

Prologue

Phoebe

Eighteen years earlier

Phoebe McFadden, seventeen and wise to her dad's fondness for the horses, tilted her head to watch her only parent straighten the new sign on the front entrance of the racetrack. His strong, lithe frame stood silhouetted by the sun, and she knew his red fringe would be plastered to his forehead under the tattered Akubra. The rest of the hair under that hat would be wet curls.

She'd inherited those curly waves and glints of red from her dad, though hers were long, but sometimes she wished her hair was black like her mum's had been.

'Looks good, doesn't it?' her dad called down.

BIRDSVILLE RACE CLUB INC. ENTRANCE. The green letters stood out brilliantly against the cream corrugated iron and wooden frame.

'Yep.' The sign looked smashing, and pride swelled in Phoebe's chest. Her dad had made that sign. He could make anything. Except, of course, money. Clever, wonderful, exasperating, financially bereft Dad. Sometimes she felt like the parent.

But he'd been her hero since she was old enough to stand up and gawp at him and nothing would change that.

Dad, so tall with his big hat and his heeled boots, ruggedly handsome when he smiled that winning smile. They didn't have much in the way of extras at home – never had, Dad said, since Grandpa made that infamous bet on a long-gone Birdsville Cup and they'd lost the family station – but they had enough.

Dad said he'd inherited Grandpa's luck, which she believed, while she'd inherited her dad's hair. But despite relying on lady luck, Dad always made her feel special and loved. That said, Phoebe remained determined to save her own nest egg for a better life.

From when she was little Dad's blue eyes would crinkle when he crouched down to say, 'How's my princess? You're so clever. So pretty.' And always, 'Dream big, baby. You can do anything.' Yes, she could. And would. And she'd look after him.

Today, he called down from his high ladder next to the old crane arm, 'Is that straight, Phoebe?' Like he did every year when she watched him do repairs to the racecourse buildings.

She laughed because she knew he had his own spirit level up there and didn't need her input. Dad was a gifted carpenter, a sign writer, opal miner, sometime training jockey, barman and a bookie's assistant. On race day, when the tiny outback town could swell from around one hundred residents to thousands of tourists, he was an excited racegoer.

Dad was her world, her small world, since her mother had died when she was little. Otherwise there was only her cousin, Scarlet, Scarlet's parents, and her other aunt – and school in Charleville, of course.

The year before, she *had* made friends – despite their age difference – with a young kid when his family ran the pub for a while. Atticus had only been ten, so there were more than six years between them, but the things he'd come out with! He was fun. Yes, she missed the little jerk. He'd been like the younger brother she'd never had – not that they would have become friends for real, if she hadn't spectacularly stacked her bike in front of him the first time they met.

He'd almost made her forget the scrapes on her knees and hands when he picked her up, telling her stories of the spectacular disasters he and his older brother, now in boarding school, had had. His dad had taught them both first aid – they needed it so often.

She'd laughed, shakily, while he offered his handkerchief for the blood, realigned her bent front wheel, and dried her tears with the back of his hand. So grown-up for a kid.

He'd walked beside her, pushing his own bike, when she'd been too sore to ride home, and handed her over to her dad.

After that, Atticus paused to chat whenever he ran into her, and she'd humoured him – she'd even shown him her wreck of a car she would fix one day, the Desert Lizard, in all its disastrous glory and wonderful potential.

He was almost as tall as her despite the difference in their ages, with a smile that could show how glad he was to see her from across the street. She often wondered what happened to Atticus after his family moved on.

She'd run into him a lot when she was at home from school for a weekend or holidays – Birdsville was a very small town – but if her cousin was with her, Scarlet told him to push off. She said the older brother, Dali, was hot, but Phoebe wasn't drawn to him at all, despite him being closer in age to her and Scarlet than Atticus was.

She'd been sad when he said his family were leaving. Sad for the loss of her little mate – almost cried, though she'd hidden it. She'd never told Scarlet that story. Her cheeks heated at the thought of what Scarlet would have said.

She never fancied any of the boys at high school; she was too busy at her aunt's Charleville truck-stop, where she boarded during term time. There, she and Scarlet had learned to cook fast, clean well, and save their money. Auntie Daph believed in women standing on their own two feet – *she* wasn't relying on Grandpa's luck – and Phoebe took those lessons to heart. Any boys at the truck-stop were either petrol heads or cowboys with no manners, and none were funny or kind like her dad, so her heart was never at risk. Besides, her dad was her hero.

Dad, Scarlet's parents, Auntie Bee and Uncle Rob and Scarlet were such a big part of her life that she couldn't imagine not living here in Birdsville when she wasn't at school. She'd be with them forever.

Any time she could, Phoebe hitched a lift home with the cattle transports coming through Charleville Friday night on their way to one of the big stations past Birdsville. Mrs McKay had made it possible. She owned five of the stations in the channel country and she'd told Dad she'd arrange it. And she had.

Phoebe would always choose the chance to sleep behind someone's seat compartment if she could go home – even if it meant ten hours trucking Friday night and the same back on Sunday night – waking with just enough time to shower and head to school Monday. She missed home too much. Seemed sensible to travel since she had to sleep anyway and waking up at home made it all worthwhile.

But schooldays were spent at Charleville High along with Scarlet, coming back to Birdsville for the holidays. Soon she'd have her driver's licence. She'd be able to come home any time, then, with only a year to go before she could get a proper job back home.

It was holidays now; she was back in Birdsville before her last term of year eleven, and she'd already worked at the bakery when they were short. Hopefully, she'd get a few days at the caravan park too, and maybe a shift or two at the fuel depot shop if they needed her.

She'd been saving to repair the Desert Lizard, a Land Cruiser, for what felt like forever.

'The paintwork is so beaten it looks like she has scales,' Dad had said, and yes, the outside was a bit rough, though he said he'd help her panel beat and repaint when it was ready to be registered.

The old beast had been a present from one of Dad's friends on her fifteenth birthday. Dad had been broke that year and his mate had stepped in. A throwaway gift that turned into a savings goal she focused on with the intensity of a hungry kookaburra watching a snack-sized snake. Phoebe's red 80 series needed the engine rebuilt. Her good luck that Dad's mate couldn't be bothered selling the rest of the vehicle for parts.

But, for a smile from her, the boys from the garage had promised to help Phoebe get it up and running when she had her licence and could afford the components needed. With her own calculations – and she hadn't counted the stash under her bed since she came home – she was almost there.

Two years of saving. Two years of loving the interior of the car while it sat in Dad's shed, her humming a country song as she polished the old leather seats and wiped away the dust that had accumulated in the weeks she'd been away. That was the saying – *The dust never settles in Birdsville* – and it was true.

She'd saved good money this year because she and Scarlet were both clever in the kitchen and at the cash register and worked hard doing jobs for people. Both stashed coins and small notes away with weekend work. And especially, this month, in the kitchens at the once-a-year Birdsville Races. There was great money to be made this weekend.

Since acquiring the Desert Lizard she'd even saved the present money Dad gave her, often well after the birthday or Christmas, whenever he finally had cash to spare. Sometimes the dosh might come two months late, but always, eventually, he'd give her something. And she'd save it. She could be determined like that.

'Not like her mother or father,' Dad said with pride. 'You're a saver.' He always laughed at the fact he seemed permanently broke. Told her if it wasn't for the horses, they'd be rich. Yet, he'd always covered their needs.

Yesterday had been a big day. Dad had taken her out into the desert again in his car and, after watching her manage the sand hills, had pronounced her capable to drive. She'd already booked an appointment with the police office to go for her test as soon as her birthday came. Couldn't come quick enough.

'You wool-gathering down there, Phoebe?'

She was.

'Hold the ladder, would you, love?'

She gripped it firmly as Rusty began his steady descent from the roof of the entry gate. He looked down and smiled his million-dollar smile.

Such a shame, his daughter thought fondly, we can't bank some of that charm.

Phoebe pushed the ladder firmly against the brown rail to steady it and let go as he landed. Her gaze travelled over the empty ticket lines. So hard to imagine right now, but several thousand tourists would be here for race day, buses dropping them off at the gate, guiding them towards the open yard before the covered public area, where they'd mill around the stalls selling mementos and drinks.

Dad stepped back to examine the sign and Phoebe grinned at him. 'Looks great.'

'That it does.' But his gaze drifted over the long rail stretching around the huge red-dust circuit. He said, 'Two thousand metres in circumference. Did you know Birdsville remains one of only four tracks in Queensland that operates in an anti-clockwise direction? Like the Melbourne Cup.'

'Yes. I did,' she said. 'You tell me every year when we check the ticket office is fine.'

'Do I? Must be a true story.' He grinned at her and she grinned back.

She wondered who he was going to blow his money on this year. No way would she bet hard-saved money. Excitement fizzed. Soon it would all pay off. 'This week I'm going to get my stash and ask the mechanics to fix my car. Get it ready for my P plates.'

Rusty's face froze, along with his body. His gaze pinged back to her and away. Dark brows furrowed, and his mouth pulled down even as he forced it back up with a smile. His eyes slid away again, not meeting her suddenly intent gaze.

She didn't know why, but Phoebe's stomach sank. Were they broke? Did he need her money? He'd promised he wouldn't be silly this year. And the race wasn't even here yet.

Her heart began to pound, and she felt that cold skitter of fear, scurrying like a tiny gecko had slipped into the neck of her shirt to run down her back, leaving a dew-damp trail.

Rusty cleared his throat. 'That's exciting. How about we go to the bakery for a celebration?'

Phoebe's skin chilled more despite the heat. The bakery? That's where he told her he didn't have money for her birthday. A tiny cake in front of her. An excuse on his lips.

As if she wouldn't cry while the staff watched. It worked. She never did.

She narrowed her eyes. 'How about you tell me what happened now? Here. In private.'

She watched him swallow, his Adam's apple bouncing up and down, and she could feel her mouth pull tight as the gecko inside turned cold and dark and stopped in her stomach. Coiled, ready to bite.

He blew out a breath and screwed up his eyes as if he couldn't watch her face. 'I'm sorry, love. I had to borrow it, Phoebe. Your money's gone. But I'll pay you back.' He looked stricken. And ashamed. And lost.

Phoebe opened and shut her mouth. Trying to understand. Trying not to understand.

Suddenly she was more hurt, more horrified, more humiliated than she'd ever been. He borrowed it. Took it? From under her bed? Without asking.

She couldn't grasp the concept.

No. He'd always lost his money but never had he taken hers.

She struggled to get the words out. Had to swallow twice. 'Did my money go on the races?' Had he actually gambled her hard-earned cash?

His face paled and he clenched his hands. Didn't meet her eyes. 'In a way, yes.'

'In what way?' It didn't even sound like her voice. More of a soft croak of horror. So hard to comprehend. Then, not waiting for the answer, she whispered, 'It's all gone? The money for the Desert Lizard repairs? You took it all?'

'Yes. I had to. But I can explain.'

Explain? The hurt closed her throat until she struggled to breathe. She dragged in a breath. 'How could you?' Her eyes stung but she wasn't going to let him see her cry. It wasn't even the money: it was the fact her own dad had stolen from her. He'd cared more for the excitement of a race tip than for his own daughter.

Heck. She'd just been proud of him! Had thought that would never change. What a joke. 'You know what?' She wished she could just walk home but it was too darn hot. She'd melt before she got there. 'I'll wait for you in the truck.' And she turned and walked back to the old truck and opened the door.

That weekend after the races, Phoebe left Birdsville for her aunt's house. For good. She was never coming back.